Captured

A Demon Kin Novella Double

Tori Minard

Captured
A Demon Kin Novella Double

Tori Minard

Cover by Tori Minard with photos by © Dmitry Pichugin

Copyright 2015 Tori Minard

Enchanted Lyre Books

Taken By Storm

Chapter 1

He needed sex. They wouldn't allow him to have it. They had put him here, stuck him in a cage as if he were an animal, laughed at him, taken his clothes, strapped a metal cage over his cock so he couldn't touch himself. Couldn't get even that much relief from the need that pounded at him, clawed him.

Demanding. All the time. Every instant of every day and night, when he was awake, when he was asleep, until he could hardly eat and sleep eluded him. Until he couldn't remember his own name.

He leaned against the door of the tiny, gray cell they called his room. He could smell the humans in the equally gray corridor, even though a powerful reek of disinfectant tried to cover it. There were no females in that group. He could smell others of his kind, males, somewhere nearby but not close enough for him to hear. Not close enough for him to speak to them.

Were they being treated the same way?

His fingers brushed the skin at the back of his neck and found the tiny rectangle they had inserted under his skin. Somehow, that little rectangle kept him from knowing their thoughts. It kept him from influencing his captors with his mind. It made him as weak as they were.

He didn't understand anymore what the rectangle was. He'd forgotten the word, just like he'd forgotten his name. But he knew that if he didn't have it, he could force them to release him. He could force them to do whatever he wanted. But they'd put it in him when he was unconscious, and now he was helpless against them.

He growled at the thing. It needed to come out. Now.

His fingernails were dull and short, but they were the only weapons he had. He would have used his teeth, except he couldn't set them at the back of his own neck. So fingernails it was.

He dug them into the skin on either side of the rectangle and kept digging until they pierced his skin. He gritted his teeth at the extra burst of pain, his fangs on full display. Blood flowed from the wounds he'd made.

His skin turned slippery. Still, he kept digging. Farther in. Deeper. Deeper. There—the hard edge of the tiny rectangle. He pinched it between his fingertips and carefully pulled.

A weird electric bolt of painful energy surged through him, as if some invisible person yanked on all his nerves at once. His hand locked in place as he shook all over. His limbs, his whole body, it was all out of his control.

His teeth chattered loudly from the shaking. His legs trembled and quaked until they shook him right off his feet and he landed on the smooth, cold floor of the cell. The electric shocks continued to surge through him, one after another, until he was blind with agony.

Somewhere, a wild animal was screaming and roaring as if it were being tortured. No. It wasn't a wild animal. It was him.

A burst of cooler air hit his skin. The smell of humans flooded him. They were talking—their voices buzzed incomprehensibly around his screams, but he couldn't understand what they said. Several sharp stabs penetrated the electric torture that consumed him, their sting barely perceptible.

Blackness washed through him and he sank into it, grateful for its oblivion.

❖ ❖ ❖

To love and obey, *as long as ye both shall live.* Mercy Wheaton had sworn those words years ago, when she'd married her husband, Cletus, and she'd meant them at the time. She'd never expected it to be quite so hard, though. Maybe she hadn't loved Cletus, or even liked him much, but her parents had chosen him as her husband and she'd trusted their judgment.

Yet her marriage had led her to this place, the Novus Vita Planetary Prison For Women Number One.

Cletus Wheaton stared across the table at her, his thin lips drawn so tightly they all but disappeared. His small, blue eyes looked even squintier than usual in the harsh light of the prison's visitor chamber. His gaze traveled over her rough, gray prison gown and the shackles on her wrists with undisguised contempt. She was his wife, yet he'd never had anything but contempt for her.

"The divorce is final," he said, a subtle note of satisfaction in his voice.

Not his wife anymore, then. Mercy leaned forward, the shackles bumping the thick, wooden table between her and her former spouse with a loud rattle. "Cletus, you know I'm innocent. Why are you doing this?"

"It's Mr. Wheaton to you, whore."

"I'm not a whore and you know it."

He drew himself upright, puffing out his scrawny chest. "You were duly convicted of adultery in a Novus Vitan court of law and that's good enough for me."

"I know this is about Ronilda. You want to get rid of me so you can marry her." That way, he could keep Mercy's dowry and have Ronilda's too. The fifteen year old Ronilda would make exactly the sort of meek little wife Cletus would like, and she'd probably pop out a dozen offspring in as many years, unlike Mercy, who seemed to be barren.

Cletus turned red at her accusation. "That's not true." He shoved his chair back and got to his feet. "You are a whore. You were nothing but trouble from the day I married you. Always arguing, always with every man in the village sniffing around your skirts. Well, I'm done with you and good riddance."

He spun on his heel and stomped to the visitor chamber door. The male guard on duty opened the door for him, his expression inscrutable. Mercy watched her now-ex-husband leave her without a backward glance, the ugly overhead light shining off the bald spot on the back of his head and his wispy dishwater-colored hair.

She covered her face with her hands. She wouldn't miss Cletus. Not even for a minute. Their marriage had been a nightmare from the beginning. But she'd harbored a foolish hope that he would see she'd been wrongly convicted and take her out of this terrible place.

Why had she ever thought that? He'd been the one to find her in flagrante delicto with Marcus—never mind that Marcus had forced her. Cletus didn't care about that.

The female guard assigned to take her to and from the visitor chamber jabbed her in the back with a powered-down shock stick. "Time to go, Wheaton-5."

Mercy dropped her hands to her lap. The guard poked her again. She got to her feet, stifling the glare she wanted to level at the other woman. Glaring was considered a minor infraction, a show of disrespect that would probably earn her a real shock with the shock stick. The pain of electric shock was an experience she'd do almost anything to avoid. Once had been more than enough.

The plain ugliness of the visitor chamber gave way to even greater bleakness as they walked—Mercy in the lead, the guard with shock stick at the ready—into the main hallway. Beyond was corridor after corridor of nothing but unadorned concrete walls and floors, stained with decades of use and punctuated only by the occasional metal security door where the guard had to produce passwords so they could continue.

It was vital to maintain a high level of security. After all, they wouldn't want their whores, female debtors, beggars, and petty thieves to escape. Who knew what awful havoc they would wreak if they ever got loose in society?

Several security doors later, they entered Mercy's ward. As far as she could tell, it looked exactly the same as every other ward in the prison. Even the prisoners looked much the same, and not only because they wore identical gray gowns. They all had the same shorn heads, the same pale, resentful, frightened faces, the same hollows in their cheeks and beneath their eyes.

She'd seen herself in a mirror once, after she'd been in prison a few weeks. She'd hardly recognized herself. Her luxuriant black curls were gone,

4

reduced to a fuzz of black velvet on her scalp. Her normally mocha-colored skin had turned a weirdly bleached-looking tan, her lips so pale they almost disappeared. *She* had almost disappeared. This place was toxic to her.

As the last security door crashed into place behind them, a trio of men in the company of another female guard came around a bend in the hall ahead of them. The men had horns on their heads. Long, serpentine tails with furry poufs at their tips swayed gracefully behind them.

Dear Maker. Demon Kin.

Mercy stopped short on a gasp. The guard slammed into her back.

"What in hell is wrong with you, Wheaton-5?" she snapped.

"W-who are those m-men?" They obviously belonged to the conquering race that had ripped control of her homeland away from her people. She'd heard of the Demon Kin, but only ever seen one.

About ten years earlier, at the young age of fourteen, a handsome Demon Kin male had turned up in their remote farming community. He said he was adventuring, traveling to faraway corners of the galaxy before taking up his responsibilities in his homeland. That, at least, was what he'd told her. Right before she helped the village elders capture him and hold him prisoner until soldiers could come to take him away.

He'd seemed so beautiful and exotic, and she'd been fascinated by him. But the elders, and their local Teacher, had explained to her how evil the Demon Kin were. Mercy hadn't wanted to hurt him. But she hadn't wanted to allow evil to flourish, either. She hadn't wanted to be a bad girl.

He was the only one of his kind she'd ever seen until now. She'd been hidden away in a jail cell by the time the conquerors had made their way to her small community.

The guard peered around her and chuckled. "Those are your new masters. Hadn't you heard? The Demon Kin are taking over administration of this prison. That's the new warden and his assistants taking the grand tour. Would you like to meet them?"

Mercy flushed at the woman's sneering tone. "No."

"No? That's all right. I'm sure you'll have plenty of opportunity later. I hear the Demon Kin are short on females. They're going to have a rousing good time with all you inmates."

Short on females. That was one way of putting it. Their planet, Malefica, had been afflicted with a plague that had wiped out most of their women. The Teachers said it was a judgment sent by the Maker for their evil ways.

While she and the guard had been talking, the Demon Kin had closed half the distance between them and the women. They walked with animal grace, their bodies moving with a slight rolling gait that reminded her of Cletus's favorite barn cat. All three men had fixed their gazes on the women, as if they couldn't look anywhere else.

They must be profoundly short on women, if Mercy and the ugly female guard could mesmerize them so easily.

Mercy's breath grew shallow and fast. Her palms began to sweat. "What would they want with us?"

The guard laughed outright. "Are you joking? What do you think they want? And they'll get it, too. I hear they get up to all kinds of nasty perversions." She laughed again, maliciously.

She stopped talking as the three Demon Kin bore down on them. The one in the lead, a tall man with hair the color of ripe wheat, stopped in front of Mercy. He stared down at her with an enigmatic smile. She trembled as she looked up at him; he reminded her so much, so painfully, of the one she'd betrayed.

The blond one smiled more broadly, showing the fangs possessed by all Demon Kin. "Who's this?"

"Wheaton-5, sir," the guard said. "We're on our way back to her cell."

"What's her crime?"

"Whoring, sir."

Mercy went hot with shame. She couldn't look at the man anymore, so she stared at the cracked concrete floor instead.

"She seems an unlikely whore," the Demon Kin said. He caught her chin and tipped up her face.

Mercy gasped at the contact. Her eyes remained downcast.

"Look at me, Wheaton-5," he said.

Reluctantly, she raised her eyes to his. They were blue.

"I'm looking for women who would like to get out of prison. In exchange, they would agree to mate with a Demon Kin male of our choice. Would you be interested in such a proposition?"

Was he talking about marriage? To a Demon Kin? That would have to be even worse than her union with Cletus, and that had been horrible. At least Cletus was human. At least Cletus wasn't a member of the race that had beaten and subjugated her world.

"N-no, sir," she gasped. "I-I couldn't."

"Is that so?" He sounded disappointed. "Well, the decision may be taken out of your hands. Just know that those who join us of their own free will can expect a much better reception than those who have to be forced."

"This one likes to be forced," the guard said.

Mercy flushed all over her body. The bitch lied. She didn't like being forced, but no-one cared what she had to say about the matter. Not Marcus. Not Cletus. The fact was, a man other than her husband had lain with her. Whether she'd wanted it or not was immaterial.

"I think we'll be seeing each other again soon, Wheaton-5," the golden-haired man said. He nodded to her guard. "Carry on."

They passed the woman and disappeared through the thick metal security door. Mercy's guard jammed the shock stick in her back with gleeful force. "Get moving."

They rounded the corner. Here the hall was lined with cells, their barred doors offering no privacy to the inmates. Women huddled at the backs of their cells, as far as they could get from the doors and the easy reach of the guards, who liked to walk by at random moments. The closer an inmate was to the doors, the more likely she'd get a shock or even have her fingers broken by a passing guard slamming a stick against her hand. Or worse. There was always much worse.

None of those things had happened to Mercy. Not yet. She kept far away from the doors, kept her head down, spoke little. But it was only a matter of time.

The guard unlocked her cell door and shoved her into the tiny room. "Sleep tight, Wheaton-5."

She hurried to the back of her cell and climbed onto the hard cot that served as her bed. The room was as chilly as ever. Mercy pulled her thin, scratchy blanket around her shoulders and waited for the guard to leave.

Chapter 2

The cage normally strapped over his cock was gone. They'd removed it. The cage kept him from touching himself, prevented him from achieving an orgasm. The only time he was allowed to climax was when they provided him with a woman, and that didn't happen very often.

It would happen soon, now. They'd taken off the cage, and that could only mean one thing. A woman was nearby and soon he'd have her.

They stood at the door of his room and aimed a hose at him. In his weakened state, the spray of water was almost powerful enough to knock him off his feet. He clutched the bars on the door to keep from falling over.

Everything in his body ached, even his bones and horns and tail. He couldn't remember the last time he'd eaten. Food wouldn't stay in his stomach. But they were going to give him a woman soon. Once he'd had the woman, the pain would ebb and he'd be able to eat again. For a while.

He might not remember his own name, might not be able to form words anymore, but he could remember that. His people needed sex the way most creatures needed food and water. Without it, his mind would fail and then his body. Eventually he would die.

The water hurt. It was too forceful. But it was good. Its arrival meant that soon he'd have a woman and the torment in his body would ease for a while.

He should not go to her. He should allow himself to die. But he knew, from past experience, that any attempt to hold himself back would fail. His instincts invariably took over and drove him to the female, no matter how he tried to prevent it.

Where was she? He couldn't smell her over the scent of the deluge of water. Soon, though. Soon, they'd release him and her into the corridor and he would chase her and take her.

The punishing flood of water stopped, the remaining liquid sluicing off his bare body and running across the floor and down the drain. He continued to clutch the bars on his door, breathing heavily. The human on the other side of the door laughed and spewed words he couldn't understand. Then the human left.

Alone again. For a while. He leaned against the cold, hard metal and closed his eyes. They'd made him go longer between women this time and he'd been having dizzy spells lately. But he would get the woman. He had to get her. Failure was impossible.

A slight puff of the stale air in the place teased his nostrils with the scent of human female. He straightened, his nostrils flaring. She was here.

What would she look like? What would her voice sound like? How would she taste? Smell? They never gave him the same woman twice.

He could smell her fear. Painfully sad, that fear, like a sharp knife hidden inside the lust that pounded in his belly. He didn't want her to fear him, but he had to get her. Take her. Why were they always so afraid of him? Didn't they know he would never hurt a female?

The bars on his door shivered. Metal screeched inside the opening mechanism. He stepped back and watched as the door slowly raised, pulling up into the ceiling. His heart began to pound ferociously and he trembled.

The opening was now at waist height. He ducked beneath the door as it continued to rise and stumbled into the corridor. The woman's scent was stronger now, nearer. He turned toward it.

His cock stood out like a pillar of rock in its eagerness. It ached unbearably. Soon he would quench it in the woman's body and he would be sane. For a while.

He ran down the corridor, his feet sinking slightly into the squishy gray padding on the floor. His legs felt stiff, unresponsive. They made him stumble. His shoulders bumped into the padded walls, first on one side and then the other.

The corridor bent around and around, turning corners at random, every new stretch of hall looking precisely the same as every other, but his Demon Kin sense of smell told him exactly where he was. Where she was. Just around this next bend, he would find her.

He careened around the corner and stopped. There she was, huddled against the wall, trembling. Her long, blond hair covered her face and much of her naked body.

He took a deep breath, savoring the smell of her. Even with the reek of fear, she smelled intoxicating. He walked toward her.

The woman whimpered. She tried to press herself into the wall, as if she could disappear that way. He extended his arm, his hand palm up.

"Shhh," he said.

She made that whimpering sound again.

"Shhh." *No hurt. Never hurt.* But his words wouldn't come.

He took a careful step toward her. The woman's trembling increased, grew so powerful her teeth began chattering. He was close enough now to touch her, so he did. His hand stroked along the yellow silk of her hair.

"Shhh. Shhh."

He was trembling, too. The ache in his bones, the weakness throughout his body drove him onward, forced him to continue touching her in spite of her terror of him. He needed her. If he could only tell her why, maybe she wouldn't be so afraid. But he'd lost his words.

"Shhh," he said, and lifted the length of her hair to reveal her naked breasts.

◆ ◆ ◆

The images on the vid screen made Promise shudder. They made her feel strange inside her body, bringing aching and hot sensations into parts of her she'd never even noticed before she'd accepted this assignment. The senior Angels had warned her it would be a difficult job, that it would change her. That it would take everything she had, all her faith and strength, to avoid being corrupted by it. Exposure to evil can tempt even an Angel, they'd said.

She'd been so sure she could handle it. She was one of their young stars, one of only two young women who'd risen to powerful positions in the Angel hierarchy in spite of their ages and their gender. The other one, Catherine, was being groomed for politics, especially interplanetary relations. Promise's unusual background in life sciences made her the perfect candidate for this assignment at the Novus Vita Life Studies Center.

"When's the new shipment due?" said one of the guards.

A second guard—Chisholm was his name—cleared his throat. "We're picking them up tonight. They should be ready to start by tomorrow at the latest."

"Heh," the second guy gloated. "I'm looking forward to that. This bunch is getting tired. I'm sick of looking at the same tits and ass all the time."

"I don't know," Chisholm said. "This one is pretty fine. But we could use some new meat."

The guards, all male, leered and snickered at the pictures of the Demon Kin prisoner and the human female.

"Yeah," one of them said. "I'd love to give it to her. Too bad they're off limits."

"He's taking his damn sweet time," one of them said.

"Just stick it in her!" Chisholm remarked to the vid screen.

Promise's face burned. They sometimes forgot she was present and spoke far too freely. She cleared her throat.

The guards exchanged embarrassed glances. "Sorry, Angel Promise," Chisholm said stiffly.

She nodded as graciously as she could manage. Yet she imagined there was resentment as well as shame in their averted gazes. They didn't like having a human female around—at least, not one who wasn't a prisoner.

Being so exposed to the Demon Kin had probably corrupted them all.

The Demon Kin on the vid screen freely touched the woman's naked body, even though she cringed away from him in fear. He was beyond caring what the woman thought, since the Life Studies Center personnel had prevented him from any sexual expression in several weeks.

The Demon Kin were a barbaric and evil race, created millennia ago on Old Earth as sexual slaves to human perverts. They had a sex drive so strong they began to go crazy if deprived for more than about a week. She and her staff kept the males even from pleasuring themselves, so they would have the maximum level of desperation when they were confronted with an available female. By that time, they were in such a frenzy they didn't know or care what their victim thought about the encounter.

Except, if that were true, then why was this Demon Kin being so gentle? Before arriving here, Promise had assumed they would be violent, that they would hurl the women to the floor and mount them immediately. Yet that had never happened during the time she'd been here. They always took the time to caress, even to seduce.

She curled her lip. A gentle rape was still rape. Besides, she didn't care what the victim thought about the encounter, either. The women's responses were irrelevant. Their role in this experiment was simply to provide sexual release for the males.

Chapter 3

In the middle of the night, they unlocked the door to Mercy's cell. At least, she guessed it was the middle of the night. There was no window in her cell, but she felt like she'd been asleep for a while, several hours or so.

The screech and clang of the metal door woke her, and she sat up on her cot, her heart slamming against the walls of her chest. The prison reduced the light in the corridors at night, but there was more than enough to illuminate the faces of the two night guards—both women—who entered her cell with shock sticks drawn.

"Get up, Wheaton-5," the first one said.

"Why?" Her mouth was so dry it was hard to get out any speech.

"You're wanted."

"Wanted? Who wants me?" No-one wanted her.

The guard chuckled unpleasantly. "You're being moved. Now get up and come along. We don't have time to chat."

"But I—I don't understand. What's going on? Where are you taking me?"

The guard advanced on her with a hard expression on her flat face. "Get up now or you'll get a dose of this." She brandished her shock stick.

Mercy got up.

"That's better." The guard snapped a set of shackles on her wrists. "Get going." She pointed toward the door, where her colleague stood waiting.

Mercy's mouth lost any drop of moisture still remaining. The rest of her broke into an icy sweat. She moved to the door, but her feet felt as if they had heavy stones tied to them.

"Is this about the Demon Kin?" she said faintly.

"Don't know. Don't care. We're to deliver you to the gatehouse. Now go."

"What about my things?" They'd confiscated all her personal belongings when they'd booked her into the prison, but they should still have them in storage. Shouldn't they?

"What about 'em? Get moving." The guard lifted the shock stick, as if she wanted to blast Mercy with it.

Mercy hustled to the door. The guards escorted her down hallway after hallway, past the visitor chamber and through the last security door into the gatehouse. It wasn't really a gatehouse, just a set of rooms used to process inmates into and out of the facility. She hadn't seen it since the day she'd arrived.

12

It was just as ugly as the rest of the prison, with hard concrete walls and floor that made it cold and drafty and loud. A group of men dressed in unfamiliar gray uniforms stood in the middle of the inner processing area, along with a line of female inmates all chained to each other.

The inmates didn't look at her or at the guards. They didn't look at anything except the floor. Were they as afraid and confused as she was? She wanted to demand an explanation, but then the guards would have an excuse to shock her.

They brought her to the end of the line and connected her to the woman ahead of her.

"Last one," the guard said.

"All the documents have been approved and submitted," one of the men in gray said.

"Take them away, then." The prison guard turned away as if bored with the whole procedure.

The man in gray had the end of the women's chain in his fist. He moved toward the outer door of the prison and the line of women slowly followed him, the chain clanking and jangling along the whole row of them.

Outside, there was snow on the ground. She hadn't smelled or felt snow in years, not since her arrest. A cold wind bit right through Mercy's thin gown. They hadn't given her shoes to wear. The snow and ice on the pavement seared the soles of her feet.

A few paces away sat a shuttle, its engines roaring and its doors standing open. Mercy's stomach gave a nauseous lurch. Were they taking them off-world, then? Why?

The men gave no explanation. They herded the women into the shuttle, where they sat in crude bucket seats along one wall. The men buckled themselves into their own seats. The doors slammed shut and the shuttle lifted into the air.

Mercy sneaked sideways glances at the other women. They were all staring at their laps. Did they know what was going on?

One of the men was staring at her. His dark eyes had a polished look to them, as if they were made of some kind of smooth, black stone. He had a square jaw and cruel, thin lips. A name badge sewn to his uniform announced him as Chisholm. No first name.

There was something in his face, a kind of gloating satisfaction, that made her even more uneasy. All the other guards had their gazes trained elsewhere, on other women or in their laps or focused on the impersonal wall of the shuttle. Chisholm simply stared at her.

She cleared her throat. "Excuse me, sir." She looked him in the eyes. "Can you tell me where we're going?"

His hard gaze rested on her without expression. "Shut up."

"But I only want to know—"

"You're going to a new prison. That's all I can tell you. Now shut it or I'll gag you."

She bent her head. A new prison. It didn't make any sense. The uniforms the men wore didn't look like any prison guard or police uniforms she'd ever seen and the insignia on their shoulders was completely unfamiliar. She couldn't read them from this distance, but they all looked identical, so they probably identified the men's employer.

We've been sold.

She'd heard of that, of the prisons selling prisoners off as slaves. Workers were hard to come by, even now that the war with the Demon Kin was over, and sometimes they used prisoners to fill the gaps in the workforce. That must be what was going on here.

At least they wouldn't be going to Demon Kin males.

But how did she know that? She didn't. She was making assumptions, baseless ones at that. For all she knew, these men were deputized by the Demon Kin to provide females to them. The new warden had warned her she could be forced into such a relationship, but she hadn't ever thought it would happen so quickly.

The ride seemed to last forever, but Mercy estimated it was actually around two hours long. Two miserable, cold, hungry, sleepless hours. They left Novus Vita's atmosphere, its gravity well, and moved out into space. Since the shuttle had no artificial gravity, her stomach began to float in a nauseating manner and Mercy had to shut her eyes and breathe slowly to keep from vomiting.

The other women remained silent the whole time, apparently as afraid as she was of the guards and what they would do if the prisoners attempted conversation. If these men worked for the prisoners' new owner, their behavior didn't bode well for the women's future.

Finally the shuttle landed. Since it had no windows in the passenger area, she couldn't tell where they were. They sat in their seats, waiting with dull, beaten-down acceptance for the next phase of whatever it was that was happening to them.

The shuttle doors slammed open and the men got to their feet. They ordered the women up and herded them out into a huge, echoing docking chamber. She'd never traveled on a shuttle before and could only guess where they were. In space? On a ship? A station?

The dock had ceilings so high she almost expected to see clouds clinging to the higher reaches. Noise echoed around the hard walls and floor as men rushed back and forth around the shuttle and a few other vehicles parked there. Everything here was some shade of gray, except for the warning signs in

14

bright yellow and red.

The guards conducted the women through the dock and into what appeared to be a storeroom or warehouse of some kind. Rows of open, gray metal shelves held packages and crates labeled with identical white stickers, all of which bore the same insignia as that on the men's uniforms.

She craned her neck to the side to get a better view of one of the stickers. It read Novus Vita Life Studies Center. That sounded relatively innocuous. But what kind of studies did they do here, and what did the women have to do with any of it? Maybe they were here to help with the support work. Sorting all those packages, for example.

The guards brought them to a room just big enough for all of them to find a place to sit on the hard industrial carpet that covered the floor. Then they locked the door, leaving the women alone.

She glanced around at her companions. Most of the women kept their gazes down, just as they had in the prison. They sat with their knees drawn up, their arms clasping their shins, eyes trained on the floor or their own knees. No-one looked back at her. No-one seemed to have the slightest curiosity about the place or their purpose here.

She lowered her own head and closed her eyes, dozing.

Over the next hour, male guards returned to collect one woman at a time, unlocking her from the communal chain and taking her away. Still no-one spoke. No-one asked any questions. The women simply disappeared from their group, one by one, while the rest of them waited in silence for their turns.

The door to the room opened. Chisholm entered. He stared at the remaining female faces with utter detachment, as if they weren't even people in his mind. The gloating was gone, replaced with this inhuman blankness.

"Wheaton-5," he barked.

Mercy jerked in shock, even though she'd known this moment was coming.

His hard gaze latched onto her. "Are you Wheaton-5?"

"Y-yes, sir."

"Get up. It's your turn."

For what?

She glanced at the women to either side of her. Neither would return her regard. Did they think if they ignored her, if they pretended none of this were happening, that it somehow wouldn't happen to them? Or maybe they simply didn't care. Maybe their capacity for emotional response had been beaten out of them in the Novus Vita Planetary Prison For Women Number One.

She unfolded her limbs and stood on shaky feet. Chisholm marched into the room and produced a key which he used to detach her from the line of chain. He took her elbow in a titanium grip, a whiff of cologne escaping his clothes and making her nose wrinkle. That cologne seemed so weirdly out of place on a man like him.

"Come with me." His voice was as hard as his eyes.

She let him lead her from the room with no protest. What would be the point in fighting him? There was no place for her to go and no-one to help her. But she sent him sneaky sideways glances, studying his cold and unsympathetic profile as he marched her down a long, narrow corridor whose walls and floor and ceiling were as gray as the dock had been.

"Where are you taking me?" she said in a low voice.

"Your room."

"My room? Does that mean I'm not a prisoner anymore?"

"No, you're not a prisoner," he said, his voice completely free of any inflection that might give her a clue as to what was really going on. "You're a guest of the Novus Vita Life Studies Center."

"I see. And what do they study here?"

"Life."

Life. Right. Obviously he wasn't going to give her any real information. Of course, he probably could have talked her ear off about whatever it was they did here and she wouldn't understand more than one word in ten. She had no advanced education. On Novus Vita, women barely learned to read, making someone like Mercy an anomaly. She did read, voraciously. But she'd never had access to much in the way of science, and she suspected this place was some kind of science center.

Did they run experiments? Oh, God. Maybe they were going to experiment on the female prisoners.

They came to a heavy, locked door made of some kind of synthetic material in a deep gray color. Chisholm produced another of his special keys and the door made a soft click as it unlocked. He opened it and escorted her through, his hand an uncompromising clamp on her elbow.

The corridor beyond was different than the one they were leaving. All the surfaces seemed to be upholstered. The floor sank slightly beneath her every step, as if cushioned in foam, and the walls and ceiling had a soft, padded look to them. Soft, dove-gray fabric with a napped look like some kind of velvet covered them. It was beautiful, if monotonous. But something about it made alarm bells clang loudly in Mercy's mind. Padding could protect from harm. It could also muffle sound. Why would they need to muffle so much sound they'd upholster every surface of the corridor?

"We're subjects, aren't we?" she said, watching him closely for his reaction.

He blinked. Frowned. Then his brow smoothed and he assumed the expressionless expression he'd worn before. "I don't know what you mean."

16

Chapter 4

Her scent was everywhere. It boomed in his nose, pounded him, clamoring for him to chase her, take her. Now. Now. Now.

Sweat poured off his freshly hosed body. He trembled. He hurt, his throat so dry he struggled just to swallow. But the door to his cell remained closed.

He slammed his fist against the surface of the door. It boomed too. The sound banged around the hard surfaces of his cell, assaulted his eardrums, reverberated in his empty, aching body. He roared.

Where were they? Why wouldn't they open the door? It had to open. Open. Now. Now. Now.

Then he heard her voice. High-pitched, frightened. Shouting.

Her words meant nothing to him, nothing but noise. Her fear and anger set his teeth on edge, made his trembling worse, made him hit the door again. His knuckles hurt and the door boomed, yet no-one came and the door remained closed.

He roared a second time. The bellow seemed to tear something in his throat. Savage pain. Agony in his hand, agony in his throat, agony in his muscles and bones and hair.

She would take it away. She would make the pain disappear. She was relief and solace and nourishment and joy and everything that was good in his world. He needed her and they—*they*—refused to give her to him.

A growl boiled up from deep inside him. What he would do to them if he ever got close enough, if he could just get his hands around their throats....

Kill. Tear. Bite. Blood and more blood, running into his mouth, down his parched throat, down his face and his neck and his chest, over his belly...

If he ever got close enough...

The door made the soft clicking noise that meant it was about to open. His heart leaped into a hard, pounding rhythm and he began to pant. Soon now. Soon.

The door rose noisily toward the ceiling. He fell on his belly and crawled under it, into the corridor. The woman's scent filled the air so powerfully he wasn't sure where it originated. But he'd find her soon enough. He'd find her. There were no places to hide.

* * *

The cell they'd given her was a lot more comfortable than the one she'd left behind on Novus Vita, but it was still a cell. They could call it a "room" all they liked; Mercy knew the difference. Guest rooms weren't locked from the outside. And they didn't have windows in their doors. Barred windows.

Everything here was gray, just like on Novus Vita. Except it was a soft, lush gray that seemed intended to be soothing rather than punitive. The blanket on the bed was soft, too, and plush. Warm. The shower was hot, the food they finally gave her was at least edible, unlike the nasty sludge they'd fed her on the planet.

What a strange prison.

The door made a soft, repetitive clicking sound. She stared at it, wondering what it was doing. Then it began to rise, slowly, the top portion receding into a slot in the ceiling. What was going on? Where were the guards?

She approached cautiously, bent down and peered under the bottom of the door and into the corridor. Empty. No guards anywhere that she could see.

"Hello?" she said in a barely audible whisper.

There was no answer.

Should she leave her cell? Maybe this was a test of some kind. Were they trying to find out how compliant she was?

If she left, she'd be demonstrating that she wasn't completely broken yet, that she was willing to take the risk of leaving her cell. Or maybe leaving was what they wanted her to do. Maybe leaving would show the greatest compliance. After all, they'd opened the door. She hadn't broken out.

She bit her lip, considering her options. Could the open door be a mistake? Could there be a computer error somewhere? In that case, staying put might be the smartest thing to do, because if they found her wandering around, they might punish her.

Yet if she left, it was possible she could find out something about this place. Some clue to what they were doing here. What they wanted with her and the other prisoners. Maybe that would be worth the risk of punishment.

Mercy stepped into the corridor. The squishy floor felt strange under her bare feet. She stood in the hall, heart racing, trying to decide which direction to take first.

The door slammed shut behind her with a loud clang. She whirled, staring. It had risen so slowly, she'd assumed she'd have plenty of time to change her mind if it started closing again. Obviously she'd been wrong.

They wanted her in the corridor. That seemed like the most probable explanation for the slow opening and quick closing. They'd wanted to tempt her out and then had closed the door quickly to prevent her from going back in.

Her stomach gave a queasy lurch. Something about this set-up made everything in her want to run and hide. But where would she go?

A thundering bang exploded from somewhere nearby. Mercy jumped, a squeak escaping her mouth. The sudden noise felt like an attack, as if some invisible assailant had punched her.

"Hey!" she yelled. "Hey! Let me back in! I want to go back!"

No-one answered.

"Hey! Can you hear me? I want to go back in my cell!"

A second boom answered her shouts, followed by a metallic squeal. They seemed to be coming from her left. She ran toward the right, hoping to find someone who would help her. Or even a place to hide. A storage room or cupboard. Something. Anything.

Feet thudded on the floor. Something large bumped into a wall somewhere behind her. It growled.

Mercy gasped and stumbled. She picked herself up and ran, sweat pouring from her body. The creature behind her was growling continuously now. It sounded like a wolf or maybe a large cat. Some kind of huge predator. They'd cast her out into the corridor in order for that thing to hunt her.

What would it do when it found her? Kill her, no doubt. Maybe eat her.

She muttered a prayer as she careened along the hall. Doors identical to her own—except their windows were covered with solid metal shutters—lined its length. It turned a sharp corner, revealing more faceless doors. Everything was gray. Floor, ceiling, doors, all gray.

The rhythm of the feet following her sounded...human. Human? That couldn't be right. Why would a human chase her? Why would a human growl like a wild predator?

She turned another sharp right corner and came up on a dead end. Ugh. Terrible choice of words.

The corridor ended just twenty feet away. There were no doors in this little niche. It seemed to have no practical purpose, except maybe as a trap.

Mercy whirled in the direction she'd come. A figure filled the corridor, blocking her exit.

She screamed.

He was tall. Horned. Demon Kin. Naked.

Aroused. His fully engorged cock stood straight out, thick and long, its size horrifying. Cletus hadn't looked like that. The one time she'd managed to catch a glimpse of her ex-husband's sex, it had been so much smaller than this Demon Kin's that it almost looked like a different organ entirely.

She had to get away.

She knew there was no way out of this section of corridor, but something primitive in her brain forced her around, forced her to run to the end of the hall as if she might find a hidden door there or something. All her actions did was trap her against the wall. She turned to face him.

He was tall, pale-skinned and black-haired. His black tail whipped back and forth behind him, the way an agitated cat would snap its tail. His hair was dripping wet and long, past his shoulders; black scruff covered his jaw. And his eyes...oh, God, his eyes. They were fixed on her with a terrifying, predatory gleam she didn't understand.

Demon Kin didn't eat humans, did they? Did they?

Of course they don't eat us, ninny. He wants to mate with you.

Oh, God. No, no, no.

He stalked toward her. His movements seemed stiff and clumsy for a Demon Kin. He bumped into the wall on his left and stumbled before catching himself.

Maybe he was sick or hurt. Maybe she could dash past him. Maybe he wouldn't react quickly enough to catch her.

She bolted toward the main corridor, trying to stay on his left where he seemed weakest. A powerful arm shot out and snagged her around the waist. With a fierce growl, he yanked her against his naked body.

Mercy screamed again. She wasn't normally a screamer. These sounds simply tore their way out of her, as if she had no control over herself.

She flailed and writhed in his grip, her legs and arms banging frantically, uselessly against him. He seemed to be made of stone. Some kind of high-tech synthetic stone that was impossible to break.

His free hand traveled over her, touching her through her gray prison gown, stroking her back and hips in long caresses. Even when her blows connected with him, he kept touching her, as if he couldn't feel her hitting and kicking him.

Chapter 5

Mercy kicked and flailed wildly. But it was like fighting with a wall. The Demon Kin simply ignored her, holding onto her and letting her strike him as if he couldn't feel the blows.

She knew it was useless, yet she couldn't stop herself. Something else, something ancient and primitive and desperate, had taken over her mind and body, driving her to battle him no matter how ridiculous that was.

He lifted her effortlessly in one arm and descended to his knees. No. No! He was going to lay her on the floor and then he'd...he'd...

The Demon Kin lowered her to the padded floor and stretched himself on top of her in one smooth operation. Mercy shrieked, her movements becoming even wilder and more desperate. But his weight pinned her and his arms and legs gathered hers in, trapping her, forcing her to stop striking him.

He would destroy her. She had to get away, had to get away, had to get...

"Shhhh," he murmured, his voice low and even. "Shhh."

Mercy's shrieks continued, high and mad, one after the other like a wild beast. Her voice was like something outside of herself, something that didn't belong to her. She couldn't stop it.

"Shhh," he said again.

"No! Please, please, please don't. Please don't."

"Shhhh."

His big hands stroked her side, her arm, her upper leg. He was petting her, like she might pet a frightened and unmanageable horse.

"Let me go. Let me go." She wriggled beneath him.

He let out a loud, shuddering groan. Mercy froze in place. All her struggling was only exciting him more, rubbing against his erection in a way that he probably found provocative. Maybe he even thought she was doing it on purpose.

"Oh, Maker," she whispered, pinching her eyes shut as a hot flush of mortification covered her skin.

She could feel the hot length of his stiff rod pressed against her belly, pushed into her flesh by the weight of him on top of her. Her scratchy prison gown provided a layer of protection between her and his sex, but it wasn't much. It didn't stop her from being painfully aware of how aroused he was.

His stroking continued, venturing up to her shorn head, skimming along the column of her neck. She couldn't move, couldn't get away from him. All she could do was lay there and tremble as he touched her.

He smelled of male sweat, a spicy scent that seemed to have a strange effect on her. It made her tingle in odd places. She'd always hated the way Cletus smelled, especially when he got sweaty from working in the fields. Marcus, too. They'd smelled like old, dirty socks and oppression.

But this Demon Kin...he smelled like enticement. Like the promise of some secret pleasure she couldn't understand or anticipate. That made no sense. He was a rapist, an evil freak of some ancient gen-tech lab where they'd bred creatures like him for the amusement of human perverts.

But the heat and weight of him above her began to soak into her, to seep into her bones and muscles and force her to relax.

She found that she no longer wanted to scream. Her voice fell silent. She trembled beneath him, waiting, waiting to see what he'd do next.

Mercy expected the nameless Demon Kin to shove up her gown and rut on her immediately. She couldn't escape. He was so much stronger than her that he could do anything he wanted to her, anything at all, and she could do nothing to stop him. He could use her whenever he wanted.

Yet he continued to do nothing more than stroke her, pet her. She lay, exhausted and still, while he explored her. His touch was gentle. His other arm, which he used to prop himself up so she wasn't taking all his weight, was hard and immovable, but not brutal. It made a warm sort of cage to hold her in without hurting her.

That enormous erection she'd seen, now sandwiched between their bodies, pressed insistently against her belly. She knew he was going to push that thing inside her eventually. She began to shake.

She'd heard rumors, mostly in prison, that some women enjoyed sex. That seemed frankly unbelievable. Men got pleasure from the act, but women? What was there to enjoy? Mercy had always been thankful when it was merely tiresome and not painful.

This, with the Demon Kin, was going to be painful. She knew it. She couldn't help being afraid.

Then she noticed something strange. He was shaking too.

Shudders ripped through his big body. The hand roaming her curves trembled. He cupped her ass, and his breath caught. He bent his head toward hers with a low groan.

Was he simply overcome with lust or was something else going on?

She didn't want to look at him, didn't want to see his face in any detail. Looking at him would make what was happening seem more real. But his expression might give her some clues to his inner state. So she tilted her head back and looked.

He was beautiful. So beautiful. Sharp, angular jaw with sculpturally high cheekbones, a straight nose, gorgeously chiseled lips, thick black hair sliding

22

forward like a pair of silky curtains. And his eyes. She'd noticed them before, of course, for their intensity. They were so dark brown they were almost black, large and gracefully shaped and rimmed with the heaviest black lashes she'd ever seen.

They were full of pain.

The Demon Kin had the lines of strain and the hazy expression of someone in agony. She'd seen that look before on men injured by farm equipment and women in childbirth. He was suffering. But why? He looked whole enough.

He lifted his hand to her face and cupped her cheek. "Shhh." His voice was soft and low, soothing. He was comforting her?

This was so confusing.

"Shhh," he said again, his thumb stroking slowly back and forth along her cheek.

The caress felt good. His hot, hard body pressing against her felt good. That was wrong. She shouldn't enjoy contact with this man, or any other man for that matter. They'd called her a whore, but she wasn't. She was a good, pious Novus Vitan woman who did her best to follow the Teachings and this...this treacherous spreading warmth in her body was wrong.

Mercy trembled in his embrace. He was an attacker, wasn't he? How could she respond to him with anything but fear and disgust? What was wrong with her that she could take pleasure from the hot column of his body against her?

Yet she couldn't lie to herself. Something in her wanted him. The place between her legs, a place she did her best to never think of or notice in any way, ached and tingled in an unfamiliar way that she couldn't name. What was that sensation? It felt pleasant. It made her want more of him.

He was going to hurt her, even if he didn't mean to. There was no possibility that he could put his...his male organ into her body without injuring her. It was simply too big.

What are you thinking? Are you really considering submitting to this? Are you thinking you desire...are willing to have...conjugal relations with a stranger, a man who isn't even human?

His long fingers slid down to cup her chin as his gaze focused on her lips. He was going to kiss her. This was really happening and she could do nothing to prevent it. Something brushed against her legs and she realized it was his tail.

His tail. Mercy whimpered.

"Shhhh," he said. "Shh. Shhhhh."

Why did he keep saying that? She wasn't making much noise in the first place, now that she'd stopped screaming.

His head tilted as he lowered his lips to hers. She stiffened instinctively, her head turning until he cupped the back of her skull with his hand to position her and keep her in place. His mouth pressed lightly to hers.

The touch was so gentle, so soft it didn't even feel like a kiss at all. There was almost no pressure. No hard, thrusting tongue. No teeth. Just whispery caresses of his mouth, his lips over hers.

This was torture. She wanted it over, done. Wanted him to put it in her so he could finish and leave her alone.

She pulled her head back long enough to force out a few words. "Just get it over with."

"Shhh." He kissed her again.

He lightly sucked her upper lip into his mouth. Then her lower lip. His tongue flicked out, teasing her without insisting on entry. At the same time, his tail continued to swish lazily against her skirt, first on one side and then the other.

He wasn't hurting her. When would it start? When would he pinch and bite and force his way into her body?

The kisses continued, soft and warm and light. A sigh escaped her. His encircling arm began to feel more like support and less like a prison.

She found herself softening against him. Her left hand found its way to his upper right arm. His skin was hotter than she'd expected, and smooth as the finest velvet. She stroked him slowly, experimentally.

He sighed against her mouth as a shudder wracked his body. His trembling hadn't eased at all; if anything, it had increased. Something distressed him.

Perverse woman to feel sympathy for a creature like him; non-human, and a rapist to boot. And yet...and yet...

Before she knew it, her lips parted and he slipped his tongue into her mouth in a long, hot, wet glide of flesh against flesh. And it...it didn't hurt. His tongue was as gentle and coaxing as his lips, his hands.

He slicked that tongue across her teeth, up against the roof of her mouth, places she'd never been kissed before. And Mercy found her lips, her tongue moving in return. Her other hand settled on his left arm. Distantly, she noted the hardness of the muscle beneath his warm skin.

Another kind of hardness thrust against her belly, reminding her of what was going to happen soon. She ought to be terrified, but with him kissing and stroking her all she could think of was how good it felt. She'd gone so long without any kind of touch at all, and longer than that without the comfort of loving touch. Certainly, Cletus had never made her feel this way.

The Demon Kin's hand on her ass squeezed, molding and shaping her flesh in a rhythmic pattern that had her sighing and arching into him. He moaned into her mouth. The sound made the aching and tingling inside her even more intense.

Was it fear causing those sensations? Fear had never felt like that before. Usually it made her sick to her stomach. Her heart was pounding, her breath was shallow, she trembled, but the aching warmth in her belly was pleasurable.

Maybe this was a form of madness. Maybe they'd drugged her food. That might explain why her reaction to this alien and his unwanted advances was so abnormal for her.

Yes. They'd drugged her food.

He reached down the side of her leg and drew up her skirt. Mercy went still beneath him, her stomach icing over in sudden dread. This was it, then. This was where everything got ugly. He was going to do it to her and it would be just like back home, only worse, and she couldn't...she couldn't seem to...oh, Maker...

"Shhh," he murmured. Was that the only word he knew? It wasn't even a real word, actually.

His fingers skimmed over the skin of her thigh, the touch no more demanding than any of his other caresses. She trembled, waiting for him to force her legs apart. Instead, he merely continued stroking her, his hand traveling down to her knee, massaging the thick muscle of her thigh, stroking intimately along the inner plane of her leg but staying away from *there.*

After a few minutes of this, some of the tension in her body released. Whimpers she hadn't realized she was making ceased. A sigh escaped her.

He drew the skirt higher until he had it rucked up around her waist. But he still didn't force her legs apart, he still didn't pinch or bite her, although his broad masculine hand persisted in shaking as he petted her.

He ventured up, under the loose bodice of the prison gown, his fingers spanning the whole side of her rib cage. His fingertips brushed the bottom curve of her breast. Mercy gasped, her body jerking.

"Shhhh," he said again.

Her whimpers returned. She bit her lip to keep from making that stupid noise, but it worked its way out of her anyway.

The Demon Kin brushed his thumb along the bottom curve of her breast before circling around the top. He repeated the action again and again, but it didn't have the same relaxing effect on her as his other caresses. All she could think of was the moment when he would grab her nipple and twist.

Finally he palmed her whole breast, his fingers curving around her. He gave another of those broken groans, his head dropping down until his face was nestled in the nook between her head and neck. His lips touched the skin on the side of her neck.

Now his whole body was shaking so badly his teeth started to chatter. His touch became frantic, moving over her in swift, hungry passes, yet he still didn't pinch or bite or do anything else to hurt her. When was he going to get to it? How long was he going to make this last?

His hand returned to her thigh. Mercy braced herself. He pushed at her leg, and she allowed him to spread her wide. What would be the point of resisting? He'd do whatever he wanted no matter how she fought him and she'd likely get hurt in the process. So she let him open her.

Chapter 6

He slid down her body, his hands now curved around her thighs like manacles. Suddenly she found his head between her legs, staring at her most private place. She tried to clap her own hands over herself, but he beat her to the target and buried his face in her sex.

Mercy yelled in outrage and shock as he kissed her there. How could he? She'd heard the Demon Kin were perverse, but this...

The long, wet slide of his tongue on a place for which she had no real name stopped her breath in her throat. She couldn't yell anymore; she could only gasp and twist beneath his ruthless assault. What he was doing to her...it didn't hurt...it was...it was...She couldn't think about what it was.

Perverse. Monstrous. Hideously pleasurable.

Then he rearranged himself above her and fitted his cock in her entrance.

Once again, she braced herself, her entire body going rigid. He sucked in a breath as he breached her. He was huge. He wasn't going to fit. Couldn't he see that?

But he pushed forward and her body stretched to accommodate him. He was only inside her a few centimeters, and already he burned her with a ferocious onslaught of sensation.

Mercy gave a helpless gasp. He pulled back, then thrust forward, more deeply this time. She gasped again as the burning, stretching, piercing, pleasure-pain invaded her further. Cletus and Marcus had never felt like this. She'd never imagined anything could feel like this.

He lifted her thigh, forcing her to bend at the knee, then draped her leg around his waist. Inside her, he sank more deeply, so deeply he felt like he was bumping up against her navel. She gave a wild cry. Her hands clutched at his upper arms, her nails digging into his skin.

Mercy ventured a glance at his face. His coffee-colored eyes were almost crazed, his teeth bared in a strange grimace that looked more pained than aggressive. The contortion of his features made him no less beautiful. Even the silver-gray horns protruding from his ebony hair couldn't make him less beautiful.

He flexed his hips. She cried out again. Something in him seemed to loosen, some control fell away, and he surged into her over and over, a series of rough groans emerging from him as he took her. He threw his head back and roared, his hips jerking as hot moisture flooded her.

He went limp on top of her, although she could tell he was keeping his full weight off her by propping himself on his elbows. Mercy sighed. It was over. In a minute he would pull out of her and leave her here alone.

Alone.

But he declined to withdraw from her. Instead, he wrapped his arms around her and rolled onto his back, bringing her with him so she ended up splayed across him. His hands roamed again, up and down her back, squeezing the globes of her ass, petting her hair and tracing the curve of her ear. He still wanted her? Cletus had never done more than pat her shoulder afterward, and Marcus...he'd simply adjusted his trousers and left. This Demon Kin wanted to stay with her. How odd.

He took one of her hands and pressed it to his naked chest. She blinked, staring down at him. He'd lost some of the pain lines and tension in his face, yet his gaze still held the focus, the intensity she'd first seen in him. He took her hand again, moving it back and forth over his skin.

He wanted her to stroke him the way he was stroking her.

Mercy had never touched a man before. Not so intimately, and certainly not such a great expanse of naked skin. But he kept dragging her palm across him and instead of fighting him she went along with it.

Black hair grew in soft whorls across his chest. Not a lot of hair, just a dusting. And he had nipples. They were not like hers. They were small and hard, their color lighter. They felt like tiny pebbles beneath her palm.

This man had kissed her in a place no other person had ever seen. He'd joined with her. Ejaculated into her. They were still joined. She didn't know so much as his name, yet he'd been more intimate with her than any other male—any other person—she'd ever known.

Buoyed by the loose warmth caused by whatever they'd used to drug her, Mercy freely stroked and petted the broad, hard planes of his chest, his shoulders, his upper arms. She slipped her hands up and ran her fingers through his hair. His eyes closed; his head angled into her touch. He sighed.

The drug must be giving her this false sense of closeness, even tenderness. With no way of turning off the effect, Mercy simply surrendered to it. The Demon Kin hadn't hurt her. He'd never once pinched, or bitten, or grabbed her hard enough to leave a bruise. He'd given her pleasure, astonishing pleasure.

Although she hadn't wanted it, had tried to reject it, she couldn't help feeling almost grateful. After all, he could have done anything at all to her. No-one would have stopped him. He'd chosen to show her gentleness instead of brutality.

He urged her down and took her mouth with his. There was a strange, tangy flavor on him. Mercy realized with a shock that it was her own taste, still on his mouth.

His kiss turned hot and desperate. His sex, still buried inside her, was growing stiff again. Mercy's eyes went round as he resumed the ancient rhythm of mating with her on top of him.

People did it this way? With the woman on top? How peculiar.

He grasped her hips, pumping her up and down on his enormous cock, sliding ruthlessly in and out of her. Her breasts bobbled with her movement. The cream of his earlier ejaculation made the motion easier, smoother. Exquisite sensations, brighter and sweeter than before, shot through her with each stroke. She rose and fell on her knees, unconsciously mimicking his motions, meeting his hips with thrusts of her own.

Every time their bodies came together, a soft explosion of delight burst through her pelvis and out, into the rest of her. And each time he withdrew, the slide of his cock on her passage walls brought a moan from her throat.

He thrust faster, his hands gripping her more tightly. Mercy's breasts bounced under the scratchy fabric of her gown. She braced herself on his chest as she rocked on him and the pleasure built and built, driving her onwards to some goal she could only sense but couldn't see.

Then it all coalesced inside her, drew to a tight, hard point and burst into abrupt, flooding release. Something in her seemed to break, to fall apart as shudders of ecstasy racked her body. She screamed.

He ground her onto himself, shouting, his mouth wide, head tilted back, eyes rolled up into his head. He looked as transported as she'd felt a moment ago.

Was that what had happened to her? She'd had a crisis, a climax? But that never happened to women. Did it?

She'd always thought women incapable of climaxing. Nothing in her prior experience had made her think anything different. Maybe it was the drug they'd given her. It was giving her some male characteristics, such as desire and orgasm. Maybe that was the purpose of the experiment.

They lay entwined in each other's arms, breathing hard, shudders still coursing through them. His fingers stroked her short hair and lingered on her ear, rubbing her ear lobe in such a sensual way that she moaned.

Someone cleared his throat. Mercy gasped, her whole body jerking in the Demon Kin's embrace. He kept his arms around her, a nasty growl rumbling in his chest.

She turned her head to see the guard Chisholm standing in the middle of the junction between their nook and the main hallway. His eyes glittered as he stared down at her.

At her bare ass.

Mercy jerked her gown over herself, every inch of her skin burning with humiliation. Chisholm smirked. The two men standing behind him laughed.

The Demon Kin's growl grew louder, his grip on her tighter. Chisholm pointed some kind of hand weapon at them and the Demon Kin snarled.

"Let her go," Chisholm said. "Your time is over."

But he only held her tighter, the growl turning vicious. Mercy clung to him, burying her face in his chest, as if he were her ally and not her attacker. Then he twitched under her, his breath catching slightly. A moment later, his arms went slack and he released her.

The guards swarmed up, grabbed her by her arms, hauled her off him. His eyes were glazed, almost empty of expression. He wouldn't even look at her. What had they done to him?

"Come on, Bambi," Chisholm said. "You're done here."

Bambi was Novus Vitan slang for whore. "My name is Mercy Wheaton," she snapped. "Not Bambi."

"You could've fooled me. Looked like you were having the time of your life a few minutes ago."

All three guards laughed as they dragged her from the nook. The Demon Kin lay passively on the floor, his dark eyes half closed, his hands resting loose by his sides. A dart stuck out of the sole of his right foot.

They'd shot him with a drugged dart, probably to make him more manageable. Demon Kin were powerful creatures and three human men would have been no match for him if he'd been awake and alert.

"You drugged me," she said. "You're to blame for all this, not me."

Chisholm laughed. "We didn't drug you."

They hauled her along the corridor toward her cell. She stumbled. They yanked her upright again, sending shearing pain through her armpits and into her arms and shoulders.

"You're lying." She glanced over her shoulder, but the Demon Kin was already hidden from her.

"Why would I lie?" Chisholm said. "Face it, Bambi, you're a natural whore. It's what you went to prison for, remember?"

No. It couldn't be true. If they hadn't drugged her, then her response to the Demon Kin was natural. And that couldn't be. She'd never felt those things with any man before. She'd never enjoyed sex, had only tolerated it because it was required of her.

She followed the Teachings.

And now these prison guards, these bullies, were telling her she hadn't been drugged, that her wild response to the Demon Kin male had been her own. It couldn't be true.

They arrived at her cell. She only knew it was hers because the door had begun to rise as they approached it. There was nothing inside the little room to indicate that she or anyone else occupied it. No personal belongings, no trace of individuality.

"Take a shower, Wheaton-5," Chisholm said. He gave her a little shove into the room.

Mercy stumbled toward her bed. The door slammed shut behind her and she was alone.

The men's voices came to her through the little window in the door, but they were muttering among themselves and she couldn't make out what they were saying. They padded off down the silent hallway, leaving her behind in her cell.

She sat down on the narrow bed. Moisture leaked from her body. His moisture. She'd mated with a Demon Kin and she'd enjoyed it.

Maybe she really was a whore.

He'd been so gentle, almost sweet. He'd made her feel good. But she'd said no and he hadn't listened. Had that been a rape? Had he raped her?

At the beginning of the encounter, she would have said yes, unequivocally. It was rape. But now she didn't know. If she'd wanted it, then it couldn't be rape. She was so confused.

Either something terrible had been done to her or she'd offended the Maker with her whorish nature. Was she a victim or a criminal? Both choices were awful.

Pain descended on her, sudden and choking. Mercy wrapped her arms around herself and shook in silent misery.

Chapter 7

They were being watched. Mercy glanced up at the smooth and shiny patch on the ceiling of her cell, then quickly looked away as if there were nothing significant in it. As if it weren't a camera put there so her captors could spy on her.

She might put her suspicions down to paranoia, except they fit so well with the situation. Looking out through the window of her cell door, she could see more of the shiny spots in regular intervals along the corridor ceiling and wall. They were the same gray color as the rest of the corridor, so it was easy to overlook them at first. But now that she'd noticed them, she couldn't stop thinking about them. About what they might mean.

Cameras. It must be part of whatever experiments they were running here.

How do you know they're experimenting?

She didn't, not for sure. But her gut told her she'd been turned into a lab rat, and the Demon Kin male as well. They were subjects in some kind of study.

A study that involved sex. The sex drive of Demon Kin? The ability of the Demon Kin to mate and produce viable offspring on human women? Or maybe their almost supernatural ability to make pious women into shameless, whore-like wantons with no self-control. Whatever it was, they were using both human women and Demon Kin males against their will.

She didn't believe for one instant that her Demon Kin attacker had signed up for this treatment. It might soothe her ego to think he'd gone after her of his own free will, but he was a prisoner, the same as her. The way he'd reacted to the guards and the fact they'd shot him with a tranquilizer was all the proof she needed of that.

But why hadn't he spoken? That part didn't make sense to her. He'd made plenty of vocalizations, so his voice worked. He simply hadn't formed words.

"Wheaton-5," Chisholm barked from outside her cell. "Exercise time."

She turned her head slowly, refusing to give him the satisfaction of seeing her jump at the sound of his voice. He was a bully. It was her bad luck he'd been assigned as her personal guard. Or maybe he'd put himself in that position. He seemed to have an obsession with her.

Sometimes, he simply stood outside and peered in at her through the window. Not speaking, just watching. The windows were supposed to be closed all the time, but Chisholm liked to open hers so he could stare at her. She

32

always pretended she didn't know he was there, but it made her nervous.

He could come into her cell anytime he wanted. And he could see anything she did just by looking through that stupid window. Even something as innocent as scratching her back drew suggestive remarks from him.

Mercy straightened and stood up, moving slowly toward the door. It began to rise. Chisholm's foot tapped impatiently at the padded floor. She could see his shiny black shoes under the gap created by the opening door.

He took her by the elbow as soon as the door cleared his head. The new uniform they'd given her had short sleeves, so his hands touched her bare skin. She wrestled with the urge to try yanking her arm away. It wouldn't do any good if she did. She'd already explored that option; he'd merely clamped down harder, leaving a bruise on her skin.

"Hurry up," Chisholm said.

"What happened to the other women who came here with me?" she said as he hustled her down the corridor. She hadn't seen them since that awful night, and it had been at least ten days since then. Maybe more. She'd lost count.

"They're incarcerated, just like you," he said.

"Are they...did they...have any of them met any Demon Kin?" She flushed hot.

Chisholm chuckled. "Why? You like to watch?"

"No!"

"Looking for professional tips, huh, Bambi?"

"I'm not a whore," she said between gritted teeth.

"Sure you're not. I can give you all the practice you need." He leaned close, his breath hot and sour against her cheek. "I'll teach you everything you need to know, Wheaton-5."

She kept her head down, declining to reply. He laughed.

They reached the warehouse area where she and the other prisoners had been sorted, passed through the shelves of supplies and into a large greenhouse on the other side. Another prisoner, her arm clamped in the meaty hand of a guard, passed her in the doorway on her way in. Mercy tried to catch the other woman's eyes, but she wouldn't look at her.

The air in this room felt warm and moist, and there were grow lamps shining brilliant light down upon her and the plants. There were row upon row of lettuce, carrot, tomato, onion, vita greens, jeshli, and even a couple of citrus trees growing here. It must be a kitchen garden.

She suspected they were on a space station of some kind, maybe situated on a moon. She'd seen no windows to the outside. A ship wouldn't have room for a garden of this size, and probably wouldn't be a good place for experiments. Not the kind they were conducting, anyway, the kind that required long mazes of corridors for Demon Kin to chase their human prey. It seemed to her that a space station was the likely answer.

But why? Why would Novus Vitans be experimenting on humans this way? Or Demon Kin, for that matter. What did they hope to accomplish?

The face of the Demon Kin male floated up in her consciousness. He was never far from the surface of her mind, haunting her dreams and her waking hours with the same intensity. Sometimes she found herself longing for his touch, aching with the need to feel him against her. Inside her. Then the rage and shame would come and she'd pound the mattress on her bed until she was exhausted and breathless.

Chisholm marched her up and down the rows of plants. Something in his demeanor suggested he was thinking of dragging her behind a screen of leaves and fucking her. But soon another prisoner and her guard would be along; she could only pray that would be enough to keep him from attacking her.

They repeated this every day. He escorted her through her fifteen-minute walk, leering at her and making suggestive remarks the whole time, making it impossible for her to enjoy her brief period outside the cell. Then back to her prison, where she never knew when she'd glance up at her window to find him there, staring.

"What happened to the Demon Kin male?" she said.

Chisholm gave her a startled glance. "The Demon Kin?"

She'd never initiated conversation with him before, and he probably didn't know what to think.

"Yes. The male you...um...put me with." If her face got any hotter, it would catch on fire.

"Why would you care what happens to him?"

She gave her shoulders a careless lift. "I don't. I was only curious."

"He's in his cage, like all the other monsters."

There was so much contempt, so much naked hatred in his voice, that she turned her head and looked straight at him. "If they're such monsters, then why are you doing this? Why are you putting them with human women?"

Chisholm's jaw clenched. "It's not your place to ask questions, Bambi."

"It's not right."

"Shut your trap." His hand tightened so hard on her arm she knew she'd have another bruise by the next day.

She pinched her lips together. She shouldn't have provoked him in any way, and showing even a hint of sympathy for the Demon Kin had been a mistake. But she'd wanted to press him, to see what he'd do. She'd wanted to know why she was here; why the Demon Kin male was here.

What was his name? Why didn't he speak? How long had he been here?

She had so many questions about him and no way to get answers. Did the other women feel as curious as she did about their male counterparts? Did they understand that the Demon Kin were prisoners too?

Maybe her Demon Kin was the only one here.

No, she didn't believe that. There were too many women for only one male. Even a Demon Kin would have trouble keeping up with that many females. There had to be more of them around.

She and Chisholm reached her cell. He pressed a control he kept in his pants pocket and the door began to rise. Mercy half expected him to make a grab for her breasts, given the way he kept sneaking glances at them. But he just shoved her into the cell and closed the door, walking away without a comment.

She was alone again with nothing to do but wait. They wouldn't give her a happy link or even paper and a pencil to pass the time. She had no window. Nothing. No-one spoke to her.

To keep from going insane from lack of stimulation, she'd turned to singing all the songs she knew and inventing new ones. She made up stories about the people in the prison. She planned imaginary houses she wished she could own and imaginary dresses she wished she could sew, parties she'd like to give, places she would visit, if not in reality then at least in her mind.

And she thought about him. She remembered the taste of his mouth, the hot smooth skin beneath her palms, the silk of his hair. The way he'd shuddered and moaned when she touched him. The way he'd tried to calm her, comfort her, even while he did something she fought against.

Then she'd stopped fighting.

Something inside her was broken, or perhaps missing. Maybe she'd been born without a normal sense of feminine decency. How else could she explain her yearning for a man who'd so wronged her, a man who'd forced her to feel things no good Novus Vitan woman should ever feel?

But then she wasn't a good woman of any sort. She knew that now.

She despised him for his part in it. Maybe he hadn't volunteered, but he'd still gone after her. He'd touched her, tasted her...Mercy shivered. Sometimes she could almost feel his tongue on her flesh again.

They shoved her dinner through the tiny slot in the bottom of her door. Tonight it was some kind of ground meat formed into a huge ball, then baked and sliced and served with gravy. There were boiled potatoes on the side, and some wilted lettuce. The whole thing tasted like stale grease and salt and sat heavily in her stomach, although she only picked at it.

Sometime after her meal ended, but before they'd collected the dirty tray, her door rose. Mercy jumped off her bed and stared at it, her heart zooming crazily. They were sending her out into the corridor again.

Would it be him? Or would she get someone else? Her heart pounded even more heavily and her palms grew moist at the thought of seeing him again. She began to tingle and ache the same way she had when he'd pulled her against him.

What would happen if she refused to emerge? She didn't have to leave her cell. She could just sit back on her bed and wait.

But the Demon Kin would undoubtedly come and get her if she did that. She might as well go out and save him some trouble.

Chapter 8

Mercy took a hesitant step into the corridor. "Hello? Are you here?"

For a moment, there was nothing. No sound except the breath sawing unevenly in and out of her own lungs. Maybe she was wrong and this wasn't about the Demon Kin male. Maybe something else was going on. She didn't even want to speculate what that something else might be.

Then she heard someone stumbling and thumping his way along the corridor in her direction. Was it him? He sounded even more uncoordinated than the first time. It was probably the Maker's judgment on him for what he'd done to her.

Judgment would arrive one day for Mercy, too.

Since running would be pointless, she walked toward the noise. Her own steps made almost no sound on the padded floor, but he continued to thunder toward her like a drunk elephant.

Mercy rounded the first corner and stopped in astonishment. It was him, she was sure of it. Same height, same silvery horns, same long black hair. But he looked different. Ill. His hair seemed dry and lifeless and his gorgeous eyes were sunken, shadowed with such dark rings they looked bruised.

Every rib stood out in sharp, ugly relief. His cheeks were sunken, his face skull-like, the formerly beautiful muscles of his body wasted to nothingness. Beneath his short, scruffy beard, his jaw looked sharp as a blade. He looked like he was starving to death.

She stood frozen in shock as he staggered forward and dropped on his knees before her. He threw his arms around her waist, pressed his face against her belly and breathed in deep, his skeletal frame shuddering.

She ought to despise him. She did despise him. She did. But she remembered the lines of anguish on his face the first time, and how they'd eased a little after they'd had sex. Now he looked even more tortured and she had a horrible suspicion that sex had something to do with it.

Was it the Maker's judgment? Or something else? Something related to this despicable experiment?

Her trembling hands rose and rested on his bony shoulders. "What did they do to you?"

He answered with an animal groan, rubbing his cheek against the fabric over her belly. His hands kneaded the muscles of her lower back. Low sounds emerged from his throat, incoherent noises full of yearning and pain.

Suspended somewhere between hatred and compassion, Mercy hesitated, hands still on his shoulders. Clearly something terrible had been done to him.

Clearly he needed comfort. Help.

She didn't owe him anything. He'd done the unthinkable to her, and worse, he'd made her enjoy it. Their encounter had torn her apart, taken the last shred of belief she'd had in herself and trampled on it.

And yet...

She sank to her knees. His arms stayed around her. He drew her against his bare torso and bent his head to the crook between her neck and shoulder, nuzzling her.

Tears stung her eyes. She put her arms around him, feeling the hard projecting ridges of his spine, the bony cage of his ribs.

He lifted her gown and she did nothing to stop him. His hands hungrily skimmed her legs down to her ankles and then up, up to her thighs. His thumbs brushed her sex. She gasped, her whole body jumping at the touch.

He moaned and pressed his face between her thighs.

He was absolutely without shame and gently relentless in the way he pursued her.

She allowed him to lay her down on the soft floor, to spread her thighs apart, to kiss her already throbbing secret place. Her eyes rolled back in her head and she cried out at the stroke of his tongue.

Then he was over her, pushing inside her, and she wasn't ready but she accepted him anyway. She bent her knees, instinctively giving him more room to come into her. He felt unimaginably big, and male, and invasive. His sex dragged against hers, inside her, over her, pressing on sensitive spots that sent bolts of pleasure so intense it was almost pain through her whole body.

She grabbed onto him, scraping her fingernails across his skin. With a hoarse cry, he plunged all the way into her. His hips moved, thrusting in a desperate, inelegant rhythm, so fast and hard it nearly hurt. Yet the pleasure—the unholy pleasure overrode any pain, any desire she might have had to escape.

She could do nothing but hang onto him and endure. This was not at all like her experiences with Cletus, or Marcus either. It was brutal, but there was a savage joy in it that her earlier experiences had completely lacked.

Her hips worked against his as if they had a mind of their own, meeting him thrust for thrust, taking him deep. Soft, high-pitched gasps and whimpers escaped her throat. She couldn't help herself. There was something in her, something ancient and powerful that overrode the Teachings as if they'd never existed, and that something wanted him.

A blinding wave of ecstasy crashed through her and she screamed as it dissolved her. There was no warning. One instant she was caught in a rising swell of delight and the next she was coming apart.

The Demon Kin groaned and shook in her arms as he reached his own climax. Once again, he flooded her with ejaculate. Would she conceive a child by him? What would the Novus Vita Life Studies Research Center do with such a child?

Mercy's heart contracted. If she did conceive, she couldn't allow them to have the child. She'd rather die, rather the child died, than be raised by those men.

The Demon Kin relaxed on top of her, keeping most of his weight off her but otherwise going limp. His head bowed as he panted. Mercy found her hands rubbing his emaciated back, up and down in unconscious caresses. She was treating him like a husband. Like a lover.

No, that wasn't right. She was treating him the way she'd dreamed of touching a husband, not the way she'd ever interacted with Cletus.

Would they come and drag her away now? She had no idea how much time she'd have with him.

He pressed his lips to her forehead, the kiss almost reverent. Then another to her cheek. The other cheek. Her lips. She put her arms around his neck and opened her mouth to him.

The kiss seared her with its intimacy. The taste of him, the slide of his tongue over hers, his deep moans as he explored the interior of her mouth, it was all so much *more* than anything she'd ever had with the other two men who'd claimed her body. And she didn't even know his name. Didn't know if he could speak normally at all.

Was he mentally incapacitated? The way he'd looked at her suggested he was not. He seemed intelligent, and yet he didn't speak.

He thickened, lengthened inside her despite his recent climax, and began to rock his hips again. The long slides felt slick from all the moisture he'd already put into her. She moved with him, giving herself over to the passion, the joy.

Afterward, he gathered her against him the way a child might hold a soft, stuffed toy at bedtime. There was no sense in fighting him—she couldn't win. But for him to hold her after he was done with her—what did it mean? Bemused, Mercy let her head rest against his shoulder. Her left arm fell across his chest, her fingers brushing his rib cage. His heart beat loud and fast, his breath still rough from his exertions.

She rubbed her fingers across the taut cage of his rib bones, the sunken flesh between them. They must not be feeding him. Inexplicable anger rose up and tightened her throat at the notion they were deliberately starving him.

She didn't know why she cared about this alien creature who'd so wronged her. It was probably a sign of her moral weakness. Whatever the reason, she found it impossible to condemn him, impossible to look at his condition and not rage on his behalf. Yet the warmth of him soothed her and as her breath slowed she found her eyelids drooping.

Sometime later, she blinked sleepily and raised her head. She and the Demon Kin were entwined, arms and legs tangled together. He lay on his side now, facing her, his harshly beautiful features slack in sleep. He looked vulnerable that way. Almost innocent.

They'd slept together. The only other male she'd ever slept with had been Cletus, and that had never involved holding or cuddling.

Mercy lifted her hand and touched the fullness of his bottom lip with the tip of her forefinger. So soft.

Thick, black lashes fluttered. His lids slowly lifted. His gaze, hazy at first, sharpened, focusing on her. He gave her a lazy smile that revealed the tips of his fangs.

Her breath caught. Emaciated as he was, fangs clearly showing, his smile was dazzling. She flushed, her lips curling up to answer him.

"Hello," she murmured.

His eyes narrowed. "Heh...heh—low." His voice sounded rough and uncertain.

"You can talk?" she said, her eyes widening.

"Tah—"

Maybe not. Or maybe whatever they'd done to him had temporarily destroyed his ability to speak.

She pointed to her own chest. "My name is Mercy. Mercy."

"M-m-muh—" he repeated.

"That's right. Mercy."

"Muh—see." His large, male hand cupped the side of her face, almost dwarfing her skull. He smiled again, almost tenderly, his thumb stroking her bottom lip. "Muh—see."

She opened her mouth to ask him his name. But his head came up, his eyes focused on something she couldn't see. They were certainly alone in the gray corridor, so what was he looking at?

The Demon Kin sniffed. He looked down at her and grinned.

She smiled back uncertainly as he unwound himself from her and stood. When he extended a hand to her, she took it and let him draw her to her feet.

"What is it?"

He sniffed again and pointed down the hall.

"I don't understand."

The Demon Kin tugged on her hand, urging her to follow him. All right. She didn't know what he was doing, but there was nothing else for her to do, so she went along with it.

They passed her cell...she thought. It was difficult to tell one cell from another, but she sensed they'd passed the one she normally occupied. Several turns took them past the nook where they'd first...encountered each other.

40

Mercy glanced at the little dead-end hallway and shivered in memory. But he didn't stop there.

He led her through a couple more turns until they arrived at another cell, a bigger one this time. Its door was wide open. Inside was a much larger bed, one big enough to easily sleep the two of them, plus a table and two chairs, and a bench shoved against one wall. Two bowls sat on the table top.

She glanced at him. He sniffed and pointed into the room.

Mercy frowned. "You want to go in there?"

He tugged at her hand, still pointing.

"You know that's what they want us to do, right?"

The Demon Kin let go of her hand and walked into the cell, seeming completely unconcerned with the possibility he could be trapped inside. He sat down in one of the chairs, picked up a spoon and dipped it into the bowl, his long feline tail curling around his lower legs. After taking a bite, he looked up at her and motioned her toward him.

Mercy glanced first to one side and then the other. Of course, no-one was there. They were alone in the hall. No, *she* was alone in the hall. He was alone in the cell in front of her.

If she joined him, they could well be trapped together. But if she stayed out here and the cell door closed, they would be separated. Was that what she wanted?

Joining him would mean she accepted him on some level, that she wanted to be with him. He was unholy. A rapist. He'd made her do things, things she shouldn't want. He'd taken her from herself.

Yet just a moment ago, she'd been busy trying to get his name, as if they could be friends. Friends! A Novus Vitan could never be friends with a Demon Kin.

He made her forget who she really was, who she was supposed to be.

Her weight shifted from foot to foot as she pondered that. Was it better to be companion to a Demon Kin or better to remain alone?

Chapter 9

The station's night hours were arbitrary, but humans needed a day/night cycle that imitated that of their planet of origin as closely as possible. Demon Kin did, too, but their needs were largely irrelevant to Promise and the other Angels. The test subjects must only be kept alive long enough for the Life Studies Research Center to obtain the data they needed, so the day/night cycle really had little to do with them.

It was all for the staff. They had to remain healthy so they could carry out their duties and keep control over their test subjects. For health reasons, the majority of the guards slept during the night part of the cycle.

That left Promise alone when she found sleep unobtainable. She liked being alone. The offices, the control center, the greenhouse were all so quiet and peaceful when everyone else was asleep.

The monitors were still on tonight. Someone must have forgotten to turn them off. She padded over to them in her slippers. It was a waste of precious energy to leave them on like this and she'd have to speak to the staff in the morning. They had a strict budget here.

Most of the monitors showed empty gray corridors and darkened cells where the test subjects were all sleeping. She flicked them off one by one instead of returning to the main control panel where she could have dealt with them all at the same time. Why not walk around the room? There was nothing else to do, and moving around might help her get back to sleep.

The last monitor showed movement. She peered at it a little more closely. In the lower right hand corner, something that looked like a pair of feet twitched and moved. The feet seemed to be resting, as if their owner were laying down on the floor.

The cameras were supposed to move automatically to pick up any action in the corridor, so that test subject behavior didn't always have to be monitored by individual staff members. Someone needed to do a little adjustment to the program. Otherwise, they'd lose valuable data. She'd assign someone to that tomorrow; Promise didn't have enough knowledge of the programs they used to be able to do a good job of it.

This particular angle on the test subjects would be lost for now, but other cameras would pick up the event anyway. The Center had plenty of back-up.

It was late and Promise was tired. She ought to shut down the monitor and go back to bed. There would be another long day tomorrow, just one in what felt like an endless string of long days. She needed her rest.

Yet she sat down at the chair and adjusted the angle of the camera so it picked up its subject more completely.

There. A Demon Kin male, black-haired, with one of the new human females they'd acquired from the Novus Vitan prison system. He wasn't laying down; he knelt before the clothed female, his arms around her waist. Promise flinched at the sight of his naked body and their intimate embrace. Sexual behavior or thoughts were forbidden to the Angels, and entirely foreign to them. Angels did not have sexual feelings.

But he wasn't...taking her...as Promise had expected. He'd buried his face against her belly. There was anguish in his features.

She pressed her lips together. The Demon Kin was no doubt feeling quite sorry for himself at the moment. He was definitely showing the effects of long-term sexual deprivation on his species—mental derangement, appetite suppression leading to emaciation, loss of coherent speech, body-wide pain. The Center could only guess at the pain, since they couldn't get any answers directly from their Demon Kin subjects, but the males' behaviors certainly supported the idea that the deprivation caused them discomfort.

Promise would never cause any decent person pain. The Demon Kin were anything but decent, however. And this one had been a soldier, if she remembered correctly. He deserved, richly deserved, all the agony the Center could provide. All his kind did.

The woman wasn't fighting him. Usually they did everything they could to avoid being taken, and when it became obvious there was no escape they submitted with trembling and terror. This one looked more sad than fearful. She touched the male's bony, starved body as if she felt pity for him.

Promise shook her head. Perhaps confinement in the prison had affected the woman's sanity.

The male drew up the woman's ugly test subject gown and caressed her naked brown skin. She didn't protest. She made no attempt to flee. In fact, she touched him in return.

It was such an anomalous response compared to other subject pairings she'd seen that Promise checked the subjects' identification numbers and test history. Hmm. These two had been together before. They were part of the new phase of the experiment, in which the subjects had repeated exposure to each other, in order to promote enchainment, an addictive pattern of behavior sometimes seen between Demon Kin and their lovers.

Maybe the repeated exposure was what allowed the female to be unafraid of the male, although Promise herself would have been even more terrified the second time around. But perhaps there was some hormonal attraction, some kind of pheromone the male released that pacified the woman. They'd have to consider this new behavior when they designed the next phase of the experiments.

Promise leaned forward, watching intently as the two subjects kissed. She'd observed kissing behavior before, of course, both on Novus Vita and here at the Center. But this was different.

On Novus Vita, kisses were usually circumspect and brief, if they happened at all. Especially kisses between grown men and women. Public displays of affection were inappropriate. They caused forbidden feelings and thoughts, both in the people participating and in anyone who might see them.

She had no idea what grown men and women did together when they were alone, since she'd entered the Teacher training program at the age of six and hadn't had the opportunity to be courted.

Here at the Center, kissing occasionally happened between the Demon Kin males and the human females. More than occasionally. In fact, now that she thought about it, there had been kissing in every video recording she'd seen. However, she hadn't seen very many, since her work here was primarily administrative. It wasn't her job to actually watch the recordings. That was work for scientists, not administrators.

Still, nothing she'd seen so far had prepared her for this. The male laid the woman down on the cushioned floor, still kissing and touching her. They were holding each other as if they couldn't let go, as if they both wanted to merge together completely. The woman's fingers buried themselves in the man's hair. His hands traveled restlessly over the woman's body, squeezing her bare buttocks, her thighs, stroking her back only to pause to cup her full breasts.

The sight of those big hands on the woman's small body made something clench deep inside of Promise. She should not be seeing this. It was wrong. It was corrupting her—just like that other time, with the Demon Kin named Cain—even though she'd only watched this particular display for a few minutes.

And Cain—she must not think of him. Ever again. She must go on as if that kiss had never happened.

Promise could not look away from the monitor. The male now had the woman's dark nipple in his mouth. He was sucking on it, the way a baby sucks on its mother. The woman's head fell back, her lips parted, her lashes fluttering. Her hands clasped his head to her, as if to encourage him. Her moans were easily audible on the sound pick-up.

She wanted what he was doing to her. She liked it. There was no other explanation for her behavior.

The woman was a slut. Promise's quick perusal of her records had told her that immediately. She'd been convicted of whoring, so it should come as no

44

surprise that she enjoyed the illicit touch of this male.

It was disgusting. Did the woman have no pride? Did she have no spiritual inclinations whatsoever? It was bad enough to whore with her own species, but with Demon Kin? She must be entirely beyond redemption.

She—Promise—ought to look away. She really ought to look away. Watching these vids was not in her job description, so there was no reason for her to put her soul in danger by exposing herself to them.

She continued watching as the male worked his way down the female subject's body until he was nestled between her thighs. The woman simply opened her legs to allow him access, with not a hint of modesty or reluctance. She seemed eager to accommodate him.

He pressed his big hands to her inner thighs, spreading her even more. And then the most astonishing, unspeakable thing happened. He lowered his head and placed his mouth right between her legs. On her...on her sex.

Promise's own mouth fell open and stayed that way. She bent forward even more, narrowing her eyes at the screen in revulsion and fascination. No, not fascination. Disgust.

Yes, she was disgusted.

Was he biting her? The female test subject cried out, her head falling back, her mouth open. Her hands remained on his head, cradling him. Then she reached between her own thighs, her fingers pressed to her own flesh. She seemed to be spreading herself even more.

And then Promise knew. He was licking the woman's sex. It was the most perverted, bizarre act she'd ever seen or even imagined. And she could never have imagined this, not in a hundred million years. Who would do such a thing?

The Demon Kin, of course.

Heat flushed Promise's whole body. Her heart pounded and her body tingled with the weirdest sensations she'd ever felt. It was like the way she used to feel as a girl when something extra special was about to happen, like on the morning of a feast day. Like excitement, only different.

What was happening to her? What was wrong with her?

The Demon Kin continued licking and kissing the human in unspeakable ways for a long time. He seemed to enjoy what he was doing, if his enthusiastic-sounding groans were any indication. What would it be like to put one's mouth on another human's—or Demon Kin's—private parts? It didn't seem like the kind of thing any sane, normal being would enjoy.

The viewing should have become monotonous, yet still she couldn't look away. She found every movement of the subjects fascinating, every noise they made. And when the woman's moans turned to loud, frantic cries—they sounded almost like cries of pain, yet she made no attempt to escape him and even seemed to be encouraging him to continue—a penetrating, throbbing ache invaded Promise's body. Right between her legs and in her lower belly. Almost as if she...

No. That could not be true. She didn't want what he was doing to that other woman. She didn't want any of it.

He crawled back up the female's body and sealed his mouth to hers. His unclean mouth, foul with the residue of whatever he'd been doing to her sex. The thought of him kissing her after that...

No. What Promise felt was disgust. Not excitement. Not yearning. Never yearning.

The woman seemed to be helping him mount her. She had a hand between their bodies, as if guiding him into her. That made Promise frown. Why would she help?

Idiot. Why do you think? She obviously likes all this revolting carrying-on.

They both yelled as he sank into her. Promise's hands clutched hard at the edge of the desk. Her body ached insistently, asking for something she couldn't even name. She suspected. But she would not name it.

It was time to leave. Time to turn off the monitor, to vacate the office.

She kept watching.

The Demon Kin rhythmically flexed his hips, driving himself into the woman's body again and again. The woman wrapped her legs around his narrow waist and her arms around his shoulders. She moved, too, pushing upward against him. They looked ridiculous. Awkward, animal, ugly. It should have made Promise sick with revulsion. And yet she continued to watch.

The male threw back his head and roared as he climaxed in the woman's body. She seemed to take a bizarre pleasure in this, watching him, moaning, moving with him as he shuddered above her. How could she?

She's a criminal. A whore. She's not a decent woman.

But then he lowered his head and kissed her, and there was something in that kiss that made Promise's heart ache. His hand cupped the side of the woman's head. Her fingers dove into his hair. He drew away just far enough to press his lips to her forehead, her nose, her chin, as she continued to stroke his hair.

Tenderness. They displayed tenderness toward each other and it baffled her more than anything else she'd seen so far. She'd expected something else. Triumph on his part, shame on hers. Not tenderness.

It was over and the spell was broken. Promise turned off the monitor. She could leave now.

But she knew those images would never leave her. They'd be engraved on her mind forever.

Chapter 10

Mercy walked into the new cell. As soon as she'd cleared the door, it slammed down behind her. Although she'd expected it to close, the loud sound made her jump anyway.

The Demon Kin calmly continued eating his soup; although his hands still shook, he seemed unaffected by the door's closing. He must have expected it too. Or perhaps he simply didn't care anymore whether or not he was locked in a cell or loose in a hallway.

She glanced around, at the table with its two chairs, the huge bed, the soft-looking padded bench against the wall opposite the table.

He looked up, gave her a half-smile and gestured her closer. With a hard swallow, she went to him and took the empty chair. This was it. This was her accepting her fate, accepting that she wasn't the person she'd thought.

Now that she was at the table, she could smell the savory aroma of the soup. That must have been what had caught his attention and drawn him to this room. She'd heard his kind had a remarkable sense of smell, but she'd never seen it in action until now.

He pointed to her soup bowl, then to her. He wanted her to eat? Mercy shook her head. She had no appetite, and he looked like he needed it a great deal more than she did. He'd already finished his own portion. She pushed her bowl toward him and pointed at him.

"You have it," she said.

He raised his brows in an unvoiced question. She nodded, smiled a little, pushed the bowl toward him again. He pointed to it, looking at her and raising his brows again as he pulled it toward him. Mercy nodded.

His gaze softened. He reached out with his free hand and took one of hers, squeezed it gently. Although the touch was platonic, it aroused a flood of pleasure in her and she blushed.

There was so much feeling in the way he looked at her. She didn't know what to do with it or how to respond. The only thing she could think of was to squeeze his hand in return.

He kept hold of her while he ate, his manners impeccable although it was obvious he hadn't eaten in a long time and his spoon clinked randomly against the bowl from the shaking of his hand. The soup was thin, mostly broth with a few tiny bits of meat and vegetable floating in it. He ate it with so much relish it could have been ambrosia.

If only he could tell her his name, where he'd come from, why he was a prisoner.

When he'd finished the second bowl, he stood up, her hand still clasped in his, and led her to the attached bathroom. This one was more than twice as big as the tiny closet she'd had in her cell. He went to the shower and turned on the water, holding his hand under the stream to check the temperature. He still had her other hand in his.

The water adjusted to his satisfaction, he led her into the stall. Mercy had taken a shower that morning, but given his extremely sensitive sense of smell, maybe she offended him. On the other hand, he didn't look or smell as if he'd bathed with soap in quite a while.

Was bathing together some kind of Demon Kin ritual? If so, what did it mean to him?

She stood under the generous stream of hot water and stared up at him, wondering what he expected her to do. He simply stared down at her, a faint smile curling his lips and warming the deep brown of his eyes. His hands weren't shaking at the moment. The soup must have done him some good, then.

She turned to find the soap. He restrained her with a hand on her shoulder, reaching across her to take the soap for himself.

Mercy flushed. She'd never bathed with a man before, but she ought to have known it was proper for the male to go first. That was how everything worked on Novus Vita, and apparently it was true on Malefica—no, they called it Belleren, didn't they?—as well.

Then he set the bar aside and lifted his soapy hands to her neck, massaging the muscles on either side of her spine gently as he washed her skin. Her mouth opened as she stared up at him. He was washing her. Why would he do that?

"Muh—see." His voice was deep and low, and it seemed to vibrate inside her, making her achy and hot.

She pointed at him. "You? I am Mercy. You?"

His beautiful eyes narrowed. He shook his head. His hands continued washing over her shoulders, her arms, down to her hands. He lifted each one and carefully soaped her fingers one by one, massaged her palm and between the bones of her hand.

A slight tremor began in his hands as he reached again for the bar of soap. Mercy caught his wrist.

"You don't have to wash me," she said, holding her palm up for the soap.

He shook his head. He lifted his hands, his eyes fixed on hers, and cupped her breasts. Her face flushed as a bewildering mixture of shame and arousal flooded her. She arched her back without even thinking about it or noticing at

48

first that she was doing it. She pushed her breasts more deeply into his palms, a barely audible moan escaping her.

The Demon Kin brushed suds across her curves, her sensitive nipples, drawing another gasp from her. He molded her flesh, squeezed, then brushed the tight, deep-brown buds of her nipples again.

If they hadn't drugged her food, then he must have cast some kind of spell on her. This wasn't the way she behaved. It wasn't even something she could have imagined herself doing before she'd met him. Yet every time he touched her or even appeared in her field of view, she reacted this way to him, as if she were made of lust.

Maybe this *was* the way she behaved. Maybe she'd never really known herself.

He washed her belly, the indented curves of her waist, the planes of her back, all his movements slow and appreciative, almost worshiping. Then he dropped to his knees and picked up her right foot.

The soft brush of his fingertips there tickled. She giggled, twitching and trying to pull back when he touched her sole. He smiled up at her, but he didn't release her. He was just as relentless with her feet as he'd been when he'd taken her.

She tried to pull away a second time. He shook his head at her.

"Shhh," he said. "Muh—*Mer*—see. Let."

Let. That was a word. A real word in Galactic Standard. He was starting to talk.

She put a hand on his shoulder to communicate how glad she was to hear his words, but he didn't seem to notice. All his attention was focused, lavished, on her foot and from there upward to her ankles, calves, thighs.

He rubbed soap suds over the generous curves of her ass, his strong fingers digging gently into the tense muscles beneath her skin. And then between the cheeks of her ass, one finger sliding up and down, slick and soapy. The forbidden touch seemed unbearably erotic to her. She had to place her other hand on his other shoulder to keep from falling to the floor at the wave of longing that crashed over her.

Finally, there was only one place on her body he hadn't washed yet. He slid soapy fingers into the creases at the tops of her thighs, sliding back and forth the way he had in that other crease. His big hands nudged her thighs apart, and she let him.

Something about the gentleness of his touch, combined with his insistence on washing her, made tears spring up in her eyes. No-one had touched her this way, with such sweetness all tangled up in persistent eroticism. No-one but she had ever taken care of her body at all since she was a very small child.

He rinsed her sex and stood, his brows puckered as a hot tear ran down her cheek. A low sound escaped his throat. He tipped up her chin and kissed her, a brush of his lips against her mouth.

"Mer-see," he murmured. "Mer-see."

The kiss moved deeper, his tongue invading her mouth and sending a terrible pang of yearning right to her core. Mercy grabbed for his shoulders as her knees buckled. He cradled her head, his touch controlling yet tender. How did he do it? How did he make her want him so much without using any of the brutal tactics she expected?

He wasn't anything she could have expected.

He'd taken everything from her, yet paradoxically he'd also given her so much, things she'd never imagined before she'd met him.

She reached blindly for the soap. It slipped out of her hands and fell to the floor, where it slid toward the drain. He didn't seem to notice. He was too busy devouring her, one large hand splayed across the small of her back, the other still holding her skull.

Mercy drew back, tugging against his attempt to keep her in place. He shook his head at her.

"Mer—see," he said in his slow voice. "Let."

She bent and snagged the soap, holding it up for him to see. He reached for it, but she yanked it away from him, rubbing it quickly between her hands. It smelled resinous, yet sweet, like some kind of mountain herb.

With her hands soapy, she placed them on the still-impressive muscle of his chest. "Let me wash you now."

He watched her soberly as she slid her hands across his skin. Without words, she had no idea what he was thinking. But words didn't always reveal people's thoughts; they concealed them as often as not, with lies and misdirection. Glancing up at his face, she saw tenderness and yearning there, even more than lust. Or maybe that was her own wishful thinking.

Chapter II

The words refused to come to him. They were there in his brain, piling up like rocks in a landslide in his throat, his mouth, wedging themselves one against the other in their eagerness to escape him. He could say nothing.

She was so...so...sweet. Perfect. Lovely. Exquisite.

Her eyes, large and dark and long-lashed, watching him warily like a rock-deer startled at some mountain spring. Her slender legs and the extravagant curves of her hips, the glorious fullness of her breasts, the smooth pale-cocoa of her skin. Even the strangeness of her cropped, brush-like black hair charmed him.

Her tiny hands hesitated at his chest, as if she feared to touch him. And he remembered, knew without knowing why, that she was afraid because he was male and she didn't know him well and he was of a different people than hers. She had no horns, no tail. He did.

He terrified her.

That thought made him croon to her, low in his throat so as not to frighten her even more. They'd joined together twice now, but she still did not believe he would never hurt her. She still feared.

She swallowed. Her small, pink tongue emerged to wet her lower lip, making his cock twitch and jump to attention. He needed her touch, needed it desperately. Orgasms weren't enough to restore him now; he needed as much contact as he could get and for a sustained period of time in order for his body and mind to heal. But he couldn't rush her.

So he waited, trembling inside and out and fighting not to let it show. She needed to believe in him, have faith that he wouldn't leap on her and simply take what he wanted. His tail twitched, wanting to lash back and forth in excitement, and he stilled it, forced it to remain expressionless.

She rubbed soap suds across his chest and up to his shoulders, lingering when she crossed his collarbones. Then up to his neck, his throat. He bent his head so she could wash his face.

Her touch was light there, like a whisper, but he felt it all the way to the soles of his feet. She explored him with her fingertips, rushing over his forehead and cheekbones, lingering across his brows, his nose, his temples. She reached his ears and pinched an earlobe gently between her fingers, rubbing. A low moan escaped him.

For an instant, he stopped breathing. His display had probably scared her, even repulsed her. She was of a people—the word...what was the word—who hated sexuality, hated the body, hated any kind of affectionate display.

Yet she didn't seem upset. Her beautiful face bore a look of wonder as she continued to touch and explore him.

She collected some shampoo and he leaned down so she could rub it into his scalp. Her fingers in his hair felt so good his eyes drifted shut. The sense of pleasure and connection between them deepened with every stroke of her hands, soaking into the fibers of his body and gradually saturating his mind and soul. She brought healing to him, profound and sweet.

If only he could get them both out of here. Wherever here was. He couldn't say the words, couldn't even find them under the rockfall that his speech had become. But he didn't need words to know this was a bad place, a cruel and evil place of torment and humiliation and eventual death. He could smell it in the air, sense it in the energy fields of the station. They'd crippled him, psychically, yet no implant could disguise the aura of malice and despair that permeated this place.

Mercy...her name meant something important. He would know what it was if only he could decipher the scrambled noises people made when they talked.

She finished with his hair and resumed washing his skin, moving down his back and skimming lightly over his ass. When she touched him there, she gasped and jerked her hands away, blushing. He smiled at the bashful look on her face and caught her hands, guiding them back.

She stared up at him, her lips slightly parted. Did she think he wouldn't want her touching him there? He dug around for the correct word to reassure her.

"Good," he finally managed. "Mer—see touch. Good."

"Good?" she whispered. Her fingers slid hesitantly over the sides of his hips.

"Good." He nodded. "Good."

Her breath caught as her fingertips brushed the base of his tail. His breath caught too. That was an exquisitely sensitive area she was exploring. He wanted to encourage her, so he kept himself utterly still as she petted his tail, her eyes going perfectly round.

A rush of words spilled from her mouth. He couldn't understand more than a handful of them. She sounded...agitated. Angry? No, not angry. Excited, maybe.

He wished she would touch his cock. But she wasn't ready for that. He would scare her if he tried to put her hand there. Instead, he let her pull away and hand him the soap, and he finished the job of washing his body on his own.

They were here in a cell together now. Maybe they would have time later for further exploration. The jailers might allow them to stay together for a time. Not for long, though. He knew he couldn't keep her. They could come to steal her from him at any moment.

* * *

The Demon Kin toweled her off with more of that speechless tenderness that seemed to be natural to him. Then he picked her up and carried her into the front room and laid her on the bed. He lifted her so effortlessly, even though he was emaciated. What could he do if he decided to hurt her?

She didn't think he would, though. Maybe it was stupid of her, but she was beginning to trust him. He could have done anything he wanted to her and no-one would have stopped him. Would they? If he struck her, would guards appear and shoot him with another tranquilizer? Or would they simply watch through their damned cameras and do nothing?

Maybe the potential for violence was also part of the experiment.

He was everything she was supposed to fear and hate. He bore the horns and tail of a devil. His entire race had been named after a breed of evil spirits from Old Earth, and the Teachings clearly stated they were aptly named. They stood for gross licentiousness, for laziness and violence and lust and greed—nearly everything the Teachings and the Maker Himself forbid.

They were the embodiment of evil.

Yet he hadn't hurt her. He'd caused her no pain. No injury. In fact, he'd done everything he could to ensure she wouldn't be afraid.

He only did that to keep you quiet so he could have an easier time of taking you.

No, she told her inner voice. That wasn't true. He could easily have pinned her, forced her, without raising a sweat. He was Demon Kin and she was a puny human. Overpowering a human woman like her would be no challenge for him. His motives in calming her had to stem from something else.

Mercy glanced up at the ceiling. There was a camera immediately over the bed, its black shiny surface staring down at them like an unblinking eye. Were they watching even now?

Probably.

Loathsome, evil men. She despised them. Before she'd met her Demon Kin, she'd thought she despised his people. But that sense of resentment and fear was nothing compared to the implacable hatred she had for the people who ran this facility. At least the Demon Kin were honest about what they were trying to do. The researchers here used human women, their own women, in their experiments and couldn't even be bothered to inform them what they were studying.

They caused Novus Vitan women to be raped by aliens. They starved men like her Demon Kin, abused them so badly they lost their ability to speak. For surely he couldn't be the only one of his kind in the facility. She had no proof, but she was sure in her gut that there were more Demon Kin. Probably many more, all kept in cells and starved and abused and set as rapists on human women.

What kind of monsters would come up with a plan like that?

The Demon Kin paused in nuzzling her neck. He lifted his head and regarded her with a puzzled frown, stroking her hair from her face.

"Muh—*Mer*—see?"

She almost voiced her suspicions out loud. Her mouth opened to tell him what she saw, but she stopped herself just in time. She didn't want *them* to know she was aware.

So she pulled his head back to hers. "They are watching us," she whispered, slowly and carefully.

"Mer-see?" Although he only repeated her name, he managed to invest that single word with all his bafflement.

She was reasonably sure he was telling her he didn't understand.

"Camera," she whispered. "Ceiling."

He shook his head.

Mercy sighed. His language skills weren't yet up to a real conversation. She could only hope he'd recover enough for them to have a talk before their captors forced them apart again.

He buried his face against her neck again, nibbling at her skin. "Mer-see. Let m-m-me."

His hand left her upper arm to cup her breast. She gave another sigh, this one of growing pleasure and excitement as he massaged her sensitive flesh. So they were watching. So what? They'd done it before and she'd survived. How much more humiliated could she become? She'd probably reached the bottom already.

He latched onto her nipple, suckling with tender ferocity. Mercy clutched his head to her, burying her fingers in his wet hair, moaning and wriggling helplessly beneath his sensual assault. He did everything to her he'd done before, but more of it. He tormented her breasts as if he could spend the rest of his life there, pleasuring her. His teeth closed on her aching nipples, yet the slight pain they caused only deepened her arousal.

Her womb contracted in longing as the sweet, nearly unbearable tugging and biting went on and on.

When she thought she could take no more, he left her breasts, kissing and licking his way down her belly. Was he going to...kiss her...there? Again?

She opened her legs so he could settle himself between them. He looked up, along the length of her body, and smiled at her. That dazzling smile. She couldn't resist it, any more than she could resist the rest of him. She smiled back.

He pushed her legs farther apart, opening her completely to him. This time, Mercy didn't bother trying to cover herself. She knew he wouldn't let her. And the truth was, she didn't want to. She waited in quivering anticipation for his mouth on her.

When he finally licked the very tips of her folds, she cried out and her eyes rolled to the back of her head. Such a delicate touch to create a mind-boggling response.

He growled softly and licked her again. She hadn't known there could be so much pleasure in the world. Before him, she'd never guessed this shameful part of her could provide pleasure at all. And he licked her, tasted her, gazed at her, all as if there were no shame. As if that part of her were a temple and he worshiped there.

His tongue was like liquid joy. He probed and caressed every nook and cranny of her sex, making her aware of herself in a way she'd never been. She hardly touched herself there. She always kept a cloth between her hand and the embarrassing landscape of her sex so that she might not know any more than necessary about it. And here he was, outlining every curve and undulation with the ecstasy of his mouth.

He found an exquisitely sensitive spot and teased it mercilessly until she shattered with loud cries, her fingers grasping frantically at the covers of the bed.

Then he covered her, his mouth devouring hers, tasting of her body. Mercy wrapped her legs around his waist and reached between them to guide him into her. Maybe what they were doing was wrong. It was definitely against the Teachings. She didn't care. This thing they shared between them had taken hold of her and she never wanted it to end.

They both climaxed screaming. Then they fell asleep in each other's arms. This time, she didn't hesitate to snuggle into his embrace and close her eyes. This time, it didn't seem foreign or childish. It seemed necessary.

Chapter 12

When she awoke, he was sitting at the table, staring at the wall, his gaze far away. Mercy sat up, rubbing sleepily at her eyes. She felt she'd been asleep for hours, possibly all night.

He didn't seem to notice she was awake. She watched him for a while, wondering what he was doing. He never moved except for his black tail slashing back and forth. He hardly blinked. But the corners of his mouth were curled downward and his eyes drooped, as if dragged down by a terrible weight of sorrow.

She slid out of bed and walked to him. Put her hand on his shoulder. His body stiffened, as if in self-defense. He looked up at her, and she could see the pain in his eyes.

"M-my n-nn-name...is...Storm," he said, the words emerging with agonizing slowness.

"Storm."

"Yes. Storm."

"You can talk!"

He snorted. "M-mm-maybe."

Mercy stroked the back of his neck. "You look upset. What is it?"

He shook his head.

"You can tell me."

Storm glanced at her warily. "You...hate. You *sh-should* hate...me."

"I don't hate you."

A line appeared between his strong, black brows. "You should."

"Why?"

His mouth turned down even more. "Mercy. You...ask? You know. Why."

"Because we...because you took me?" Her face burned at her bold words, but she wouldn't take them back. They'd done everything together and there was no further reason to be ashamed.

"You...did not...want. Me." He turned his face away from her.

"Why did you...you know...." She waited for an answer, but he gave her nothing. "Storm, why did you take me if you knew I didn't want it?" And more to the point, why was he feeling guilty at this late date?

"H-hhad to." He grimaced. "M-mm-made mme."

That sounded unlikely. "They made you? How did they do that?"

He shoved his fingers through his hair until they bumped into one of his horns; then he grabbed the strange, curling form projecting from his skull and tugged on it. "S-ss-starved m-me. N-nn-need sex."

She frowned, confused. "Don't all men need sex?"

That was what she'd always been told, anyway. Men needed sex and it was a woman's duty to provide her husband with what he needed. Her needs were irrelevant.

"N-nn-not like us." He growled. "W-words. H-have n-nn-no words."

He projected more shame, frustration, and self-loathing sitting in that chair, tongue-tied and struggling to communicate despite his problems, than anyone she'd ever known. The evidence of his non-humanity was right in front of her, unmistakable and impossible to ignore—a long, black tail that lashed from one side to the other in clear agitation, and a pair of curling gray horns that should have made him look like a terrifying devil. But she didn't see the devil anymore. Somehow, all she could see was a man who suffered.

She took his hands. "You don't have to explain it all to me now. Your speech will get better and you can tell me then."

He looked up at her, his fingers lacing themselves through hers. Then he yanked her against him, burying his face in her naked breasts with a soft groan. His arms enfolded her as she released his hands. She touched him, put her hands on his head, in his hair, brushed her fingertips against the bases of his horns. His tail brushed against her naked legs. It was as soft as a cat's tail.

His shoulders heaved. He made a strangled sound in his throat, almost like a sob. What could cause a man like him so much agony? Why would he regret what he'd done with her, when he'd been so insistent on pursuing her in the first place? Nothing she'd ever heard about the Demon Kin had given her the notion that they had any standards or restrictions on sexual behavior. They did whatever they liked, whenever they wanted to. But he obviously hurt over something having to do with their sexual encounters.

❖ ❖ ❖

Storm fought back the weakness and tears that threatened to overwhelm him. The last person on whom he could unload his guilt and shame should be Mercy. She was his victim; she shouldn't be expected to comfort him.

He didn't deserve comfort.

She'd already been far more generous than he deserved. She'd cooperated with him, reciprocated some of his kisses and caresses, even contributed her own. She'd given herself over to him once she'd gotten over her initial terror. That was much more than he could ever have expected, much more than he was entitled to. Yet still she let him cling to her like a little boy.

She was an exceptional woman, no matter her planet of origin.

If only he could tell her everything, explain what they'd done to him and why it had forced him to behave so shamefully. But his words still jammed up against each other, sticking in his mouth and throat so he couldn't get out more than a few two-word phrases.

The soft click of a door panel opening caught his attention and he turned his head toward the entrance. This luxurious cell had the same small opening in the bottom of the door as all the other cells, and someone outside was pushing a tray of food through it. The smell of coffee, eggs, and freshly baked bread instantly perfumed their small space.

"Breakfast," Mercy said. "It smells incredible." She smiled at him. "They're spoiling us."

He raised his brows at her, trying to communicate without words.

"All I've had here for breakfast so far is sticky, overcooked oatmeal," she said. "You?"

He grunted and nodded. He was like some damned primitive beast, forced to rely on grunts and pointing fingers. Sometimes he hardly recognized himself in the captured animal he'd become.

She climbed off his lap and went to pick up the tray, bringing it back to the table. "Can you eat?" she said. "I don't want you to make yourself sick if your stomach is all shrunk."

Storm shrugged. "Eat. G-get s-ss-sick. Cares?"

She stared at him for a moment, her hand poised over the coffee carafe. "I care."

That made him frown. "W-why?"

"I don't know. I guess it doesn't make any sense, but that's how it is. I don't want you to get sick."

Storm rose, stalked to her, kissed her forehead. "Mercy. G-good." He kissed her again, wishing his damned stupid words would obey his orders.

Her smile wobbled. "Come on," she said in a shaky voice. "Let's eat something."

His stomach was still not back to normal and he could only pick at his food. Mercy did little better. She managed a full cup of coffee and a small portion of eggs along with one of the rolls the guards had sent. He got about three bites of egg and a few sips of coffee before his stomach rebelled and he had to stop.

He glanced over at his companion. She wasn't like other Novus Vitan women he'd met. She seemed more educated, better read, and much less hostile to him. Most Novus Vitan females treated his kind as if they were walking nightmares, hissing and flinching if they had to pass him on the street, making furtive gestures of protective magic when they thought he wouldn't notice. They seemed even more hateful most of the time than their men. But Mercy was different and he wondered why.

He set his fork down and caught her gaze. "Mercy. Y-you tell. W-where ch-ch-child?" The last word almost refused to emerge.

"I don't have any children," she said sadly, her head beginning to droop.

"N-no. *You* child."

"Me? You mean where did I grow up?" She seemed surprised, as if she couldn't understand why he'd want to know such a thing.

He nodded.

"Oh. Um, well, it was a little town in the mountains in Northern Novus Vita. We raised goats and sheep." She smiled bashfully. "I'm just an ignorant farm girl."

He shook his head forcefully. "No. N-not ig-ignorant."

Her lush lips pressed together as she blushed. "I got in a lot of trouble as a girl for reading when I was supposed to be doing chores. My mother couldn't understand why I wanted to overtax my mind by reading books. That was what she called it." She gave a charming giggle. "Overtaxing my mind."

Storm smiled at her. "Glad."

Her doe eyes went even rounder. "You are?"

He nodded again. "S-smart."

Now she blushed even more brightly. "Women aren't supposed to be smart. Or educated."

He reached across the table and caught her hands. "S-smart. Sex-sexy. Beautiful."

She ducked her head. "No. No, I'm not. I'm too small. And my h-hair—it's all gone—" She broke off with a shake of her head.

"M-mercy. Still b-beautiful." He let go of one of her hands to reach out and stroke the crown of her head.

She shook her head, her eyes pained. "No, Storm. I'm not. I'm ugly. My hair is ugly and inside—inside, I'm ugly too."

He stood up, pulling her to her feet. "Mercy, you n-*not* ugly." He cupped her face. "Let m-me sh-sh-*show*."

She allowed him to take her to the bed, to sit her down and put his arm around her narrow shoulders. He traced the arc of her delicate, black eyebrow and the straight run of her little nose. "Eyes," he said. "Beautiful."

She gave him another wobbly smile.

"Nose. Beautiful." He brushed across her lower lip, then her upper. "Mouth, beautiful. M-most beautiful wo-woman, Mercy."

Those lovely eyes glistened as she watched him.

Storm drew his fingertip down the column of her neck, across her collarbone to the beginning of that intriguing valley between her breasts. He tapped lightly. "Heart. Beautiful. S-sweet."

A tear escaped and tumbled down her cheek.

"Oh. N-no. Shhh." He brushed it away. "Mercy, shhh."

She turned to him and flung her arms around his neck. His heart struggled between pangs of sadness that people—life itself—had caused her to feel so bad about herself and joy that she embraced him willingly and on her own.

The soft crush of her breasts against his chest was almost more than he could bear without lowering her to the mattress and mounting her. They were already bonding, perhaps even on their way to enchainment, a condition among Demon Kin and their partners that often followed repeated sexual activity with a single lover. He'd never been enchained before, had never desired that. He'd avoided anything more than brief sexual encounters for that reason. Until now.

If they were enchained, then the gods help them when their captors separated them again. Enchained partners could not withstand more than a few days of separation without severe pain, both emotional and physical.

He should separate them now. He could sleep on the floor and they could refrain from touching each other. Maybe then they could hold enchainment at bay and avoid the agony of being parted. Because he was sure beyond any doubt that the jailers would soon be back to tear them away from each other.

But then she lifted her face to his and he found himself drowning in another all-encompassing kiss, and he knew. It was too late. They were already enchained.

Chapter 13

Promise's favorite place on the station was the greenhouse. They only grew fruits and vegetables there, nothing especially decorative. But that was how she, as an Angel, liked it. Decorative plants were vain, frivolous, useless things that took up space better allotted to food crops.

It was probably frivolous of her to love the place so much, given that she had no practical reason to be there. That didn't stop her from sneaking in every chance she got, when she needed a break from her work or on her infrequent off-hours. She liked the brilliant light used to grow the plants, and the quiet, when the gardeners were gone and she could be alone with the green.

Plants never made demands. They never criticized. They never made filthy remarks about women's bodies and then sent her sidelong glances as if to see if she'd noticed.

She'd just taken a few deep breaths of plant-scented air when the greenhouse door opened. Promise stiffened, turning around in irritation she couldn't quite hide. Had she made a mistake reading the schedule or were these interlopers the ones who'd made the mistake?

Her body tightened even more when she saw who it was. Chisholm and one of the female prisoners—er, test subjects. The guards took the women for daily short exercise walks in the greenhouse. Promise had been sure she'd chosen a time when no walks were scheduled; she must have been wrong.

She got up from the bench she'd been occupying and walked down an aisle of lettuces toward the two. Staying here with them around would not be relaxing; it would probably make her even more tense than usual, so she'd leave instead.

The woman had extremely long, blond hair she wore in a single braid that hung down her back. She had a strained expression that implied Chisholm was not especially pleasant company. Promise pinched her lips together as she approached the female. The tramp wouldn't be here if she hadn't been living a disreputable, dissolute life, so it served her right if she was unhappy with her situation. The Maker always brought just desserts to those who deserved them.

The woman's blue eyes fastened on Promise's face. Her shoulders straightened and she took on an air of determination that made Promise cringe inwardly. She didn't care for that woman's look.

"You're that Angel they talk about," the prisoner—er, test subject—said. "Aren't you?"

"Yes, I am," Promise said in a chilly voice.

"Are you really in charge?" The woman sounded disbelieving.

Novus Vitans rarely put women in charge of anything except housework, so Promise couldn't hold that against her.

"Yes, I am," she said.

"Oh, Miss." The blonde laid a hand on Promise's arm. "Please, I need a word with you."

She glared pointedly at the hand, but the blonde either didn't notice or didn't care. "I don't give private audiences to prison—uh—test subjects."

"But I must speak with you. Please, I'm begging you." The woman pleaded with her big, blue eyes.

"No. You can say anything you need to say right here."

The test subject glanced at Chisholm. "Can he wait outside?"

Chisholm shook his head, his thin lips nearly vanishing in disapproval. "I wouldn't recommend that, Angel Promise."

"Thank you, Chisholm, but I can make my own decisions."

This made Chisholm scowl and the young blonde light up in so much hope it was painful to see.

"He stays here," Promise said. "What is it you wish to say?"

The blonde deflated. "I only—I just—"

"Well, what is it? I don't have all day."

The test subject raised her head, her hand clutching painfully at Promise's arm. "Let me go. Please, Miss Angel, I haven't done anything wrong. There's been a terrible mistake. I can't stay here; it isn't right!"

Promise peeled her hand off her arm and frowned at her as sternly as she could. "The Maker doesn't commit mistakes."

"The Maker?"

"We do the Maker's work here and we have His full blessing. He does not make mistakes. Therefore, it must be right for you to be here."

"But—no! That isn't true!"

How dare she question an Angel? Did she put herself above her Teachers? Did she think she had even a tenth the understanding an Angel had, after a lifetime of study, contemplation, dedication? She was a profane creature to say such a thing, especially to the Angel's face.

Promise glared down at her. "You commit blasphemy, girl. I suggest you think twice before you open your mouth to me again."

The blonde paled, her already light skin going pasty white. "I'm sorry, Angel. I didn't mean it."

"Didn't you?"

"No! I'm not bad. I'm not. But I don't belong here. Do you know what they're doing to us? They're setting Demon Kin on us. Why? Why are they allowing this?"

Chisholm laughed. "You're talking to the wrong lady, Kerin. Angel Promise helped design the most recent stage of this program, along with Dr. Gliptrout. She thinks it's a grand thing you're here."

Kerin gaped up at Promise. "Is that true?" she said in an appalled tone. "Did you help design this? Whatever this is?"

Promise shot a glare at Chisholm. He'd once been extremely reliable, which was why she tolerated him in spite of his sliminess. But he'd grown more and more openly resentful of her lately, and now he'd just spilled the truth, that there were scientists here with a designed program involving the Demon Kin and the women. If the blonde—Kerin—were smart, she could figure out for herself they were conducting experiments. And the program was supposed to be a secret.

Never mind. Kerin will never leave here, except as a corpse, so it doesn't matter.

"Yes," Promise said evenly. "It's true. We're conducting important work for the future of Novus Vita. You should feel honored to be included."

Kerin's face twisted. "Honored," she spat.

"Yes. Honored."

"You're a woman. Don't you have any pity for other women? You're just like me. How would you feel if someone did this to you?"

Promise drew herself up to her full, rather impressive height, her jaw clenched. "I am not in any way like you, Kerin. I am nothing like you. Now get out of my way. I have nothing more to say to you."

Chisholm pulled the blonde aside and Promise swept past them, head held high.

"You bitch!" Kerin yelled. "You're no Angel."

"Shut up," Chisholm barked.

The smack of flesh on flesh told Promise that he'd slapped her. Good. She needed to learn some manners.

Chapter 14

There was nothing to do in this cell except talk, eat, sleep, have sex. After another round of love-making, Mercy and Storm fell asleep in each other's arms. But they awoke apart again.

She opened her eyes to find him sitting on the gray padded bench their captors had left pushed against one wall. He was staring off into blank space again, with that same look of abstracted anguish on his beautiful features. She wondered if anyone had ever told him his heart was beautiful, sweet.

Watching his pain hurt her. She felt as if her soul had somehow become connected to him by an invisible chain or cord that she couldn't sever. She wouldn't sever it even if she knew how. Was that love? Did she love Storm? It was so soon.

She got out of bed and went to him, resting her hand on the top of his head, right between his horns. "You're torturing yourself over things you couldn't control."

"That does...not...make it b-better."

Mercy rubbed her fingertips against his scalp, eliciting a sigh from him. "You told me you had to do it."

He propped his elbows on his naked thighs and put his head in his hands. His broad shoulders bowed, as if weighted down with unbearable pressure. "Yes. I had to."

"Why?"

"M-my kind need sex. Mercy. My kind go m-mad without it. W-we l-ll-lose our speech. Our r-ration-rationality."

She stood there with her hand on his shoulder, stunned and unable to respond. Demon Kin needed sex to maintain their sanity? So he'd been forced...

"They wouldn't allow you to have sex?" she said.

"No. Not even m-my own hand."

That admission made her blush again. He said it so bluntly, didn't seem the least bit ashamed that he pleasured himself, a thing forbidden on Novus Vita.

"And then they set you on me," she said.

He bowed his head even more deeply. "You. And others."

"Others?" An irrational surge of jealousy spiked through her. These others—had he done the same things to them that he'd done to her? The image of him with his head between some other human woman's thighs made her

64

furious. Made her stomach churn.

It was the most nonsensical part of this whole experience, that she could be jealous of other victims. She had no claim on the Demon Kin...on Storm. He wasn't hers. He could never be hers. Except she suspected she loved him...and didn't that make him hers after all?

Perhaps not. Perhaps she was his, but not the other way around.

"They would...make me wait," he said, his words still painfully slow. "Until I was n-nearly mad. Then they would set me f-free in the corridor with a w-w-woman." He swallowed heavily. "I tried to stay away fr-from them. But I couldn't."

Her own voice felt small and tight. "Why couldn't you?"

"Because I stopped thinking l-like a civilized being." He finally raised his head and met her gaze. "I couldn't sleep. Couldn't eat. All I knew was I had to have a woman. I'm s-sorry, Mercy. Truly sorry."

His eyes looked glossy, as if tears were gathering and threatening to spill over. She couldn't be angry with him when he seemed so remorseful, so pained by his own behavior. She'd given up on being angry with him anyway. At some point during the night before, she'd come to recognize her own desire for him, had accepted it.

"It wasn't your fault," she said.

"I could have done something. I should have done something."

"Such as?"

"I don't know." He shook his head. "Killed myself, perhaps."

Her whole body twinged with pain at the thought of him dying in any way, let alone by his own hand. "No. Storm, don't say that."

"It would have pre-prevented a lot of pain." His voice sounded rough now. Ragged.

She laid her palm against the side of his jaw. "Storm. You wouldn't have prevented anything. They would have found someone else."

He looked up at her. "What do you mean?"

Mercy hesitated. She resisted the urge to look over her shoulder at the camera. Instead, she bent down and pretended to kiss his ear. "They are running an experiment," she whispered, nuzzling him, her body responding to his nearness despite the awkward conversation. "We're their subjects. They have cameras in the ceiling."

He put his hand over hers, whispering too. "Even here?"

"Yes. They're all over the place. In the hallway. In here. I think they've been watching us...you know..."

"Having sex."

"Yes."

"I'm ashamed I didn't figure that out on my own," he said, shaking his head.

"Don't your people have psychic powers?" That was part of their terrifying mystique, after all.

"They did something to me to prevent me from using them." He lifted her hand and placed it on the back of his neck. "There's an implant under my skin."

She rubbed her fingers lightly over the area until she felt it—a tiny, rectangular lump over his spine. "Could you tear it out?"

"I'm not sure I would survive," he said. "I tried when I first got here and I went into convulsions before I got it even half-way out."

"Oh, Storm. They crippled you. Those bastards."

He brought her head down to his and pressed his forehead against hers. Then he drew her onto his lap, wrapping his arms around her middle and holding her there. They sat together, not speaking, just holding each other.

Maybe she ought to hate him for what he'd done to her, but she couldn't. He was just as much a prisoner as she, just as compelled to acts he didn't want to perform. And she, fool that she was, had fallen in love with him. She looped her arms around his neck and closed her eyes, breathing in the scent of him.

"I hate what I've become," he muttered. "I'm not the man I thought I was. I had so many ideals, and it feels like I've broken and betrayed every one."

"I know how that feels," she said.

He laughed, an unhappy sound. "You shouldn't. You're the victim in this."

"You could have hurt me, but you didn't. You could have done whatever you wanted to me and paid no attention to my needs. But you didn't."

"I made you respond to me," he said. "I did everything I could to get you aroused so it would be easier."

"Easier for who? You or me?" Because her arousal couldn't have made that much difference to him. It never had to Marcus or Cletus. They'd taken what they wanted and gotten everything they needed from her, with no need for her active participation.

He made an incoherent noise. "Both of us, I suppose."

His speech had normalized. Maybe it was because of all the sex they'd already had, plus the sleep and food he'd been denied. He was beginning to heal.

"If you were trying to make it easier for me, then you couldn't have lost all your sanity. You still had compassion for me."

Storm's long fingers burrowed into the short strands of her hair to cup the back of her head. "At the time, all I could think of was I needed you and you weren't interested. I had to make you interested. But now, I remember things. About your people. Novus Vita. I know you didn't want to feel those things, that you wanted to remain pure."

She released a breath she hadn't known she was holding. "That is true," she said slowly. "But that's because I didn't know any better."

His eyes narrowed, a perplexed crease crimping his brows. "And now?"

"You realize I wasn't a virgin, right?"

His frown deepened so much it looked almost painful. "Gods of Belleren, I hadn't even thought of it. I'm an ass. I should have taken that possibility into account when I—"

"No. That's not what I was trying to say." She cleared her throat. She'd never spoken to anyone of these things. "I was married to a man named Cletus Wheaton."

"Was?"

"Yes. I—another man in our village wanted me. Marcus. He...cornered me one day and took me. I fought, but he was too strong."

He grimaced. "This man, Marcus, raped you?"

"Yes. More than once. He tried to make me his mistress. Eventually, Cletus found out what we were doing. He...he turned me into the law. He declared me a whore and had me arrested."

"*What?*" Storm drew back a few inches, glaring at her in obvious shock. "He had *you* arrested? What about Marcus?"

She lifted a shoulder. "He claimed I had seduced him. Everyone believed him and Cletus. No-one cared about what I had to say. I'm just a woman."

He growled so fiercely she tried to scramble off his lap. But his arms locked around her, preventing her from escaping.

"There is no such thing as *just* a woman," he said. "Are you aware that we Demon Kin have lost our females? Yet your people treat you like garbage."

"You're not angry with me?"

"No. Why would I be angry with you?"

"Because you growled at me. I thought something I said made you angry."

"I'm furious," he said, "but not at you. Your people. I'll never understand them." He shook his head and sighed deeply. "So they accused you of being a whore. What happened then?"

"I was convicted and imprisoned. I'd been in prison for over a year before the Demon Kin invaded."

"That should never have happened to you," he said. "Marcus was the one who committed the crime."

"When there is blame to go around between men and women, the women are always the ones who bear the burden. We are always the ones believed to be in the wrong."

"I don't believe that's always true. Before, when Belleren still had its women, they were treated with the greatest respect."

She cocked her head, trying to understand, to penetrate him with her gaze. "So your people don't believe that the actions of women brought all the evils into the world?"

Storm huffed a short laugh that sounded like disbelief. "No. Who told you that?"

"It is one of our central Teachings."

He shook his head. "As I told you, I'll never understand your people."

Her gaze fell to her lap. "You look down on us."

"No," he said quickly. Maybe a little too quickly. "Well, in some ways yes. They seem to be angry most of the time, at each other as well as everyone else."

"There is much unrighteousness in the world. Much to be angry at." But even as she spoke the words, she wondered if they were true.

Yes, there was injustice and cruelty, but Novus Vitans themselves were no strangers to cruel and unjust behavior. Look at this facility. Novus Vitan through and through, yet permeated with hatred and abuse. If anger was the answer, the antidote to all this unholiness, surely it would have reaped better results by now. And surely their government, steeped in the Teachings, wouldn't have approved such a facility as this.

These were heretical thoughts. At one time she would have crushed them without hesitation, out of fear she was straying down a dangerous path. But she'd changed. Novus Vita itself had changed her by throwing her into prison, by allowing her to be used as an experimental animal, by having her raped. They had re-created her in prison and in this facility, yet she knew they would take no responsibility for the outcome of their actions.

"Anger is sometimes the most appropriate reaction," Storm said. "But most of the time, it isn't. Most of the time, another approach would be more useful. Your people seem angry merely to be alive, to be mortal. It's as if they hate themselves and everyone else."

She blew out a soft breath. "I think you're right. They are angry all the time."

He smoothed the palm of one large hand across her cropped hair. "You're different, though. Different from other Novus Vitans I've met. Different from the other women."

Jealousy over those other women and elation that he thought her different warred inside her chest. "I am? How?"

He cupped her jaw. "Not so angry or fearful. You didn't try to bite me. And you don't hate me, although I still can't figure out why."

"Did the other women try to bite you?"

He looked sad. "Yes. I tried to tell them I wouldn't hurt them, but I couldn't find the words. I could only make noises, like an animal." He closed his eyes. "And I tried to stop, tried not to go to them, but I couldn't. I couldn't stop myself, Mercy."

She stroked his hair, hoping the caresses would comfort him even though there was nothing she could do to take away the pain of what he'd done, what had been done to him.

"I was afraid of you," she said softly, resting her cheek against his. "Terrified. But I was...aroused too. I was sure you were going to hurt me because that was all I'd ever experienced. I didn't even know women could feel pleasure during sex. And you gave me that, Storm. You showed me what my body was capable of and how it could be between a man and a woman."

His arms tightened around her until she could hardly draw a breath. "I could never be with a woman and not do everything in my power to give her pleasure. Your men don't do this?"

She snorted, an unladylike sound. "No. Pleasure is for the men."

"Novus Vitan men are even bigger fools than I'd suspected," he said.

Mercy snorted again, this time with laughter. He lifted his head, a half-smile on his sensuous mouth.

"I'm deeply sorry this thing has happened to you," he said. "But I'm not sorry I met you. I only wish it had been under better circumstances."

She kissed him. "I feel the same way."

They stared at each other silently. Something seemed to pass between them, unspoken but clear nonetheless. Some kind of understanding. That they were together now, that they were more than two strangers locked in the same cell, more than two victims of the same perpetrator.

They were together. Did that make them true lovers? A couple? Or were they simply allies against a common enemy? She couldn't tell what he was feeling, whether he loved her the way she did him. If she guessed wrong, there would be heartbreak.

His gaze softened, warmed, his thumb tracing slow arcs across her cheek, and then a long brush across her lower lip. He bent his head and kissed her mouth, his lips as soft and warm and caressing as his gaze.

Chapter 15

Mercy didn't even try to resist. She surrendered to him, body and soul, the instant their lips met. She was a fool. He wasn't her kind, wasn't even human. Yet that seemed so much less important now than the fact that he knew her, understood her in a way no other person ever had.

Besides, resistance would do her no good. She didn't have the strength to say no to the pleasure and closeness he brought her. And now that she understood his pain—now that she loved him—-she could never refuse to offer him comfort. Their captors had violated him every bit as much as they'd violated any of the women.

Storm smelled faintly of the soap they'd used the night before, yet his own unique scent still clung to his skin and hair. That tangy, male essence made her womb, her sex, contract in ardent longing. She needed him inside her.

Storm cupped her head in both hands as his mouth opened across hers, his tongue taking a long, leisurely swipe across the seam of her lips. She opened to him and he moaned as that clever tongue plunged inside her. He kissed her with so much yearning, so much desire, yet he always remained gentle, as if he were savoring her.

She slid a hand up the back of his neck and into his hair. The silken black strands of it fell over her hand, tickling her wrist. He had more beautiful hair than many women she knew.

He tasted uniquely Storm, a flavor that only sharpened her need for him. Mercy took his bottom lip between hers, sucking on him and letting her teeth score him lightly—a move she'd copied from him. Her boldness seemed to inflame him. He slipped one hand around between them and cupped her breast, squeezing her as he groaned against her mouth. Beneath her lap, his organ thickened and grew long.

His arousal fed hers. She whimpered as he pinched and plucked her nipple while he devoured her mouth. He inserted a finger inside her and she cried out against his kiss. Then he was pushing her knees apart, making her straddle him on the bench so he could position her over his cock.

She'd never heard of having sex sitting up before. But if anyone would know how to go about such a thing, it would be a Demon Kin. Mercy let him slide his big hands beneath the globes of her ass and shove her down onto him.

Their eyes met as he plunged upward into her body. She cried out again, still holding his gaze, the intimacy almost unbearable. He was looking at her, looking right into her eyes while he joined his sex with hers.

His lips parted and his eyes went half-lidded and smoky as Mercy seated herself on him. His fingers clutched at her hips and he moaned.

"You feel...so good...so perfect," he said. He lifted her up, his cock sliding slowly out until only the swollen head still remained inside her. Then he shoved her down on him, stretching her ruthlessly and sending a brutal shock of pleasure deep into her core.

"Storm! Oh, Storm!"

"Is that good, sweet?" He did it again.

"Yes. Yes, please, please..." She seemed to have no more pride, no sense of shame as she moaned and pleaded for more.

She rose and sank on him, helped by his hands supporting her ass, his arms seemingly tireless as he worked her up and down on his huge cock. He seemed made to fit her, made to torture her with this delicious agony.

Storm looked down to where their bodies joined. He groaned. "So beautiful."

She followed his gaze to see his huge shaft disappearing into her, the slick folds of her sex clinging to him as he pierced her. She'd never seen that before. The others had never savored the act the way Storm did. They'd always gotten it done as quickly as possible, usually in the dark, never watching themselves fuck her as if to celebrate every moment of the act.

The sight of his narrow hips bracketed by her thighs, his enormous shaft plunging into her over and over, sent her over the edge into wild cries of delirious climax. She watched him fuck her, listened to his hoarse groans of release as her sheath milked him dry, and she loved it.

She loved the sounds he made, the slap of their flesh as they pounded together, the wet noises of her body clasping and then releasing him. It was disgusting, filthy, and wrong, and she reveled in it. Everything that made it wrong also made it the most beautiful experience she'd ever had.

Finally they stopped moving. Mercy leaned down to rain kisses across his face. Her body shuddered in aftershocks from her seismic orgasm and she uttered soft moans as she pressed her lips to his skin. His hands moved in long strokes over her ass and up the lower curve of her back.

Mercy glanced up, one of the facility's ubiquitous cameras catching her eye. No doubt the researchers had caught the entire show, or else they had it recorded so they could watch later. Did they think they were shaming the women they had imprisoned here? She refused to be shamed.

In giving her Storm, they'd also given her things they probably couldn't even imagine. Things that would horrify them. Unbelievable pleasure, a completely new way of seeing herself, a kind of freedom—of thought, if not of body. She smiled as she kissed him and thought of all the ways those fools had benefited her when they only wanted to hurt her.

Of course, that realization wouldn't stop her from doing everything in her power to damage them if she ever got the chance.

"You are the best thing to ever happen to me," Storm murmured as she turned her mouth back to his.

"That can't be true," she said, even though she felt the same way about him.

"It is. I've never had this with anyone."

Mercy pulled her head back and gave him a skeptical look. "I'm sure you have a great deal of experience. I'm nothing special."

"Yes, you are." He brushed the side of her face with his fingertips. "And being with many partners doesn't mean I ever found anyone I wanted to bond with."

"How many have you had?" She bit her lip. "I'm sorry. That's none of my business."

He smiled wryly. "I didn't keep a running tally, Mercy. But I was a soldier and I sought out women every time I had shore leave. I managed to accumulate quite a bit of experience in the four years I fought before I was captured."

"You were on a starship, then." She tried to imagine him in the Bellerenic uniform, striding about with a gun on his hip. The militaristic image was startlingly easy to create.

"I signed up as soon as I found out about the plague."

The Demon Kin home world had been devastated by a plague that had killed most of the females. The disease had broken out not too long before they'd declared war on Novus Vita. It had always struck Mercy as odd that they'd choose to attack another planet so soon after they'd struggled through the loss of their women, but at the time she'd put it down to the inscrutable and corrupt nature of the Demon Kin.

She cocked her head. "Why did that make you want to go to war?"

He frowned. "Don't you know? Novus Vita sent the plague to us."

A sick feeling settled into her stomach. How could he think for even an instant that her homeworld would do something so terrible? If that was what the Maleficans believed, no wonder they'd gone after Novus Vita. But they were wrong. They had to be wrong.

She frowned back at him. "No, we didn't."

"You didn't. Your government did." He looked so serious, so confident.

It was obvious he had no doubts whatsoever about what he was saying. But...a guilty shiver went through her. Novus Vitans had despised the Demon Kin for so long, even before the founding of their colony. They saw themselves as the Maker's instruments of resistance against the corruption of the devilish race.

Yet she knew—or at least she refused to believe they would do something so horrible as send that disease.

"I don't believe it," she said, with more firmness than she felt. "The plague was just some kind of freak of nature."

It had to be a freak of nature. Otherwise...otherwise, she was guilty too. She'd done something...that golden-haired Demon Kin male from long ago...she'd turned him in because she believed in the Novus Vitan way.

"Our scientists analyzed it exhaustively," Storm said. "It was engineered and we traced its origins back to Novus Vita."

"I don't care." Her voice began to rise. "Your scientists are wrong."

"There's no need to shout." He sounded so damned reasonable. "And they're not wrong. They produced evidence that convinced an interplanetary council convened on the matter. How is it you never heard any of this?"

Mercy leaped away from him, refusing to be quieted. "No! That isn't true. I know it isn't true."

The tip of his tail twitched as he regarded her sadly. "I'm sorry, Mercy, but it is true. Your people sent it to us as a kind of opening shot. Biological warfare. It allowed them to attack us without making themselves vulnerable. It was supposed to kill us all."

She shook her head, back and forth, back and forth, her eyes shut tightly. "No. My people would never do something like that."

Except they would, and part of her knew it without a doubt.

"They did it. Ask our gracious hosts if you don't believe me. Who knows, maybe this facility contributed to the development of the plague organism."

"No." She could feel tears stinging behind her eyelids. She didn't know why it was so important that he was wrong; she simply couldn't take another slur against her homeland.

It was one thing to believe the Novus Vitans were cruel and unfair to women and to their enemies in battle. It was something entirely different to accept that they'd attacked the Demon Kin completely unprovoked, that they'd schemed to wipe them out of the galaxy altogether. Surely they weren't that evil.

But they were. She knew they were and she hated that knowledge.

"Sweet," he said, his voice gentle but relentless, "we know the plague originated with Novus Vita. The original plan was to completely depopulate Belleren. When they found the disease mainly affected our women, they simply hoped it would ruin our morale and make us unable to fight back when they invaded."

"Don't. I don't want to hear anymore."

"All they succeeded in doing was infuriating us. They brought their doom on themselves. We would never have come here and taken over your planet if it weren't for the crimes committed by your Teachers, your Angels. They commissioned their scientists to design the plague."

"Stop it!" She opened her eyes and glared at him. "Just stop! I said I don't want to hear it."

There had been that man, that Demon Kin who'd come to their village when she was a girl. And her people had captured him. They hadn't been at war with Belleren at the time, but he was a devil, or so the Teachers said. They'd captured him and some men from the government had come to take him away. And now she wondered whether he might have been taken to a secret medical facility like this one. If he might have become the subject of biochemical research.

Oh, Maker. She'd helped them capture him. She could still remember the way his hair had shone like burnished gold in the sun, the caramel color of his tail, the gentle way he'd smiled at her. He'd been beautiful—different from Storm, but still beautiful. And she'd helped them kill him.

"I don't blame you," Storm said. "You know that, right? I would never blame you for what your government did, or take it out on you in any way."

She struggled to keep in the tears. "Why are you telling me this?"

He stood up and walked to her, took her hands in his. "Because I want you to know the truth about our two peoples. Because I love you."

"No, you don't." She shook her head.

Only a few moments before, she'd been thinking the same thing. That she loved him. But it wasn't true; it was an illusion, a fantasy brought on by being cooped up with him in this little cell. All the sex had made them crazy.

"Mercy, they're going to separate us. You know that, don't you?"

"Yes," she said, her voice embarrassingly small.

"We're enchained. It's something that happens to Demon Kin, and sometimes our human lovers. It's a kind of addiction. Our bodies crave each other and when they split us up, it's going to hurt."

"I don't understand." She yanked her hands away. "Why are you telling me this? What difference will it make?"

"Because I love you. I want you to understand what's happening to you. Maybe that will make it less frightening."

She crossed her arms over her naked breasts, tucking her hands in her armpits to keep them away from him. "They're not going to split us up."

His tail lashed in a single back and forth sweep. "Yes, they are. You know it as well as I do."

"Well, I don't care. I still don't want to hear about the plague."

He frowned. "Why? Why does this bother you so much?"

She couldn't tell him. He'd despise her if he knew what she'd done.

74

"It's just too much," she mumbled, knowing she wasn't making any sense. "I can't take anymore."

"Oh, love." He gathered her into his arms. And she let him. She allowed him to hold her, knowing she was nothing but a viper, knowing he'd shove her against the wall in disgust if he even guessed at what she'd done.

She nestled her cheek against him, his chest hair tickling her cheek as his tail flicked against her naked calves like a caress. Where Storm was concerned, she was too selfish and besotted to say no, even if it would be for his own good.

Eventually, she'd have to tell him. She couldn't keep it a secret forever. The longer they stayed together, the more likely the truth would slip out.

She might as well get it over now and save herself some future pain. Mercy lifted her face to him, opening her mouth to begin her confession.

The door hissed open. Five guards stomped into the cell. She'd been so caught up in Storm that she hadn't noticed the sounds of the guards approaching.

Storm's head whipped toward the door. He seemed just as startled as she was. He growled ferociously, his tail lashing violently as the guards advanced on them, Chisholm in the lead.

"Leave us alone," Storm said.

Chisholm sneered. "The beast speaks."

"Go away," Mercy said, knowing it wouldn't do any good.

Chisholm laughed. "It didn't take you long, did it, Bambi? You're already wrapped around him like a vine." He nodded at the other men. "Do it."

Storm pushed her behind him, using his arm like a bar to keep her back. "Don't touch her," he snarled at the men.

He was trying to shield her, obviously, but that would only put him directly in the line of fire. He'd take everything meant for the both of them on himself alone.

"Storm, no!" She wrestled against the titanium grip of his arm.

The soldiers paid no attention to her. They simply lifted their tranquilizer guns and fired at Storm, their little poisoned darts whizzing out and thunking into his body in multiple places.

His grip on her loosened. The lashing of his tail stilled. His knees buckled and he fell to the floor.

He blinked up at her, his gaze unfocused. "Mercy...love...you," he mumbled, his voice so slurred it was hard to understand.

She sobbed, falling to her knees beside him. "Storm!" She threw her arms around him.

His eyes were half-closed, dazed, his mouth slack. She watched as his thick black lashes lowered, hiding his beautiful eyes from her. His tail no longer moved. Only his chest showed a sign of life, rising and falling in slow, shallow breaths.

"You bastards!" she screamed at the guards. "You've given him too much. You might have killed him."

Chisholm gifted her with another of his sneers. "He won't die, more's the pity. He's Demon Kin, or had you forgotten? They're animals. They can take a lot more tranq than a human."

She bared her teeth at him, growling wordlessly. There were no words adequate to express how much she despised him, the things she wished she could do to him. He might have killed Storm, and she hadn't told him the truth about her feelings for him. She might never have the chance now to let him know she'd fallen in love with him.

Chisholm grabbed her by the elbows and dragged her off the Demon Kin. Mercy threw herself from side to side to break his grip. He refused to let go. His fingers merely dug deeper into her flesh and he laughed as he pulled her away from her lover.

"She's a wild one," he remarked to his smirking comrades.

She switched tactics, going limp in Chisholm's grasp. That didn't yield any different results than active struggle had. He simply wouldn't let her go, and she had no idea what she would have done if she could have gotten free. Yelled them all to death? She had no weapons and no training in the use of the guns they carried. Besides, she was so astronomically outnumbered that even if she had managed to defeat this group of guards, there would be others soon and she wouldn't be able to kill or incapacitate them all.

She sagged in miserable defeat.

She'd never thought herself powerful. In her world, women were simply not creatures of power and agency. They were the servants, the handmaidens, of men, born to submit. But she'd rarely felt truly helpless until now.

When they'd arrested and imprisoned her, she'd been helpless then too. But it had been only her own life at stake, her own puny destiny threatened. Now, she had Storm to think about and the fact she could do nothing to defend him made her sick. The looks of smug satisfaction mixed with loathing on the faces of the guards made her sick. They hated Storm, and now he was unconscious.

"What are you going to do to him?" she shouted as two of them dragged him away by the arms. "Don't hurt him!"

"How soon a whore turns her coat," Chisholm said.

"What coat?" One of the other guards winked and laughed. "She hasn't got a coat that I can see."

"If she could kill you with a look," Chisholm said, "you'd be nothing but a cinder."

"Come on and help us," said one of the men hauling on Storm's arms.

The remaining two picked up his feet and they carried him into the corridor. Chisholm followed, his grip on her arms almost bone-breaking. She saw them cart the Demon Kin around the nearest corner, going in the opposite direction from her and Chisholm. When she lost sight of him, she began to cry humiliating tears.

"You make me want to vomit," Chisholm growled as he yanked her along the hallway. "You've only been with him for a few hours and already you're panting and crying for him. Don't you have any loyalty to your own people?"

"You're not a person," she said through gritted teeth.

He let go of her left arm in order to backhand her across the face. "Shut up, whore."

Now her face hurt too much to talk, and she was glad. The pain gave her something besides Storm to think about.

No, it didn't. The only thing in her mind was the image of them carrying his unconscious form away from her, to do the Maker only knew what. And he couldn't even fight back.

They reached her cell. The door was open, waiting for her. Chisholm dragged her in and threw her to the floor. He jumped on top of her and forced her legs apart.

She didn't fight him. What would be the point?

Chapter 16

Darkness and fog had invaded his mind, his soul. There was a world beyond, and memories, and people he loved, and places...places...things...words...jumble. Jumble. Jumble. A jumble, a rock slide...

My name is Storm. My name is Storm.

He needed to hold onto that, to hold onto the memory of *her*—no, Mercy—for as long as possible. So he wouldn't lose himself. If he lost himself, he might lose *her*—Mercy, Mercy—forever.

But the clamor in his mind, the agony in his body, it was crowding out his name, all his words. They were jumbling and falling over themselves again.

Mercy. Storm. Mercy Storm. Stormercy.

This time it had come on earlier than ever before. How long since they'd taken her from him? He didn't know. Time seemed to bend and melt and ooze all over the place like butter softened under a desert sun. He didn't know. He didn't know.

Too long. Five minutes would have been too long. They'd taken her from him, like he'd known they would. She was hurting. She had to be hurting, and there was nothing he could do for her.

His bones seemed to be crushing down inside of him from some invisible force. He lay on the floor of his cell, curled on his side, and panted. Sometimes he screamed. There were no words in his screams, just noise, just sound, just raw agony.

Ride it out. Ride it out. But there was no riding it, no surviving. This would be the end of him unless it stopped very soon.

The scream came from outside him. Outside his cell. It was not his scream. Not him. Not Storm. It was female, that scream.

Storm lifted his head, although it took every bit of energy he still possessed. He listened.

"No!"

A very female voice.

"Storm! Storm, they're—" A grunt interrupted the shout, and she went silent.

"Mercy!" he shouted.

He couldn't be sure her name sounded coherent, coming from his mad throat. It didn't matter. He crawled to his feet and staggered toward his cell door. He couldn't hear anything now. She was so quiet. So quiet.

78

Then there was laughter. Male laughter.

Storm growled. They'd hurt her. They were hurting her now. They could do anything they wanted to her and he couldn't stop them. He couldn't protect her because he was locked in this cell, crippled by the implant in his neck.

She began to cry. Storm launched himself at the door. He slammed into it with a loud bang. Yet it barely moved under the force of his body, as if it were mocking him and his impotence.

He could hear her. Crying. He could hear them, too. One laughed. Another made a kind of moaning sound that Storm knew all too well. He knew exactly what that piece of shit was doing to his woman.

He shook all over with rage. Shook until his vision went red and he roared with fury. Had to get to her. Had to get out of this accursed cell.

But how?

Powers. He'd once had powers, abilities. More than words and memories. Powers...

Without thinking, he reached behind him to the back of his neck and dug his fingernails into the flesh on either side of the implant. With a roar, he burrowed his nails into his skin and pinched the implant between his bloody fingertips. An electric shock zipped through his whole body, all the way to the soles of his feet. He ignored it. Dug farther. Ripped, tore, yanked.

New agony drove him to his knees. He gazed down at his gore-covered fingers. The implant was a tiny rectangle covered in slick red. A crude thing, huge compared to similar technologies on Belleren, but effective nonetheless. That tiny bit of—of—of stuff had prevented him from escaping. And now it was no longer in his body.

Why wasn't he going into convulsions? He glanced at the implant again. Who the fuck cared? It was gone and he was free, or near enough.

He stood up and stumbled to the cell door. Grabbed the bars on the window, stuck his face against the narrow opening between them. A scent came to him. Men. Sex.

Another ferocious growl left his throat. They would pay a thousand fold for what they'd done to her.

With his *powers* he reached through the bars, down the corridor, all the way to the human creatures who dared to hurt his woman. There were rules for the powers, rules he was supposed to follow. But he couldn't remember them and didn't care.

His powers felt like invisible fingers he could use to dig inside the heads, the minds of the human men. He grabbed the first one he encountered and pierced him, wrenched him around, forced him in the direction of his cell.

Let me out. Now.

The other men yelled. They jumped to their feet, ran after the one he controlled. One stayed on the ground. He lay on top of someone. *Her.* He moved in a suggestive rhythm, grunts escaping him, and Storm growled. He was attacking *her*, forcing himself on her.

Storm ripped into the attacking human's mind and squeezed until something broke. The human went limp on top of *her*. Stormercy. Mercy. Mercy.

She pushed him off her and sat up, her face expressionless.

Men were coming toward him. They were fighting. The one he controlled hit out at the other two, but they were stronger than him. They were winning. Storm tore into their minds as well, and sent them unconscious to the floor.

He beckoned the first one to his cell. The man appeared around the corner, his eyes even more dazed and blank than Mercy's, his uniform torn. He tapped the security panel on the outside of the door. The panel raised, much more quickly than it did when they released Storm on a woman.

He smiled at the human, showing his fangs. The human lost all color in his face.

Storm growled. The smell of piss filled the space as the human lost control of his bladder and a large spreading stain appeared at the front of his uniform trousers.

Storm reached into his mind.

"Let them out," he said. "Let all the prisoners out. Women and men."

"Let all the prisoners out," the guard repeated.

"Do it now." He shoved past the fool and bolted toward Mercy.

❖ ❖ ❖

A few moments later, he rounded a corner and found her standing over a guard's prone and half-clothed form, kicking him with vicious jabs of her feet. First one, then the other. Bang. Bang. Bang.

She nailed the human's ribs, his pelvis, his legs. His head. Animal-like growls and snarls erupted from her throat as she punished the bastard.

Her violence did nothing to blunt the force of Storm's sexual response to her. She was the one, the only one, who could take away the agony in his body and mind. She was the one he needed, the one he loved. Rage and humiliation and the sexual odors of her assaulters distorted her natural scent, yet still it filled him with desperate need.

Storm recognized the man she was kicking as the one who'd been in the act of raping her when he'd invaded his mind. Served the piece of shit right to get beaten while he was unconscious and unable to defend himself. The only thing Storm regretted was that the asshole wouldn't have any memory of who had given him the beating.

Then he remembered the cameras and smiled.

He loped forward and caught Mercy by the arm. She snarled as she twisted toward him, her fist raised. She paused, blinking up at him. The snarl faded.

"Storm?" she whispered brokenly.

"I—I'm h-hh-here."

She launched herself into his arms, wild sobs tearing and shaking her body. He embraced her, bent his head, inhaled the sweet scent of her hair. He trembled with the force of his need for her, his cock instantly rising to gigantic proportions.

Damnation, he was terrible. He shouldn't be thinking of getting inside her after what those shits had done to her. But he simply couldn't help himself.

Mercy mumbled something under her breath, the same words over and over, interspersed with more of the racking sobs. Her hands traveled frantically over his body, as if she could absorb him through their skins.

"Wh-what w-was that?" He had to force the words out, force them to stay separate from each other and not tangle together the way his brain wanted them to. He needed to be coherent for Mercy.

"Th-they—they—"

"I know." He petted the back of her head. "I know. S-saw."

"H-how?"

He showed her his bloody hand. "Pulled out m-my implant. Controlled them."

She jerked her head up and stared at him, her eyes wide. "Is that why they collapsed like that?"

Storm nodded. "Yes."

Her lips parted. "Do you think we could get out of here? Escape?"

He hadn't thought that far ahead. But now that he didn't have an implant, they couldn't prevent him from invading their minds. Theoretically, he could incapacitate every human in the facility.

"Yes," he said. "Escape."

"Can you fly a shuttle?"

"Yes. Easy." He hoped.

Mercy's gaze flicked up to the camera in the ceiling above them. "They might be watching us right now. We have to be quick."

"Quick." He nodded.

He sounded like an idiot. But until he quieted the sexual savage in him, truly coherent speech would be beyond his capability.

Mercy clung to him, still shuddering and crying. He stroked her back as he sent his mind questing, searching for more humans to control. He didn't know how many guards lived in the facility, or where their quarters were. He also didn't know if they had some other means of incapacitating him, such as poison gas. So he pushed his mind, his powers, fast and hard toward every trace of humanity he could find.

Most were female. Woman, woman, woman, another woman. Prisoners all, he assumed. He kept looking until he came across a male. One swift stab at the man's mind and the human went down, unable to protect himself. The human's ability to control his conscious, waking mind was now jelly and Storm had no way of predicting how long it would take for him to recover.

He didn't care. These so-called people had perpetrated horrible crimes against both Demon Kin males and human females. They deserved what they were getting.

He blasted through the facility, taking down guard after guard, along with a cluster of males in white coats, who he assumed were the scientists in charge of the place. Finally, all the men he could locate were knocked unconscious.

He lifted his head and took a deep breath. He was covered in sweat.

Mercy tilted her head back. "What is it?"

"They're d-dd-done."

She frowned, seeming to think over what he'd said. Then she indicated the nearby guards with a nod of her head. "Like them?"

"Yes."

"Good." She sneered at the one she'd been kicking. "I'd like to kill him. But I want to do it when he's awake."

Storm tightened his grip on her. "H-he h-hh-hurt you."

She nodded without words. Her gaze fell. She looked ashamed.

Storm tipped her chin up gently. "S-sweet. N-nnot your f-fault."

Her lip trembled. "They called me a whore, Storm. Because I l-love you."

He kissed her forehead. "Love you, Mercy."

She choked back another sob and his heart twisted in his chest. His cock was painful, it was so hard and eager. He didn't want to impose himself on her, not after what had happened to her, yet now that he wasn't searching for and dispatching humans, he could no longer ignore his need.

"M-mercy, I n-nn-need you." His voice came out so raspy and full of growl, he sounded like a wild beast.

"Y-you still want me? After—" She gestured vaguely at the men.

In that moment, he wanted to break their necks with his bare hands. How dare they make her feel ashamed at the crime *they* had committed?

He cupped her face in both his hands, trembling with the force of his longing. "Love you. Not care. Hear? Hear me?"

She nodded tearfully.

"Only want...p-punish th-them. Not you. N-never you."

"But I'm not—" She closed her eyes. "I'm not clean."

It was going to kill him to say his next words, and he couldn't be sure she would understand. But it had to be said. "M-mercy. If y-you—if no w-want...n-nn-no sex."

She looked stricken. "You don't want me."

"No! Y-y-yyou not want."

Mercy bit her bottom lip. "But I do."

He fought back a moan. "Want s-sex? With m-mme?"

"Please. I think I need it." She glanced tearfully at the men on the floor, then back at him. "I'm starving for you. Enchained. And I need to forget. Help me forget?"

"M-my love." He ran his hands up and down her back, over her ass, then back up to her neck, her bare head. "Forget. Mercy, forget."

She pressed her forehead against his chest.

Slowly, her shuddering subsided. Instead of disappearing, however, it changed. Turned passionate. Her hands, clutching him around his waist, began caressing him. She kissed his naked skin, her hips surging against his thighs. His cock throbbed painfully, his heart beat so fast and hard it seemed as if it might jump right out of his chest.

Storm groaned. "Can't w-wait."

He slipped his hands under her sweet little ass and lifted her. Mercy wrapped her legs around his waist as he turned and pressed her against the wall.

He supported her with one arm as he reached between them to guide his cock to her pussy and slid inside her in one thrust. The intimate contact sent a searing shock through his body. He'd never felt anything like it. No other time with a woman could compare to this, to his bone-shaking need on the brink of being quenched in the body of the one female who could heal him. He quaked all over, rattling so badly that for an instant he was afraid he'd drop her.

Chapter 17

She threw her head back, hitting her skull against the padded wall as she yelled Storm's name. Her nails dug into his skin and he welcomed that pain. It was healthy pain, not torment.

His hips surged, pounding against hers with no plan and no finesse, only the driving need to finish. To slake himself in her body. She jerked under him, pushing herself against him with just as much passion, if less strength. Their bodies made a rhythmic slapping sound, their moans combining into a single erotic song.

His climax boiled up in him so swiftly he didn't even feel it coming until it was already upon him. He shook and groaned and shouted her name as his body emptied itself into hers. The orgasm seemed to go on and on, pumping out everything he had, dissolving him into something mindless and boneless and nameless. In the distance, he could hear Mercy's voice raised, calling his name as she quaked through her own climax.

He should have lasted longer. His hips continued to move, to pump into her, as he tried to prolong her orgasm, to make it as good for her as possible. He should have lasted longer, but he hadn't been able to control himself. He'd been ready to explode the instant he'd touched her.

She pressed kisses to his chest, the indent between his collarbones, his neck, his upper arms. Storm bent his head to hers, breathing hard, still shuddering in the aftermath. He was covered in sweat and dripping it onto her.

The hammering need settled after his orgasm. It was still there, beneath the surface, preparing to rise up and pound at him again, but for now he could think more clearly. And the first thing he noticed was the noise.

From the corridors around them came a bewildering din of male grunts and growls, female shrieks, cries of ecstasy from both genders, feet pounding down hallways, flesh slapping rhythmically against flesh. The prisoners were out and they were having an orgy.

Mercy blinked up at him as a tentative smile brightened her face. She looped her arms around his neck. "Thank you."

"Don't." He shook his head. "I was being selfish."

"I don't care. I needed it."

"Mercy, what they did to you—"

Her smile dimmed. "I don't want to talk about it. Or think about it."

"You'll have to, sooner or later."

"Then make it later."

He sighed. "All right. But when you want to talk, I'll be here. I don't want you to feel alone."

"I know." She glanced to her right, where most of the noise seemed to be emanating. "Is that what I think it is?"

"Before I came to you, I told one of the guards to let all the prisoners out," he said.

Her eyes were perfectly round. "And now they're—"

"The males are pursuing the females." He grimaced. "I wasn't thinking when I gave that order. I only wanted to get them out as quickly as possible, and rescue you."

She disengaged from him, turning toward the sound. "Let's see what's happening."

He caught her arm as she moved to follow the noise. "Mercy, no. One of them might come after you."

She glanced back at him with a startled expression. "I hadn't thought of that."

"They'll take any females they can get. Stay close to me and we'll peek around the corner. Just to make sure no-one's getting hurt."

He couldn't think right now about the fact that some of the females might be unwilling. Unless he shot all the males with tranquilizers, there would be no stopping them from doing what their nature compelled them to do. And if he tranqed them, he wouldn't be able to get them on board an escape vessel. But at least he could ensure no-one was being injured.

As they got closer, the sounds grew louder and easier to differentiate. It didn't seem as if the women were being harmed. From the noises they made, they were enjoying it. Some of them had probably become enchained, just as he and Mercy had.

He put an arm around Mercy's shoulders and tucked her tightly into his side. Hugging the wall, they eased their way to the corner. Storm kept her on his left, preventing her from getting a good look at the action, but also preventing any of the other males from easily grabbing her. Then he craned his neck and peered around the corner.

Everywhere, up and down the narrow corridor, Demon Kin males buried themselves inside the bodies of human females. The males were all naked, mostly bearded, their hair wild and unkempt. Most of the females still wore their gray, short-sleeved prison gowns, the skirts pulled up to their waists, the tops yanked down as far as they would go, some of them torn.

A blonde just a couple meters away was on her knees, a male taking her from behind while another urged his cock into her waiting mouth. She opened for him with apparent eagerness, moaning in rhythm with the one behind her.

The sight made Storm's cock rise again, pulsing with the need to get inside Mercy.

A little farther away, a woman with cropped black hair that reminded him of Mercy's rose from the floor, where she'd been entangled with a male. She was staring even farther down the hallway, toward the place where it bent sharply to the left. Storm followed her gaze. A tall, probably once-huge but now emaciated, blond Demon Kin male stood at the corner, staring at her, his whole body quivering with tension.

Then both of them cried out and ran toward each other, stepping over and around lovers writhing on the floor, males taking females up against the walls. They came together in a frantic embrace, their mouths clinging, opening, their hands touching voraciously. The male was crying. Storm could see his shoulders shaking, see the wetness on his face.

The woman cried, too. The sounds she made traveled clearly to his ears over the wildness of the orgy.

His own eyes began to sting in sympathy. They were clearly enchained. They probably even loved each other, judging by their display of emotion. Just like him and Mercy.

"Is everyone all right?" she whispered beside him.

"Uh...they look fine to me."

"I want to see."

He whipped his head around, staring down at her in shock. She wanted to watch? Where had that come from? He'd never suspected Mercy would enjoy such a thing.

Her face glowed pink as she smiled at him bashfully. She then tried to peek around him, moving out from the safety of the corner into the open where anyone could see her.

"Hey, now, stay back where it's safe." He switched places with her, grinning. "You can watch from here. Don't let them see you."

"You don't mind?" She glanced over her shoulder at him.

"No. But you only have a moment. We've got to get some kind of vessel ready to go."

She turned back, biting her lip. Her gaze fell on the unconscious men littering the floor behind them, and turned cold. "Before we go, we should kill them."

How long had the abuse he'd witnessed gone on? How many times had it been repeated? He glanced at the fallen guards. He ought to wake them up just so he could punish them for their transgressions.

"I can do that for you," he said.

"No. I want to do it myself."

Although he'd been in the Spaceforce, he'd seen enough hand to hand fighting and ground pounding to know how brutal war could be. He'd seen plenty of dead bodies, taken many lives. Battle rage was nothing new to Storm. But regret followed the killing, like dawn followed midnight. Especially that first kill.

He didn't want to see her carrying around that kind of burden.

"I admire your ferocity, but you might regret it later if you do something like that," he said softly. "Think about it. Do you want that on your conscience?"

She glowered, first at the guard, then at him. "Don't you think he deserves it?"

"Yes, he does. But you don't. Killing him might hurt you worse than what's already happened."

Her lip trembled. "He hurt me. They all did, but Chisholm was the worst. He was their leader. He seemed to be obsessed with me."

Storm stroked her cheek with his thumb. "Do what will help you sleep at night. Not what you think he deserves." Then he paused. "Would you like me to kill him for you?"

"You'd really do that for me?"

"Of course I would." Better the murder be on his conscience than hers.

She wiped her eyes with the back of her hand. "I'll do it."

"Mercy—"

"I said I'll do it."

She disengaged from him and walked over to Chisholm's prostrate form. For a moment she stared down at him dispassionately. Then she crouched next to him and shoved him onto his back, displaying his naked and shrunken cock laying against his thigh.

Mercy reached for the man's belt. She yanked a knife from the sheath on Chisholm's left hip, just in front of the holster of his flechette gun. Her jaw clenched. She grabbed his chin and sliced his throat open.

Chisholm made a choking sound as blood welled up from the vicious cut. Mercy calmly wiped her blade on the front of his uniform shirt.

"Now we're even, you scum," she muttered as she stood up, the knife still clutched in her hand.

Storm nodded at her. She'd made her choice and he'd stand by it. "Do you have any other unfinished business with these men?"

"No." She swallowed hard. "Chisholm was enough."

"Then let's go and find a ship."

Chapter 18

Promise couldn't sleep. Again. She'd been having that problem ever since she'd arrived at the Life Studies Research Center, and her usual tactics of reading the Teachings until she felt sleepy again weren't working.

She set her media unit on her bedside table and climbed out of her narrow bed. The air in her room felt close and stale. Too hot. The monotonous gray of the furnishings, the walls, and ceiling seemed oppressive instead of soothing as they'd been intended to be.

She felt on-edge. Restless. She had the absurd sense that something big was about to happen, and that she'd be a part of it. Something terrible.

It was ridiculous, really. She had no unnatural powers, and she wouldn't want them if she did. Promise had never had a premonition in her life. She rejected such things as the evils they were. Only the Maker could know what was going to happen.

Yet she couldn't stop the thoughts whirling around in her mind. Something was moving toward her, huge and implacable and deadly, and she could do nothing to escape it.

"Don't be so melodramatic," she muttered to herself. It was only one of those middle of the night fears, the ones that seemed so convincing, so compelling in the dark hours, only to disappear like fog in the morning.

Except that here on the station, hidden on the dark side of the Novus Vitan moon, all hours were dark hours.

She was doing it again. Letting the darkness and isolation get to her, derange her mind. It was unbecoming in an Angel. She ought to be better than this. She'd been chosen by the Maker for this work, and there was no reason to fear at all, as long as she put her trust in Him and the Teachings.

The best thing she could do right now would be to go to the offices and review everything, reassure herself that all procedures were being followed and everything on the station was on track. Once she'd confirmed that the situation was completely normal, she'd be able to go back to sleep.

She pulled on her robe and stuck her feet in the slip-on shoes she kept by her bedside. Only the night guards would be awake at this hour, and they were unlikely to come into the offices, but it wouldn't do to be seen in her nightgown, even if the fabric was thick and completely opaque.

Promise adjusted the high collar of her gown as she left her room. Her quarters were just off the offices, which gave her easy access to her work, but also made it difficult to feel she had any spare time or privacy.

You're an Angel. You have no need for those things.

She pressed her lips together at her self-admonishment, and opened the connecting door to the offices. Everything looked as quiet and orderly as usual. However, a quick check of the systems would help to ease her mind so she began a circuit of the room.

The administrative work stations were all properly shut down. Promise moved into the observation room, where the cell and corridor monitors were located. Most of the monitors were turned off, since the prisoners weren't generally released during the night hours. But one flickered with movement. A nearly empty coffee cup with a couple of swallows of coffee in the bottom sat next to the monitor, as if the guard responsible for watching had gotten up for a break.

What had he been watching? She wasn't aware of any night experiments being conducted this evening. Promise sat down at the monitor.

At first she couldn't comprehend what she was seeing. There were several people in the area covered by the monitor and they all lay on the floor. One of them was half-clothed. It was a guard—Chisholm—and he lay with his eyes closed but his pants pulled down, his limp sex on shameful display. The others still had their pants on, and they were all face down on the floor.

What in heaven's name had happened there?

She peered more closely at the monitor. Chisholm's neck looked...wrong. Promise reached absently for the camera controls and zoomed in on him until she could see what was wrong with him.

A side-to-side slash in his throat made a grotesque gap in his flesh. Beneath him she now noticed a spreading pool of darkness that could only be blood. Someone had murdered Chisholm.

Promise's heart jumped into a frantic rhythm. What could have happened? Had the guards fought one another? But Chisholm had been well-liked among his fellow guards and she'd noticed no tension there lately. In fact, the other guards seemed to admire him as a leader.

The fact she'd hated and distrusted him had nothing to do with how his co-workers felt about him. They wouldn't have attacked him. She was sure of it.

An awful, impossible suspicion seized her. It couldn't be true. There were too many safeguards here at the facility for the prisoners to have escaped. But she switched on some of the other monitors in the bank just in case. What she saw appalled her.

Demon Kin males everywhere, in every corridor of the cell block. And human females. And they were...they were...mating. In pairs, in threesomes, they were mating with an abandon she'd never seen. Not that she'd seen much of this behavior in the first place.

An Angel took no interest in mating, except as a way of manipulating the enemies of the Maker's People.

The sight of all those naked and nearly-naked bodies writhing together made her pulse pound even more wildly than it ever had before. The display of animal lust was sickening in its perverse abandon. So sickening she could do nothing but stare at it in disgusted fascination for a moment.

Wait—the prisoners were out of their cells. They'd killed at least one guard and somehow incapacitated the others. She couldn't picture how that had happened, but at the moment it didn't matter. What mattered was they'd escaped and they were now in effective control of the facility.

She dashed back into the administrative office and threw herself into her chair, flicking on her vid link. Her voice shook as she gave the commands and passwords to access Novus Vitan planetary security forces. For the most part, her planet was under Malefican control, but she had contact with the most secret part of her government through the Angel House.

"Angel House security here. Caller, please identify yourself." The young male voice sounded sleepy and bored.

It was early morning on that sector of Novus Vita, not deep night as it was here. However, it was still quite early for him. He'd probably been napping and her call had awoken him.

"Angel House, this is the Novus Vita Life Studies Research Center. We have an emergency situation here. Our test subjects have escaped and we need immediate military back-up."

"Who is this again?" He sounded a little more alert now.

"The Novus Vita Life Studies Research Center. I repeat, we require assistance. Our test subjects have escaped."

"Uh...I'm not authorized to send such assistance, Miss. You'll have to wait until morning and send in your request again." Now he sounded amused.

"But this is an emergency! Who is your superior? I want to speak to him immediately."

"Maybe if you put your own 'superior' on, I could speak to someone with some authority. Miss."

Promise ground her teeth together. He wasn't taking her seriously because she was female. "I am the superior official here. Now get me your boss."

"You're the superior official." He laughed. "Who is this really? Did Bob put you up to this?"

She let out a most unfeminine growl. "Do you have any idea to whom you are speaking?"

"A girl." He snickered.

"This is Angel Promise," she said in her iciest voice. "Perhaps you've heard of me."

"Angel Promise? Yeah, I've heard of her. But I don't think you're her. Listen, girly. Do you have any idea how much trouble you could get into if the higher-ups found out about this little game you're playing?"

"Indeed." She breathed slowly in and out of her nose until she could speak without screaming. "Well, whoever you are, my security code is One-Four-Prima-Five-Novus Vita. Does that clear things up for you?"

He went silent. Then he cleared his throat. "Um...so this really is Angel Promise?"

"Yes, it certainly is. Now get me your boss. I don't care if you have to wake him up. Do it now."

"Um...yes, Miss. I'll...um...have him as quickly as possible for you, Miss."

She crossed her arms over her chest, fuming. Of course she'd encountered this problem before, but never when the stakes were so high. The stakes had never been nearly this high in the past, and she'd always had plenty of time to work around the contemptuous attitudes most Novus Vitan men had for women.

She'd been so rattled she hadn't given him her personal code immediately, as she ought to have done. That would have saved some embarrassment on both their sides. To be honest, it wasn't all his fault he'd taken such an attitude, since female leaders were vanishingly rare on Novus Vita. But that admission didn't make her any less angry.

Several heart-pounding minutes later, a sleepy male voice came on the line. "Hello? Is this Angel Promise?"

"Yes, sir." She repeated her personal code. "Our test subjects have escaped and at least one guard is dead. We need immediate assistance."

Instead of the shocked outrage she'd expected, there was only silence. Promise frowned at the monitor.

"Sir? Did you get my last message?"

"Yes, I did, Angel Promise. And I'd like to send you assistance. Please believe that I would. However, it isn't possible at this time."

What? "What? I—I don't understand."

He sighed. "We don't have anyone to send at this time."

"But—I was told we would receive assistance whenever it was necessary."

"Angel Promise, I can't send troops. I can't send anyone. The Demon Kin have made it impossible for us to defend you."

"Our food and supply shipments have always arrived without any trouble," she said, seething and trying to keep him from noticing.

"Food and supplies are easier to explain away than armed men. I'm sure you understand that we can't take the risk that the Maleficans will discover the facility."

She sat there in stunned silence. Was he saying Novus Vita had abandoned them? Had they meant to do this all along? Maybe they'd never intended to defend her from the prisoners; maybe they'd only said those things to allay her fears and make her and her staff more manageable.

"So you're saying we're on our own," she said slowly. "You're going to let them take over."

"I'm afraid so," he said gravely.

"They'll kill us all."

"You don't know that, Angel Promise."

Yes, she did. The prisoners were furious. They hated her and her staff. Given the chance, they'd cut the throat of every Novus Vitan in the facility.

Chapter 19

The guard tapped a quick code out on the office door lock and the door hissed open. The inside of the room was so dark Mercy couldn't see anything. But Storm could.

His tense posture and the alert tilt of his head told her that he could either see or smell someone hiding inside the room.

"Lights," he said in a low voice.

Overhead light suddenly illuminated the small room. It held a desk with a monitor, chair, and a woman. She wasn't sitting in the chair. She stood with her back against the wall opposite the door, her posture rigid, her hands in fists by her sides.

Her eyes traveled over Storm's tall body. When her gaze dipped below his waist, she turned scarlet and looked away. A shudder traveled over her body.

She must be the Angel. Mercy had heard there was a female Angel in charge of the Center.

The woman wore a long, gray dress that didn't look all that different from the ones worn by the prisoners, except that hers had a tight, high collar and long sleeves that ended in tight cuffs at her wrists. The body under the dress seemed thin, almost emaciated. Her cheekbones stood out in harsh contrast, her jaw sharp, her nose blade-like. Thick, golden hair had been scraped so tightly into a huge knot on the back of her head that it looked as if it pulled the skin of her face back. Yet her lips were incongruously lush and soft, her strong brows caramel-colored, her eyes huge and brilliantly blue.

She stared at them with a rage and contempt so intense it was palpable, like a vibration in the air. Her scimitar jaw tilted upward and she looked down the length of her aristocratic nose at them. Or at Mercy, at any rate. Storm was too tall for her to look down at him.

Then she turned her gaze to him, and although her shorter height forced her to gaze upward she somehow still gave the impression she was looking down.

So this was an Angel. Mercy had heard of them but had never met one. So far, she wasn't impressed.

"Get back," the Angel barked.

Storm gazed at her, his tail slashing back and forth, for a several seconds before laughing. "Or what?"

"If you come near me, you will offend the Maker and suffer the consequences." She sounded utterly convinced of her own words.

Storm simply grinned at her. "I'll take the chance."

He strode to her and took her by the upper arm.

"No!" She tried to wrench herself out of his grasp. "Don't touch me."

"I won't hurt you." He grinned at her again.

The Angel seemed to have some kind of immunity to the dazzling sexiness of his smile. Mercy shook her head in wonder as the pinch-faced woman glowered at him, apparently unaffected by his touch as well. It wasn't that she wanted Promise to respond to him the way she did. Because then she'd have to kill the woman. She simply couldn't understand how the Angel could fail to see what she did.

"You're in charge here, aren't you?" Storm said, regarding the Angel intently.

She blushed. "Yes, I am."

"You were," he corrected her. "Now, I'm in charge and I'm taking you with us."

His tail brushed the bottom of her dress and she cringed, a whimper escaping her throat. Mercy almost felt sorry for her. Then the Angel straightened her back and gritted her teeth, redoubling her glower.

"You will pay for assaulting an Angel," she said.

"I'm sure." He sounded bored. Unconvinced.

"You're already damned by our Maker, but now you'll be doubly damned. You should save yourself and release me."

He grinned down at her. "Doubly damned?"

"Yes. You'll be punished even more severely in the afterlife."

"Will I?" He began dragging her toward the door.

"You'll burn!" the Angel yelled, pulling backward against his grip. "Do you want to burn? Anyone who kills an Angel burns for all eternity!"

He glanced down at her. "Who said anything about murder?"

Promise gaped at him, looking so astonished that Mercy laughed aloud. "You're not going to kill me?"

"I would never kill a woman unless it was unavoidable," he said.

"I think you might be the one about to be punished," Mercy told her. "And you deserve it, after what you did to me and all the other test subjects."

The memory of Chisholm with his throat cut, bleeding out, roared into her mind's eye. She turned away from it. She couldn't' think of that now, or she might break down. Now she had to be strong, for Storm, for all of them.

Angel Promise gave her another imperious glare. "We chose only degenerates for our experiments. No decent people were harmed. You should be grateful and proud that you participated."

Her attitude, her pronouncements once would have crushed Mercy, feeding all her self-loathing and guilt. Now the Angel's callousness simply

94

made Mercy want to turn her over her knee and give her a good spanking.

"Really?" Mercy said. "You're going to feed me that line now?"

"We don't care what you think," Storm said. "You're coming with us. If you continue to fight me, I'll incapacitate you like I did the guards. So it's up to you. Would you rather be conscious or unconscious?"

"You degenerate, naked barbarian," the Angel spat. "Your people deserved what we did to you. I only wish it had been more effective."

He grinned down at her as he dragged her from her office, but his smile didn't reach his eyes. "I'm sure you do. And now you're going to have an opportunity to make it up to us."

The Angel's narrow nostrils flared and her lips parted. Her whole body stiffened until she was so rigid she looked like she might break at any moment. Her eyes seemed to dilate. In fear or something else?

"What do you mean?" she whispered.

"I mean that Belleren is extremely short on females. And you are female, aren't you?"

"No! You wouldn't dare."

"Hold on," Mercy said. "So it's all right for you to trap us here and force us to have sex with each other, but you're somehow exempt?"

Promise's lush lips thinned. "You know perfectly well that I'm different. If this—this monster takes me, he'll unleash all the fury of Novus Vita and our Maker."

"First," Storm said, "I have no interest in you. I belong to Mercy here. Second, I'm sure you'll forgive me if Novus Vita's fury doesn't scare me much, since you are still under our control. And third, I have my own gods. I couldn't care less what your Maker thinks of me."

"He's your Maker too," she snapped.

"Is He?"

"Yes. He created all things," she said with unshakeable sincerity.

"I thought we Demon Kin were created in a lab. And I also thought we were evil. Does your Maker create evil things?" The spark in Storm's eye suggested he was enjoying this argument.

The Angel's jaw worked. She seemed to bite back a retort. Her eyes narrowed as she chewed on her upper lip. "He does not create evil things. Your people were created by the Master of Evil."

"Ah." Storm grinned widely. "Then perhaps your Maker has no dominion over me."

Angel Promise growled in fury. "You are impossible to talk to."

They'd reached the test subject cell block. The guard stepped forward to unlock the door. It opened to reveal a corridor crowded with Demon Kin males and human females engaged in all sorts of sexual acts. Naked flesh from wall to wall. Horns and tails, bare breasts, erect cocks, women with their legs spread, men between those legs—sex in every position imaginable. And some Mercy could not have imagined.

She glanced at Promise, her own face flushed with embarrassment and arousal. The Angel seemed transfixed with horror. Her wide blue eyes were even wider, almost perfectly round. She clapped her free hand over her open mouth. She cringed back from the display even as Storm pulled her forward, toward it.

* * *

Storm had—foolishly, perhaps—expected the orgy to have calmed down by now. He'd planned to lock Angel Promise into one of the cells until they could secure a ship. But as he drew the woman through the cell block door, he realized the sexual madness would rage for a while yet.

This was a dangerous place for Mercy to be, and probably even worse for the Angel. If the prisoners realized who she was, they might try to tear her apart. The least she would suffer would be gang rape.

He turned to remove her and Mercy from the danger. A shaggy-haired blond male grabbed Promise by the ankle and jerked her off her feet. She went down with a shriek. Storm reached for her. At the same time, other males tried to take her from the blond.

They tore her dress, yanked on her hair, groped for her breasts. Storm kept one hand on Mercy to keep her from entering the fray. But his concern for her safety crippled his attempt to protect the Angel. The crazed prisoners were dragging her away.

An enraged-sounding roar came from behind him. Suddenly a huge male with wild, reddish hair and glossy black horns leaped around him and Mercy. The redhead tore Angel Promise from the blond's grip and lunged off down the corridor, swiftly disappearing around a corner, the Angel screaming in a horrible, tearing voice. The whole thing happened like a lightning strike, so fast Storm didn't understand what was going on until the Demon Kin had disappeared with his prey.

Mercy shrieked, too. Then she merely stood as if glued to his side, trembling and staring at the place where the two people had disappeared.

He could hear the pounding of the male's heavy feet. Even the thickly padded floor couldn't entirely conceal that noise. Storm jolted out of his startlement and tore after them, shoving couples and threesomes aside, Mercy's hand clasped in his. He rounded the corner, but they were gone. The pounding sound and the screaming had stopped. Damnation. Where had he taken her?

He must have brought her into one of the cells.

He could simply let it go. That woman had been instrumental in his own torture and that of many others. She deserved punishment for the awful acts in which she'd participated—or at least, over which she had presided. But rape was wrong, too, and violating her wouldn't take away the pain of her victims.

He couldn't stand by and allow her to be hurt without doing everything he could to stop it.

A slender woman with long blond hair unfolded herself from the floor and came toward him and Mercy. She wore nothing but the shreds of a test subject gown. And she looked familiar. He'd taken her, weeks ago, before Mercy had come.

The blonde laid her hand on his arm. "You should let her go."

"I beg your pardon?" he said.

Her pretty face tightened in apparent resentment. "That bitch is the reason we're here. I asked her for help and she refused me. She deserves what she gets."

"No-one deserves to be raped," Mercy said.

Storm glanced around at the Demon Kin males crowding the hallway. They were getting off the floor, interrupting their sex to move together, clumping around him and Mercy as if to prevent him from going any farther, their faces grim with anger.

"Is this true?" said a brown-haired male next to him. "Is that woman responsible for us being here?"

Storm nodded slowly. "Yes. She confirmed it."

"Then let him take her." The male glanced around at his companions. "Do I have it right? Should she suffer the consequences of her actions?"

The Demon Kin shouted in agreement, their fists raised in the air.

"We won't let you interfere," he told Storm.

He felt sick at the thought of allowing such a thing to happen, at doing nothing to stop it. "This is not the Bellerenic way."

"It is now. She owes us reparation."

Storm looked into the faces of the human women, but he saw nothing but agreement there. The women seemed to agree with the men that Angel Promise deserved what was happening to her.

"She owes us reparation."

Storm gazed into one angry, muttering face after another. Some of the men seemed capable only of growls and grunts, while others were completely coherent. But all of them looked furious, both with him and with Angel Promise.

Chapter 20

A dark-haired male near them reached out and ran his hand down Mercy's bare arm. She gasped and jumped.

Storm tightened his arm around her shoulders as he glowered at the intruding male. "Don't touch her. She's mine."

The other male grinned, showing his fangs. "We need more females. Give her over."

Mercy huddled against his side, her arm going around his waist.

"You're not having her. She's not for you." Storm backed toward the entrance to the cell block.

The prisoners had surrounded them, however, and now blocked their exit. Mercy looked up at him, her eyes wide with terror, her skin an ashen color as the crowding Demon Kin began to reach for her. Hands touched her bare legs, her feet.

"Get off her," Storm growled. "She's had enough."

"Until she's had me, she'll never have enough," the dark-haired male said with a leer.

"The guards raped her." Storm sent him a glare that should have drilled holes in his head. "Is that who you are? Are you no better than them?"

The dark-haired male faltered, his expression suddenly uncertain. "They raped her?"

"Yes." Storm took another step backward. This time the crowd allowed him through. "That's how this whole escape happened. When I realized what they were doing, I tore out my implant."

Several of the males exchanged glances.

"That's impossible," said Dark-hair. "I tried to pull mine out and I went into convulsions."

"So did I," Storm said. "But apparently enchainment overrides it. Or something." He lifted the hair on the back of his neck and twisted, displaying his wound for them.

"I'll be damned," someone muttered.

"How do you think all of you got loose?" Storm said. "The guards didn't choose to let you out. I forced them to do it."

Now they were staring at him with awe in their faces.

"What is your name?" Dark-hair said.

"Storm." He purposely left off his last name. They didn't need to know his family background; the Kelzenec name would only confuse matters here.

Someone shouted his name back at him. Another took it up and another, and within moments the males were chanting "Storm! Storm!" in deep, booming voices that filled the corridors with deafening sound. Even the thick sound insulation couldn't muffle their shouting.

It was flattering in a way, but he had more important matters to accomplish, such as making sure Angel Promise was still alive.

"Thank you," Storm said, but the others' voices drowned him out.

"Thank you!"

They continued to shout so loudly he could barely hear himself.

He raised his hands in the air. "Thank you! Now hear me!"

At last his bellowing got through to them and they quieted. He lowered his arms.

"I appreciate the sentiment," he said. "But Angel Promise has been abducted and it's my duty to protect her. Also, no-one touches Mercy. She's my mate and I won't tolerate anyone harming or frightening her."

"We respect your mate," Dark-hair said. "But the Angel's another matter."

"I agree she deserves punishment," Storm said. "But not this way. We have no idea what he's doing to her. He could murder her."

"So what?" someone yelled from the back.

"Wouldn't you rather she face a trial on Belleren?" he suggested. "Wouldn't that be more just than whatever is happening now?"

The crowd muttered amongst themselves, their faces uncertain.

"Let me through," Storm said, pressing his advantage. "Let me find her and bring her to official justice."

A few of the males stepped back as if to make room for him and Mercy. Then a few more followed suit. Storm moved into the gap. The crowd parted for him without protest and he made his way to the first cell.

The locks on all the cells had been released, so although the doors were closed it was easy to open them again. To his disappointment, however, the first cell was empty. The second one was empty, too.

The other test subjects made no effort to help him. At least they were no longer standing in his way, no longer threatening Mercy. He crossed the hall to the opposite cell and peered inside it, only to find it empty as well.

Behind them, the other subjects had stopped muttering and were making erotic sounds again. The force of enchainment and sexual deprivation was more than enough to overcome their fury at the Angel, and that was a good thing at the moment. He liked them distracted.

"I wonder how many cells there are," Mercy whispered. "He could have gone into any of them."

"We'll just have to keep looking."

"We should split up," she said. "Make it faster."

"No. It's not safe enough for you."

"Even if we stay in the same corridor?"

He shook his head. "One of the males could run in and grab you before I had time to react. We need to stay together."

She sighed. "This is going to take a while, then."

◆ ◆ ◆

The first thing he saw when he opened the door of Cell Ten, Block Three, was the male's body. The auburn-haired Demon Kin was stretched out, face down, over the woman, his brown tail making long, slow sweeps of lazy satisfaction. Beneath him lay the blonde Angel, completely naked, her bare arms and legs and a slice of her side visible under his darker, larger form.

The male turned his head to glare at Storm with pale gray eyes. Angel Promise turned her face the opposite direction, as if to hide from him.

"Get out," the male growled.

"Let her go," Storm said.

"No. She's mine. You can't have her."

Storm sighed. "I don't want her sexually. I only want to protect her."

"I protect her now."

Storm advanced into the room, Mercy at his heels. "Angel Promise, are you all right?"

She mumbled something.

"Say that again, please," he said.

Slowly she turned her head toward him, her eyes downcast, her face flooded with red. "I am unharmed."

"Are you saying that because it's true or because you're afraid of him?" Storm said.

The male growled. "I would never hurt her."

"It's true," she said. "There's nothing you can do to help me now."

There was so much defeat in her voice that he almost felt sorry for her. She was a terrible person and he despised what she'd done to so many of his fellow Demon Kin, not to mention the women of her own planet. But he couldn't let her go without making sure she wasn't being abused, that this was really her free choice.

"You can still come with me and Mercy. We'll keep you safe."

Another growl erupted from the redhead's throat.

"No," Promise said, her voice low and flat. "I would rather stay with Cain."

Storm looked down at Mercy. She raised her eyebrows and shrugged.

100

"Maybe she really wants to stay," she whispered.

"Go," Cain said.

"All right. But if you let any harm come to her, I'll take it out on your hide."

"Never," Cain said.

"I'll come back later to escort the two of you to the ship. For now, Mercy and I need to get everything ready to go."

Cain had already turned his attention back to Promise, his pale-eyed gaze completely absorbed in staring into her face. She seemed almost as rapt, gazing back at him with an expression Storm couldn't read. The only thing he was sure of was that it wasn't hate in her eyes.

That would have to be enough for now.

Chapter 21

Storm gaped at the ship's console. Around him, lights blinked and the whole bridge hummed with the life of the ship, but all he could do was gape. He wore a uniform filched from one of the Life Studies Research Center guards, yet he felt more naked than he ever had when he possessed no clothes.

"I'm sorry," he said finally. "Could you repeat that, Belleren?"

"You've been declared dead, K-Z-4500. You've been gone two years."

Two years?

"Are you sure? Two years?"

"Look, Kelzenec," the communications officer said in a tired voice. "I'm just reading the records as I see them. I don't have access to any of the higher level stuff. All I've got is K-Z-4500 declared missing presumed dead on the fifth of Travenion, 7589. That was a year and a half ago."

"Gods of Belleren," Storm muttered.

It was at least 7591 now. He'd lost two whole years of his life to the Novus Vita Life Studies Research Center. His father and brothers believed him dead. They must have held funerary rituals for him. The required period of mourning was already over.

Mercy's small hand descended on his shoulder and squeezed.

He cleared his throat. "Yes. Well, as you can see, I'm not dead. I'm requesting permission to land with fifty Demon Kin males and twenty human females."

"How many?" the officer said in clear disbelief.

"Fifty of our males and twenty human females of Novus Vitan origin. All were imprisoned on a secret Novus Vitan facility on the Novus Vitan moon."

"Um...do you have the ID numbers for our guys?"

"No, I don't."

The officer heaved a heavy sigh. "All right. You have permission to land on dock 1358. Do not leave your craft once you've landed. I repeat, remain on your craft until you have permission to disembark."

"Roger. We'll remain on the ship until we have permission to disembark."

He exchanged a glance with Mercy.

"Your last name is Kelzenec?" she said. "I thought that was the name of your capital city."

"It is. My family founded the city. It's named after us."

Her eyes widened. "Oh. Are you royalty or something?"

He laughed. "No. Not royalty. But we are pretty well-off."

"Hm." She sniffed. "I don't care about that. I'd go with you if you didn't have a single credit to your name."

That might be true, but he was glad he'd be able to give her a comfortable home. There would be no way for her to earn her own living on Belleren, since she was a Novus Vitan. Although humans in general were welcome, her kind were not. They faced heavy prejudice, even the females.

"Do you think they'll detain us?" She looked worried.

"I don't know. They'll certainly want to question us, find out everything we know about the facility."

She folded her lips inward until they disappeared. "Do you think they'll separate us?"

"No." He shook his head. "They'd never separate a Demon Kin and his or her enchained mate. Not unless they intended to torture both parties." At her frightened look, he added, "but they won't want to do that. Why would they? We're on their side."

She didn't seem convinced. She glanced around the cramped, utilitarian bridge with its dark-gray consoles, ugly metal decking, and now blank viewscreen.

"I hadn't thought this far ahead," she said, hugging herself with her spare arm. "I don't know, Storm. I'm not one of your people. They might not take kindly to me, or any of the other women."

He slipped an arm around her slim waist and tugged her against him. "Sweetheart, they'll fall all over themselves the instant they hear how much you helped me."

She frowned. "I didn't help you. You did it all yourself."

"Yes, you did. You saved me, Mercy. Your sweetness, your compassion, helped me come back from the madness so much faster than I would have otherwise. I can't tell you how much that means to me. And if it weren't for you, I never would have had the strength to tear out my implant and survive."

Her enormous brown eyes turned glossy. Storm drew her head down and kissed her mouth. "If I have to, I'll play the war hero card," he said.

She smiled, although her eyes remained tearful. "I don't think I could stand to be shoved back into prison."

He cupped her face in his palm. "You will not go back to prison. Do you hear me? That will never happen. You'll be lauded as a heroine. When we drive through Kelzenec, they'll toss flowers at you as we go down the street."

She still looked troubled. He rubbed his thumb across her lower lip, then slid his hand around to her back and urged her onto his lap. She leaned against him with an agitated sigh.

"Don't you want to go to Belleren with me?" he said in a low voice.

He wouldn't force her. It would be a huge shock to her system, trying to learn the Demon Kin culture and fit in on such a different world from the one on which she'd been raised. But they couldn't live together on Novus Vita.

Her people would never allow it. They might not be officially in charge, but forbidden relationships could still be punished. There had been a number of murders committed by Novus Vitans outraged at one of their own women taking up with a Demon Kin, even before he'd been captured. By now, the number must have grown.

If she wouldn't come with him, they would have to split up. That thought made his stomach hurt. He loved her; their relationship had grown so much deeper during the journey from Novus Vita. But if she wanted to be free of him...

"I would never force you." The words hurt his throat, but they must be said. "If you don't want to stay on Belleren, or you don't want to stay with me at all, I'll help you find someplace you can go."

"I want to be with you. It just scares me," she said.

He blew out a breath of relief. "You know I'll do whatever is needed to help you adjust," he said. "Anything. You only have to ask."

"All right." She lifted her head and kissed him on his jaw. "I love you, Storm."

"I love you, too, Mercy." He would make it right for her. No matter how difficult it was.

Chapter 22

The sunlight on Belleren was the hottest, hardest, brightest light Mercy had ever seen. Even before they disembarked from the ship, she could feel it radiating through the open hatchway and into the vessel. Then she stepped onto the boarding ramp into what seemed like a solid wall of heat.

She squinted against the stabbing glare and lifted her free hand to shade her eyes. Her other hand was still clasped in Storm's. They walked down the boarding ramp and a roar of shouting, wild whoops, and applause exploded all around them.

Mercy stopped, her heart suddenly racing. "What's going on?"

"They're just welcoming us home," Storm said. "Apparently, we're heroes on Belleren."

"You are?" She squinted up at him.

He tugged her hand as he moved down the ramp. "We both are. The media is calling us the Moon Rescue Duo."

She raised her brows. "The Moon Rescue Duo?" she said in a dubious tone.

"It sounds better in Bellerenic."

Mercy shook her head. "But I didn't do anything."

"I believe we've already established that you did." He paused to drop a smiling kiss on her mouth.

She glanced nervously at the crowd of people who'd come to welcome them. Most seemed to be Demon Kin males—not surprising since they'd lost most of their females, and there weren't many humans on this planet. It was a daunting sight, all those horned heads and waving tails, face after face of the enemy watching her, calling her name.

"Mercy! Mercy!" they chanted.

"They love you," Storm said.

They weren't the enemy any more. She wouldn't have gotten a homecoming like this on Novus Vita. They would have stuffed her right back in prison, and maybe into solitary confinement as punishment for aiding the Maleficans. No, the Bellerenics. She had to remember to use their preferred name now, since they considered Malefica to be derogatory and she wanted to fit in. This was her new home.

She looked up at Storm and smiled. "We made it. We're free."

"Yes, we are. I didn't think it was possible."

Behind them trooped the rest of the Demon Kin and human prisoners from the facility. Mercy glanced over her shoulder at them. She saw the blonde, Kerin, who'd demanded they let the unnamed Demon Kin male do whatever he wanted with Angel Promise. Kerin smiled and waved at her. Mercy gave her a lukewarm wave in return. She wasn't sure how she felt about that whole situation.

She and Storm would never have been able to save Promise, once the Demon Kin had made up their minds to let the redheaded man have her. They'd done their best to reach her, but they'd been too late. And she hated the idea that the Angel had suffered, even after what she'd done to Mercy and the rest of them.

Another glance over her shoulder and she caught sight of Promise herself. She still wore her high-necked gray dress, although it looked a bit tattered. Her long, gold hair hung free down her back. She kept her eyes downcast, but what Mercy could see of her face did not look happy. The redheaded Demon Kin male had an arm around her shoulders, and Mercy couldn't tell if the gesture was affectionate or controlling.

Then Promise leaned her head against his chest and he bent down to kiss the crown of her head. Maybe things between them were better than she'd thought. Maybe it would be all right after all.

Chapter 23

The world beyond the landing platform was difficult to make out, with all those Demon Kin crowding around. What little of it Mercy could see looked harsh, arid, and dry. But she'd expected that. Much of Belleren was desert.

She hitched up the waist of the pants they'd found on board the ship. They were too big, but better than nothing. Storm had promised her a new wardrobe when they arrived. And here they were.

He grinned wickedly at her. "We're going to say hello to my family first. But when I get you alone, I'm going to welcome you to Belleren properly."

"I certainly hope so."

Bellerenic soldiers stood at attention on either side of a walkway marked off with fancy velvet ropes. They served to make the event look more official, and to hold back the crowd of colorfully dressed and excited Demon Kin males who jostled and strained to get a look at the released prisoners and their human female companions. Everywhere she looked, there were sharp horns, curling horns, every kind of horns. And tails. Lots of tails.

At one time, that sight would have made her feel faint with terror. The strange, loose tunics and trousers they wore, complete with embroidered decoration at the neckline and sleeve hems, would have made her wrinkle her nose at their foreignness. Now, it merely interested her. Especially since the Demon Kin continued to smile and call her name.

Mercy clutched tightly at Storm's hand as they made their way along the walkway. The shoes she'd found on board the ship slipped and slid, rubbing painfully against her heels, but at least they protected her against the extraordinary heat radiating off the pavement. Petals in brilliant red, fuchsia, and white fluttered down over her head to land in her hair, on her shoulders, and on the hot pavement. They really were throwing flowers at her. She looked up at Storm in astonishment.

He grinned down at her. "I told you they would."

"I know, but—I didn't really expect—"

He raised his free hand in the air. "I see my family."

Oh, Maker. Her mouth went as dry as the desert air, while the rest of her broke out in a nervous sweat. She wasn't ready to meet his family. What if they hated her? What if they blamed her, because of her homeland, for what had happened to Storm?

Her steps slowed as she began to lag behind him. She didn't want to disappoint him. He believed his family would love her because they'd been imprisoned at the facility together, but there was so much bad blood between their people. They might not be able to overlook it.

"Are you all right?" Storm gave her a concerned look, his black brows drawn down.

Mercy pasted a bright smile on her face. "I'm fine. Just tired. And hot."

He nodded. "It is very hot. We'll get you inside as soon as possible."

He was so sweet and protective of her. She knew he loved her, and she loved him. They would make this work, somehow, even if his family didn't approve.

Three tall Demon Kin males, two younger with Storm's nearly black hair and one older with salt and pepper hair cut very short, stepped out of the crowd and slipped under the ropes, huge grins on their faces.

"Storm!" the oldest one said.

Storm let go of her hand and took the older male in a tight embrace. "Father."

His father released him with obvious reluctance, dashing tears from his eyes. "We thought you were dead."

"I heard that," Storm said. "I'm so sorry I couldn't get word to you."

His dad and the two younger men glared at him. "You were a prisoner, you idiot," the youngest-looking one said. "How would you get word to us?"

Mercy elbowed him with a smirk she tried to hide. He was being ridiculous, but it was also funny hearing his brother—was it his brother?—giving him a hard time.

Two younger males crowded around. All four men had similar dark hair and eyes and strongly chiseled features. Even if she hadn't known they were Storm's family, she would have suspected because they looked so similar.

The two younger ones clapped Storm on the back, talking rapidly in Bellerenic. They all seemed delighted to have Storm back and there was none of the stilted reserve she remembered from her home world. Here, it seemed people were exuberant in their emotional displays.

Storm turned to her and slung an arm around her shoulders, drawing her close. "This is Mercy Wheaton, my mate. Mercy, this is my father, Marcus Kelzenec, and my brothers, Linc and Gregory."

"Your mate?" Marcus said with an even bigger grin. "This is good news."

Mercy swallowed hard, suddenly nervous again. "You don't mind that I'm Novus Vitan?"

"My dear, you're female and healthy and Storm wants you. Are you happy with him?"

"Oh, yes." She beamed up at Storm, who was gazing down at her so tenderly she almost blushed. "I love him."

"Then that's good enough for me."

"Look at the two of them," Linc said with a knowing grin. "They can't take their eyes off each other."

"Enchainment," Gregory said, grinning too.

Now she really did blush.

"Don't embarrass her, boys," Storm said. He slid his arm from around her shoulders and linked elbows with her. "We need to get her inside. She's not used to this heat."

"Absolutely." His father took her by her other elbow.

"I'll clear the way," Linc said, taking the lead.

Gregory fell back, so she was surrounded on all sides by protective Demon Kin males. She'd never felt so protected in her life, actually. The ropes and the guards kept the crowd back, yet having Storm's family on all four sides of her felt much more secure.

"They love you, too," Marcus said as they approached a long, low-slung building. He nodded toward the cheering strangers. "If you weren't already taken, there would be thousands of offers of marriage for you."

Mercy shook her head. "I don't understand it. I didn't do anything."

"She keeps saying that," Storm said. "But it isn't true."

"You did something very important," Marcus said. "And you're still doing it. You love my son, even though you were taught to hate and fear him. In this war, that's a heroic act."

"They told us the war is over," Storm said, winking at her.

"It may be over on paper, but it seems both our worlds have a long way to go to achieve true peace," his father said.

"I'd agree with that," Storm replied.

"Me, too," Mercy said. The words slipped out before she realized they might not be appropriate. She'd acquired some new habits from talking so freely with Storm, and she didn't know what Demon Kin traditions might be concerning men and women conversing together.

The men didn't seem to notice that she'd said anything unusual, though. They only smiled at her as if in agreement.

❖ ❖ ❖

Storm's family lived in a large compound in an older section of Kelzenec, a neighborhood that seemed to be filled with similar residences. A high, sand-colored wall lined with tall, slender palm trees surrounded it. The driver guided the float car through a thick wooden gate painted the most brilliant shade of turquoise she'd ever seen and landed in a shaded spot next to what looked like a garage. A narrow garden occupied the space between the outer wall and a second wall that she surmised was the house itself.

A second door, painted the same turquoise and carved with an elaborate bird motif, led them into the cool and dimly lit entry hall of the house. Which was a lot more like a palace than any house Mercy had ever seen before.

The entry hall, floored with smooth green marble, led off in two different directions.

Its walls were painted vermilion, and low benches carved from dark wood punctuated its length. High windows on each end of the hall admitted filtered light through carved screens or shutters.

"Would you rather have refreshments or get settled in your suite first?" Marcus said.

Storm glanced at her, banked heat in his eyes. "I think we'd like to rest for a while. Is that all right with you, Mercy?"

"Yes, please." She wanted nothing more than to get out of the awkward and ill-fitting stolen clothes. And then, well, she already ached for Storm.

"Do I still have my old rooms?" Storm said.

"You do."

"Father couldn't bear to give away any of your things," Linc said. "Or even pack them up. The room is exactly the way you left it."

The grief implied in that statement caught at Mercy's throat. They'd felt his loss so deeply. If only she could do something to help her people understand that he and his kind were not so different, that they felt and loved as deeply, maybe even more so. But Novus Vita had built itself on a hatred of everything sensual, with a special loathing of the Demon Kin, so understanding seemed far away.

Chapter 24

Storm tugged gently on Mercy's hand. "This way. We'll come back for food when we've gotten some rest."

He led her toward a wide staircase halfway down the right-hand side of the entry hall. Behind them, the two brothers jostled each other, snickering like a couple of teenagers. They must be very young. They seemed to take a great joy in imagining her and Storm alone.

He glanced down at her with a smile. "Try not to mind them. They're not fully grown yet and they haven't seen many women."

She laughed. "It's fine. I'd already guessed."

The stairs led them up to a second floor gallery which, to her surprise, was open to the air and a central garden courtyard. Below them, a fountain trickled amid sweet-scented flowering vines and potted palms. She could see a dining table and chairs in the shade of an arbor as well.

"This house is so beautiful," she said. "I've never seen anything like it." After the gray and cold prison, not to mention the Life Studies Research Center, this explosion of gorgeousness almost overwhelmed her senses.

"It's wonderful to be home," Storm said. "And I'm pleased you like it. I was hoping you would." He paused at another carved door. "We don't have to live here, though. We can get our own place."

"Oh." She frowned. "Do we have to?"

"No. I'm sure my father would be happy to have us stay. I just don't want you to feel trapped here."

She rose on tiptoes to kiss him. "I'm just trying to take all this in. It'll probably be a while before I feel anything but overwhelmed. I'm glad we have a family place to stay, since you're the only person I know here."

"Well, in that case, we'll stay as long as you like." He opened the door.

The room was spacious. On the opposite wall, deeply embedded in the remarkably thick masonry, a pair of pierce-work wooden doors led onto what looked like a balcony. She could just see it peeking through the carving on the door.

A huge bed with filmy white curtains and canopy took up the middle of the room. Mercy stared at it in amazement. She'd never seen such a fancy bed in her life.

The frame was carved from dark wood that contrasted dramatically with the white curtains. Brightly pattered pillows were piled high. It looked like the kind of bed she and Storm could stay in for a very long time without becoming uncomfortable.

"Would you like a bath?" he said. "Or a swim? There's a pool in the courtyard."

"There is? I didn't see it."

"It's behind that screen of palms."

Mercy walked up to the bed and touched the white coverlet with a reverent hand. "I don't know how to swim."

"A bath or shower then? I could use a shower."

She nodded. "The ones on board were awful."

"They felt more like someone pissing on my head than a real shower," Storm said.

She laughed in shocked amusement. "Storm!"

"Hey, I'm just telling the truth. Let me help you get these clothes off." He grinned salaciously as he unbuttoned her shirt. "You must be awfully hot."

"Unbearably."

"We can't allow you to get even more overheated." He unbuttoned a few more buttons, his eyes growing heavy-lidded and smoky as the valley between her breasts came into view. With one yank, he popped all the buttons at once and pushed the shirt off her shoulders.

"You've ruined it," she said.

"Good. I don't ever want to see it on you again." He lifted both her breasts at once, his face reverent. "Gods of Belleren, you're so lovely."

Mercy sighed, lifting her chest and pressing her breasts more fully into his palms. "I need you."

"The feeling is mutual," he said, rubbing both thumbs across her nipples and making her gasp. "There are so many things I'd like to do to you."

She shivered at the dark tone in his voice. "Tell me."

"Hmm. I think I'll make you wait." He bent his head and captured her mouth in a wet kiss.

She moaned as his tongue plunged inside her, as he pinched and rolled her nipples. He could almost make her come just from breast play, but she didn't think that was what he had in mind.

Her hands came up to rest on his shoulders. His clothed shoulders. Mercy wrestled feverishly with the buttons on his shirt, while he continued to kiss her. She was so excited her hands didn't want to cooperate, and the buttons refused to open.

Storm pulled away from her. "Allow me."

He tore his shirt off and threw it on the floor.

"The pants, too," she said.

"I'll show you mine if you show me yours."

112

She smiled. She'd never seen such a playful side of him and she liked it.

They stripped, throwing the clothes all over the floor, kicking off shoes, kissing the whole time. When they were both naked, their bodies came together and they groaned at the press of hot skin against skin. Their hands roamed, exploring, savoring, pleasuring.

Storm drew Mercy down to the bed. He licked her to screaming rapture, plunging his tongue and then his finger into her sheath until he'd reduced her to a wordless, quivering lump of pleasure. Then he reached into the drawer of the table beside the bed and produced a small jar.

"What is that for?" she said breathlessly.

"Lubrication."

"I'm already dripping wet." Had she really said that?

"Yes, you are," he said smoothly, palming her ass. "But I want another part of you."

"You want to take me there?" She stared at him wide-eyed.

In prison, some of the women had gossiped about anal sex, but she'd never imagined she might participate. It was...dirty. Frightening. Forbidden. Gazing up at the dark look on Storm's face, the idea suddenly seemed more erotic than scary.

"I—I don't know. I've never done that before," she said.

"I'll go very slowly," he said, watching her face with an intensity she found reassuring. Storm would take care of her. He'd always taken care of her needs, even when he was unable to speak.

"A-all right." She gave him a shaky smile. "I trust you."

"Mercy." He kissed her deeply, his hand coming around to cradle her skull. "I love you."

"I love you too."

Storm opened the jar. Inside was some kind of oil or ointment. He scooped out a generous amount and reached around behind her.

"This will make it easier."

She felt his finger caressing a place that had never been caressed before. A tiny gasp escaped her, although she didn't try to get away from him. The sensation was so strange that she tensed, expecting pain at any moment.

"Relax," he murmured. "Just let yourself open up. It's all right."

"I'm trying."

He kissed her, open-mouthed, his tongue caressing hers as his finger caressed her sphincter. The kiss relaxed her, the eroticism of his mouth on hers somehow transferring itself to what he was doing to her ass. The pressure, the invasion, began to seem pleasant. Arousing.

Storm slowly pushed the tip of his finger past the tight ring of her anus and inside her body. She moaned into his kiss. The grease he'd used made him slide easily in and out of her ass, the slight friction bringing dark pleasure with it. Mercy moaned again.

She'd never imagined something like this could feel good. But it did. The forbidden slide of his finger went on and on, moving deeper, teasing her with the promise of greater invasion to come.

His other hand palmed her breast, bringing a new dimension to the pleasure in her ass. Her nipples peaked. Her sheath clenched with a longing to be filled.

He removed the finger and she wanted it back. Instead, he reached for the jar again. She watched him spread a generous amount on the stiff length of his cock. Her eyes rounded.

"It won't hurt if you relax," he said. "I'll go slowly and stop whenever you say."

"I trust you," she said.

He opened her legs and positioned himself over her.

"I thought it would have to be from behind," she said.

"Not necessarily." He rubbed the tip of his cock against her ass.

Mercy took a sharp breath. The sensation of his sex pressing into her ass was...erotic. Arousing. She wanted more.

He watched her face as he pressed inward. The hot look in his eyes aroused her even more. She bent her knees, wrapping her legs around his waist.

He groaned. "You're so tight."

"You're so big."

He laughed, pushing in a little more. "Perfect fit."

He'd used so much of the oil that, even as big as he was, he didn't hurt her at all. He stretched her, though, stretched her wide open. She groaned deeply as he penetrated her ass all the way to the hilt.

"Mercy," he said, lowering his head. "Am I hurting you?"

"Not at all." She flexed her hips. "It feels good."

"Oh, shit." He withdrew, then thrust again with another moan. "Yes, it does."

He settled into a steady rhythm of thrust and retreat that filled her ass, her whole core, with that strange, dark pleasure. The bump of his pelvis against hers brought another element to the sensations, driving her closer and closer to an orgasm.

She grabbed onto his waist. His hair slid over his forehead in a black wave. His dark eyes fixed on hers, so hot and intense that her pussy responded with a surge of aching arousal.

The rhythm of his cock inside her ass stroked nerves in her pussy as well. It was shockingly good. Then Storm reached between their bodies and touched her between her legs and she exploded in a ferocious, screaming orgasm.

Storm growled and groaned above her, shaking with the force of his own climax. Hot liquid filled her as he jerked inside her once, twice, three times. She whimpered at the weird pleasure of it, luxuriating in the intimacy.

A minute later, he dropped his head, his hair tickling her skin, his breath ragged. "So good."

"Mmm." She kissed his neck.

"I love you."

"I love you, too."

They lay together, simply breathing and holding each other, soaking in the closeness, the press of their bodies. She didn't care where they lived. As long as she was with Storm, she was home.

He sighed and kissed her. Then he lifted his head and looked into her eyes. "Will you marry me?"

Mercy blinked. Her heart seemed to skip a beat. All the ways she'd imagined receiving a proposal and none of them had looked like this.

Most of her fantasies had involved the man getting down on one knee. Cletus had proposed to her father, not to her, as her permission was not needed on Novus Vita. She'd never pictured a man proposing to her while buried deep in her body. But it didn't matter.

She didn't care how or when he did it, just that he wanted her enough to commit for a lifetime. Because she wanted him just as much.

"Really?" she said softly.

He smiled down at her, his thumb brushing her temple. "Yes, really. Will you be my wife?"

The smile that broke across her face felt dazzling. "Yes. I'll be your wife, Storm."

"Thank you," he murmured. "Thank you, thank you. We're going to be so happy together."

She knew it was true. They were going to love each other forever and raise Demon Kin children on this desert planet, and have all the joy they'd longed for but never found until the Novus Vita Life Studies Research Center. She could hardly wait to get started.

The End

Tori Minard

The Devil You Know

Chapter 1

She wasn't supposed to be here. Anne's parents had strict rules about how close she was allowed to get to the Malefican embassy next door, and inches away from the boundary was way past the limit. She was fifteen, and they still treated her as a child.

The sun beat down on her dark head, making her perspire as she walked along the gravel path at the edge of the garden. The gravel crunched underfoot, making her wince and hope that no-one from her house could hear it. Heat radiated off the stone border wall. It was really too hot to be outdoors, especially for a girl. Novus Vitan girls always wore long skirts and long sleeves, no matter the weather, making it necessary for them to spend most of the summer in the shade.

A splash came from the other side of the wall. Was it him? She'd seen him swimming in the Malefican Embassy pool every day this summer. Last summer, too. Sometimes she watched him from behind the curtains of her bedroom window, or through a knot hole in the wooden gate that led between her parents' property and the embassy grounds.

She could watch him now.

Anne went to the gate, her heart beginning to skip. It was standing ajar, the open space showing a thin wedge of shrubs and a corner of the stone pool coping. Normally the gate was locked from the other side.

She touched the green-painted wood. No-one would notice if she opened it just a little wider, would they?

Carefully she pulled the gate open another handspan. She peeked around the edge, but the thick stone wall and the gate itself blocked her view of most of the pool. And she wanted to see. She wanted to see him.

Anne slipped through the gate.

Sunlight glittered on the blue pool water, nearly blinding her. She squinted into the glare. The pool was closer to the wall and the gate than she'd realized.

"Hello." The voice was deep, masculine, the voice of a young man, not a boy.

Using her hand to shield her eyes from the sun, Anne looked toward the voice. It was him. He supported himself on his hands at the pool edge, his long, muscular legs dangling beneath the surface of the water. Water glistened on the golden tan of his bare skin.

Oh, my.

That was a lot of bare male skin. She may have watched him through a knot hole, but this was different. This was up close.

His blond hair was dark with water, slicked back from his forehead. Two cinnamon-colored horns curved up from his skull, and his reddish-gold Demon Kin tail floated out behind him. A dusting of darker cinnamon hair covered his well-developed chest. Anne tried not to gape, and failed.

His smile widened, showing gleaming white fangs. "You must be Miss Anne. You live next door, right?"

She nodded wordlessly.

"I'm Damien."

"H-hello." Her throat had gone so dry it was difficult to get out even one word.

"Would you like to take a swim?"

"Oh, no. No, I couldn't." Girls didn't swim. At least not on Novus Vita. Did Demon Kin girls swim? Did they do it naked, like he did?

"Then I'll get out." He leapt from the pool with the ease of a jungle cat.

Anne's breath caught. He was even more naked than she'd thought. The only garment he wore was a tight sort of breechcloth that outlined every contour of his bulging sex.

The bulge seemed to swell as she looked at it, as if in response to her gaze. Something in her own body ached in harmony with it, and the space between her legs grew moist. She tore her gaze away from the disturbing sight, only to encounter the flattest, tautest male abdomen she'd ever seen. She took a step backward.

"Hey," he said in a softer voice. "Don't go. I'm not going to hurt you."

She raised her gaze to his. "I've never spoken to one of your kind before."

An odd expression crossed his face, the corners of his mouth turning down for an instant. "We're just people."

She'd hurt his feelings. "I'm sorry. That was rude. It's just that I—"

"You've heard all the horror stories about us."

"Yes."

"Well, they're not true." He gestured toward a table and chairs set under a vine-covered arbor. "Will you stay and talk a while?"

Anne hesitated. If anyone should see her or find out where she'd been, she would face awful consequences. But how likely was it? Her mother was out of town visiting Anne's aunt today, and her father was at work. The servants only rarely looked this way. Damien smiled again, an inviting smile that made her want to take the hand he offered her.

"All right. I'll stay." She put her hand in his.

Damien's long fingers closed over her flesh. They were cool from being in the water, and she could feel the banked strength in them. But he was gentle as he led her to the table.

The touch of his hand on hers gave her a jolt of excitement. What would it be like to touch other parts of him? His shoulders, his face, his chest....She glanced at him, wondering if he'd read her thoughts. People said the Demon Kin could read minds if they wanted to.

"I've seen you before," he said. "You walk in the garden sometimes."

"Yes." Her face heated. Did he know she watched him? "I like to be outdoors."

"But not to swim?" He pulled out a chair for her.

"I—it isn't allowed. Not for young ladies."

"That's unfortunate. I love swimming. I can't imagine it being forbidden to me."

A horned and tailed servant, dressed in loose trousers and an exotic-looking tunic, appeared from within the embassy building. "Would you like some refreshments for you and your guest, Master Fallyn?"

"Yes, thank you."

Damien snagged a towel from the back of the chairs and dried off briskly. Then he took the seat next to Anne, just as casually as if he weren't virtually naked. The servant disappeared into the house, then returned moments later with a large tray bearing a pitcher, glasses, and a large plate of snacks.

"You don't have to go to so much trouble for me," Anne said.

"It's no trouble." Damien poured a glass of some pale, golden drink and handed it to her.

She sipped. The taste, both sweet and sour at once, was extraordinary. "What is it?"

"Lemonade. Have you never tasted lemonade?"

She'd never even heard of it. "No."

"We grow a lot of lemons on Belleren."

That was the name the Maleficans used for their world. Anne looked at him to see if he was teasing her. Of all the stories she'd heard of the Demon Kin, none of them mentioned anything as mundane and wholesome as agriculture. But Damien didn't seem to be joking. He merely poured a glass for himself and lifted it to his lips.

Beautiful lips. Most young men didn't strike her as beautiful. Damien was. Even with horns on his head, he was the best looking man she'd ever seen. When she looked at him, her belly began to flutter in the most disconcerting way.

"What do you like to do, besides walk in the garden?" He punctuated his words by offering her a pastry.

"I like to read."

"Do they let you read?" His eyes twinkled.

She smiled at him for the first time. "Not so much. Sometimes I sneak books."

"Perhaps you'd like to read some of mine. I just finished an adventure story."

"Oh." No-one ever offered to loan her books. "You'd do that for me?"

He reached out, as if to touch her hand, and then stopped. "Of course I would."

❖ ❖ ❖

A month later, Anne opened the gate one-handed and squirmed through it with her package tucked under her free arm. Damien always unlocked the gate for her now, to make their daily meetings easier. She had the book he'd loaned her, too. It was on her entertainment device, an older model with parental restrictions on what she could access from the Novus Vitan entertainment network.

Most of the material approved for her was religious. Some of the stories were interesting, but she disliked the lectures. They put her to sleep. Damien's stories were so different, it was as if they came from another world.

His books made her feel strange, on edge at the thought of a world so much larger than the one she'd been allowed to know, full of people and ideas more varied than she'd ever imagined. But they were exciting, too, like the young man who'd loaned them to her.

Suddenly the gate swung back and he was there, smiling, his hair gold in the sun. Her heart lifted. She smiled back.

"Did you read it?" he said.

"Of course." Under the covers, with only a tiny book light for illumination.

"What did you think?"

She blushed. "I think it wasn't proper reading material."

He nudged her playfully as they walked together to the shaded sitting area. "But you finished it anyway, didn't you?"

Her blush deepened. "Yes." She glanced at him from under her lashes. "Were your people really created as—as sex slaves?"

"Uh huh. Genevis Belleren and her Demon Kin lovers really established the original Demon Kin colony on our planet, too. The rest of the story I'm not sure about. It might be exaggerated a little to make it more exciting."

Anne offered him the package. "I brought you some of those cookies you liked."

"Thanks." He peeked inside the wrapper. "They're my new favorites."

They set the cookies and Anne's entertainment device down on the table. Damien was relatively clothed today, wearing the typical Malefican loose trousers and tunic. But the fabric was thin and loosely woven, and it molded to the musculature of his upper body. Anne's fingers itched to run themselves over the contours of that body.

What was wrong with her? She'd been having more and more of those thoughts lately, along with strange hot dreams that left her achy and longing for something she didn't understand. The dreams always involved Damien. And kissing. She didn't even like kissing.

She was beginning to think she was in love with him. Their friendship had begun with a definite infatuation on her side, but the more she learned about him, the more she got to know him, the more attached to him she became. He was funny and kind and he didn't talk down to her. He never treated her as if she were stupid simply because she was female.

Love. I'm in love with Damien.

"Anne," he called in a sing-song. "Are you in there?"

"Huh?" She refocused her gaze on him.

"I asked if you wanted to go for a swim."

She rolled her eyes. "You always ask that. And I always say no."

"It was worth a try."

Anne shook her head, laughing. "I'll always say no. You ought to give up and save yourself some trouble."

"I can't give up where you're concerned. You're all I think about nowadays."

His golden skin went red over his cheekbones, as if he hadn't meant to say those words. But he didn't take them back, either. He just stood there gazing down at her with those dark blue eyes of his.

Anne's face began to burn. "I—I think about you, too."

"You do?" He caught her hand, drawing her closer.

The touch of his skin on hers felt like a revelation.

"Yes," she whispered. She wasn't sure what she was assenting to.

His thumb worked in gentle circles across the back of her hand. The caresses seemed to get inside her somehow, opening her up and making her long to press herself against him.

She looked up at him, wide-eyed, as he drew her closer. His gaze caressed her face with something she could only describe as tenderness.

He leaned down and gently brushed his lips across hers. Then he did it again, with just a little more pressure. Her whole body went warm and tingly from that brief contact.

His hands splayed across her back, holding her to him as he kissed her. They were big hands, hot even through the fabric of her dress. Anne reached out, touched the warm bare skin of his forearm, let her palm glide over it.

His body felt just as hot. He was pressed against her whole length, her breasts crushing against the lower part of his chest. Anne touched her hands to the hard muscle of his shoulders, then lifted them as if he'd burned her. It was too much. The feeling of him against her, surrounding her, was so overwhelming it scared her.

But she couldn't back away, either. She wanted this even though it was wrong.

He licked her, his tongue flicking across her lower lip. Anne instinctively opened her mouth, allowing him access. And he put his tongue inside her. Instead of pulling away as she ought, she moaned softly and pushed herself against him, her hands tightening on his shoulders.

His mouth was like a world if its own, warm and wet, intimate, tasting of the cookies they'd shared and something else, something that was purely Damien. One of his hands slid downward to cup her rear end, squeezing. She trembled and sighed.

Gravel crunched under quick, heavy footsteps. It came from the direction of Anne's house, close by. At the base of the wall.

Someone was right on the other side of the wall from them. Her heart raced and her body trembled, but not from desire. Terror made her cold where she'd been so hot a moment before.

Dear God, what was she doing? If they were seen, caught, her punishment would be twice as bad as it would for merely talking to him. And he might get in trouble, too. God only knew what her father would do to Damien if he knew the Demon Kin boy had even talked to her. She jerked back.

"I can't. I have to go now." She ran blindly for the gate.

Damien called her name, but she didn't look back. She reached the gate, yanked at the heavy wood and plunged through the opening only to slam into a thick body. Anne stopped with a gasp. Her father.

He took her arm in a bruising grip. "You'll wish you'd never set foot outside, Miss Slut." And dragged her toward the house.

❦ ❦ ❦

Damien hated winters on Novus Vita. They were cold, gray, and snowy, and they froze his Demon Kin blood, froze his bones to the marrow. His beloved pool stood empty, covered against the snow. The garden looked sad and lonely, bereft of leaves and sunshine and Anne.

He ducked his head as a human woman glowered at him from the other side of an empty flower bed that fronted the tailor's shop he was leaving. She looked at him as if he were some kind of evil monster, not that her attitude was unusual. All the Novus Vitans saw him and his kind as monsters.

Then he lifted his chin. He had nothing of which to be ashamed. He was a member of a proud race, a people who had risen against terrible odds and made a place for themselves in a galaxy that hadn't wanted them.

It was the Novus Vitan who should be ashamed.

Was Anne ashamed of the way she'd left him? Probably not. She'd never returned after he kissed her. She'd left her entertainment device behind, yet she didn't come back or even send a message asking for it. He found books he thought she might like, even set them aside for her, but he couldn't share them with her.

He'd repulsed her with his barbaric caresses. That must be it.

He'd never seen such a look of horror on a girl's face, and hoped never to see another one like it as long as he lived.

The pathetic thing was how much he missed her. They hadn't known each other long, but it felt as if they'd become close in that time. She was the only real friend he'd made here on Novus Vita, and he'd allowed himself to dream. But her friendship had been false. Completely false.

He struck off toward the Bellerenic embassy. Sleet fell thickly, coating his wool-clad shoulders with ice. The wind picked up, driving the sleet into his face and making him shiver. Even the Novus Vitans looked miserable, their heads tucked into their collars, hands clutching at the openings of their coats.

He swung right into an alley a few blocks from the embassy. It was a shortcut between two major thoroughfares. It should have made his journey easier, except snow had piled up in drifts on the pavement and apparently no-one had bothered shoveling it. They'd simply made a crude pathway down the center of the narrow street, forcing him to slip and slide on the bumpy packed ice.

About fifteen paces in, he picked up the sound of footsteps behind him and turned. Five large Novus Vitan men walked behind him, their faces grim and intent, clearly focused on him. His heart slammed against his chest wall.

Whatever they wanted, it couldn't be good.

Damien broke into a run, splashing through puddles of ice melt. Freezing water splashed up onto his legs, soaking his trousers. Five more men boiled out of a couple of doorways, blocking his passage.

He paused, swallowed hard. Ten against one were poor odds, even for a Demon Kin. There had to be another way out of the alley. Up, for example.

He sprang up and clutched a doorjamb of the building next to him, trying to get purchase on the smooth stucco wall. His feet slipped, scrabbled against the stucco. Someone grabbed his jacket, dragging him down. He hit the filthy pavement with a grunt.

One of the men drew back a booted foot and slammed him in the ribs. Damien groaned. He snatched another man's trouser leg, jerking the fellow off balance. His enemy fell to the street next to him.

The rest jumped on him, punching and kicking, until he felt something break inside his rib cage. Gods of Belleren, they were going to kill him. He was going to die, and he hadn't even been able to see Anne again or tell her good-bye.

"Stop!" one of the men growled. "He's had enough."

The thugs quit assaulting him and got to their feet. Damien lay curled in a frigid puddle, trying not to make any sounds of pain. He wouldn't give the bastards the satisfaction of hearing him cry out. A warm trickle of blood ran down his cheek. He ignored it.

The icy water helped to dull the pain, at least a little. He breathed deeply through his nose. They weren't going to kill him and he wasn't going to die of pain.

The one who'd spoken stood glaring down at him. "That's what happens when one of your kind touches a decent woman. You get my meaning?"

Anne's father must have sent them. But why now?

"Fuck you," he croaked in Bellerenic. He searched for the words in Galactic Standard, but for some reason they wouldn't come to him.

The man motioned to his cohorts and they turned and left him there. It was a long time before he gathered enough strength to stand up and totter home.

Damien staggered around the corner at Anne's parents' house. And there she was, bundled in an ankle-length woolen coat, her long auburn hair pinned up and covered by a fur hat. An elderly man who looked like a servant walked beside her. It was the first time he'd caught a glimpse of her since the day he'd kissed her.

"Anne!" he called, breaking into an agonizing run. "Miss Anne!"

She didn't even glance his way. It was as if she were deaf. But that couldn't be true.

Damien caught up with them. His heart pounded so hard his vision began to blur and his breath sawed in and out of his lungs. He braced himself with his hands on his thighs.

"Anne—"

The servant tried to put himself between Anne and Damien, giving the young male an evil glare. "You are to leave my mistress alone."

"Anne, please talk to me."

She kept her eyes—those magnificent gray eyes he remembered so well—fixed straight ahead. His heart twisted. How could she do it? How could she pretend she didn't even know he was there?

"Look at me!" He reached for her arm, but the old man caught his wrist.

"Begone with you," the servant said. "Miss Anne does not consort with devil spawn."

"Anne?"

Still she didn't look at him. Damien dropped his arm to his side. The pain in his ribs dragged him down, dragged him over into a near crouch. He watched, breathing through the agony as the servant brought her up the front walk and into her parents' house. The door closed behind them, leaving him on the icy sidewalk.

He never saw her again.

Chapter 2

Twelve years later:

Damien Fallyn sat in his king's tasteful private office and thought of all the ways he could tell his monarch no. He was done being a controller. Five years of pleasuring strangers whether they were attractive to him or not was enough. And he knew this subject, or he'd known her once at any rate. Long ago. Gods of Belleren, she'd been the loveliest thing he'd ever seen.

"Are you still there?" the king said dryly.

"I'm here."

"And what is your answer?"

"No." He took a deep breath and met the king's obsidian gaze. "My answer is no."

"Damien, this is no idle request." The king steepled his fingers and gazed at Damien over their tops. His glossy black tail flicked out beyond the edge of the desk.

Damien made an impatient gesture. "Gods, do you think I don't know that?"

"I know you have a history with this young woman."

He shoved his fingers through his hair and bumped into his horns. "A history. Yes, I have a history with her. Someone else needs to perform her Soul Opening."

"The other controllers have all expressed open hostility toward Miss Paulsen. I'm not confident in their ability to perform the ceremony without causing harm to the subject. And I can't waive the ceremony without punishing her brutally for what she did, or the people will riot in the streets."

Damien held back an irritated sigh. "What makes you think I'm not just as hostile?"

King Night gave him a sharp look. "Maybe my information is bad. I was told you loved her."

Love. Was that what it was called? More like adored from afar, while she looked down her prissy Novus Vitan nose at him. Damien's own tail began to swish restlessly.

"I . . . cared for her. She didn't reciprocate. And her family...after they discovered we were friends, they ruined my father. They accused me of raping one of our Novus Vitan servants, Night. Drove us entirely off their planet, just because I'd had the nerve to—" *fall in love with her*—"enjoy Anne Paulsen's company."

126

"Do you hate her?"

"It was a long time ago." He raked his hair again. "No, I don't hate her." It would be easier if he did.

"Then you'll be better than any of my other possible choices. Besides, you're the most experienced controller I have."

He watched Night carefully. "Why do you need so much experience?"

The king shrugged as a blush crept over his face. "She's—uh—she's a virgin."

"What?" It couldn't be true. "She's got to be at least twenty-six or seven. And she's beautiful. Why hasn't she—"

"You know how these Novus Vitans are. Given her association with the terrorists, she's probably of an extreme NV orientation."

Yeah. That would fit with his memories of her. And Night expected him to make love to a frigid little stick like that? While she laid beneath him and glowered up at him in hatred and resentment.

Who are you kidding? You'd do anything to touch her again. But to have her once and then leave her would crush him.

I fucking hate being so confused.

"Do you think she knew what she was carrying?"

Night shrugged. "There's no way of telling how much she knew without doing a Soul Opening. All we know is she worked for them for six months. She claims she didn't know what kind of organization they are."

He wanted to know. Needed to know. Had Anne become the kind of person who would hide explosives on her body so they could be detonated in a public place? "I'm not sure I can do it without being enchained." He shook his head. "I still think it's better to use someone else."

"There are ways around enchainment." The king leaned forward in his chair. "We need the information from her, and the wrong controller will do more harm than good. Don't make me beg, Damien."

"Gods." He sighed. "All right. I'll do it. Just have a supply of super-codone on hand for me. I'll need it to get through the enchainment."

Night smiled, his dark eyes creasing at the corners. "Excellent. We have the chamber already prepared. The subject is waiting."

Damien narrowed his eyes. "You assumed I'd give in?"

"Not assumed," Night said blandly. "Hoped."

❖ ❖ ❖

They came for her in the morning, pulled her from her grim little cell and marched her to the equally grim shower room. There, the only female guard in the prison supervised her grooming, telling her exactly where and how to apply the depilatory cream and how to wash every inch of her body. As if she didn't know how to bathe. Afterward she rubbed scented oil into her skin, still under the hard-eyed gaze of the Demon Kin guard.

Finally, the woman handed her a loose white tunic of heavy slubbed silk. "Put it on."

"Where are the undergarments?"

The guard gave a harsh bark of laughter, her ugly tan tail lashing behind her. "You don't need undergarments where you're going."

Anne slipped the tunic over her head to hide her flush of shame. The guards in this place never lost a chance to remind her of what awaited her. And now the time had finally arrived.

She would submit sexually to the "controller," a Demon Kin male who would use her sexual arousal against her, to find out what thoughts she hid in her deepest mind. They'd let her know she didn't have to submit, but the Soul Opening ceremony was the only way she had to demonstrate her innocence. If she refused it, she would be considered guilty.

I am guilty.

They wouldn't get anything out of her anyway, because she wouldn't be sexually aroused. No Demon Kin male could possibly interest her, and besides she'd been thoroughly trained in the Teachings. She had no sexual interests at all.

The guard took her roughly by the elbow and brought her through a narrow door into a larger, dimly lit chamber. In the center of the chamber was a huge bed, piled with variously shaped white pillows and hung with white curtains. Anne stared at the bed. Good God, they wanted her to . . . to perform on that? It was like a stage.

On the opposite side of the bed, two banks of thickly cushioned chairs sat like seats in a theater. All of them were occupied by men who wore hoods over their heads, shadowing their faces. One of the men wore white, like she did. He must be the one who would . . . .

A woman with long silver hair and silver horns approached Anne and the guard from their right. She wore a flowing silver tunic that matched the rest of her. The woman held a hand out to Anne.

"My name is Lorca. I'm the Senior Ritualist here."

Anne nodded, her throat too tight for speech.

Lorca looked at the guard. "You may go now."

As the guard turned on her heel and left the chamber, Lorca turned to Anne. She lifted a goblet, which Anne hadn't noticed before. It was filled with some kind of dark liquid.

"Drink, that you may be open," she said.

Anne accepted the goblet and drank. It tasted like red wine with spices in it. How much was she supposed to have? She took a big swallow, and then another before Lorca held her hand out again, smiling.

The ritualist then went to the seated men and passed the goblet around to them. Each one drank. Did that mean they were all going to be with her? She'd thought it was only one. Her hands turned even sweatier than they were already, and icy cold.

One is enough. One is enough. One was too many.

In a far corner of the room, a band began to play soft music. It was like a parody of some romantic encounter in a vid. Anne stood next to the giant bed, feeling lost and wondering what to do next. If more than one man were to get up from those chairs, she was going to run out of here. To hell with their ceremony.

But only one man rose. He was tall. She couldn't see his face. The hood cast shadows over him, making him look even more mysterious and frightening than Demon Kin normally did. Anne nervously gripped the sides of her tunic.

Then he pushed the hood off his head and she gasped. Recoiled.

"Damien!"

It was him. Even after ten years, she could still recognize his face. He'd grown out of his teenage beauty into a man's face and form, his features more rugged and sharply carved than they'd been when she'd known him. But she remembered.

He still had those deep blue eyes, like the deepest ocean, heavily fringed with lashes, and that long blond hair hanging in waves past his shoulders. How he could have such long hair and still look so masculine was a mystery.

There was a scar on his face, though. It ran from the left side of his nose all the way down to his jawline. Her hand began to rise in order to touch it. She clenched it into a fist and willed it down to her side.

He frowned at her. "Anne. There's no reason to be afraid of me."

She lifted her chin. "I'm not afraid. But I won't participate in the ceremony with you."

"Child, you have no choice," Lorca said.

"Yes, I do." She took a couple of steps backward, toward the door. "I won't do it with him."

"Why not? You already know one another."

"Because she despises me, Lorca." Damien's gaze on her was hard as stone. Hateful. "She's always despised me. However, there is no-one else." He advanced on her.

"No!" She couldn't let him touch her. Even after such a long time, she could still remember how it had felt to have his hands on her. He would ruin her. He'd find out every secret she'd ever had.

His russet-gold tail flicked back and forth behind him, like the tail of an agitated cat. She'd made him angry. Anne turned and bolted for the door.

Damien caught her. His hand closed around her arm like a vise and yanked her around to face him. She looked up into his face, expecting to see hatred there. He scowled down at her.

"Get the restraints," he growled. "You and I, Miss Anne, have some unfinished business."

At the sound of her old name, she writhed in his grip. She leaned backward, pitting her body weight against his hold. But it did no good at all. He was far stronger and bigger than she, and he didn't seem to feel the slightest strain from all her struggling.

She'd thought that after so many years she wouldn't feel anything for him anymore. In fact, she'd never expected to see him again. Hoped never to see him again. Now here he was, preparing to take her and make a whore out of her, and there was nothing she could do about it.

Her traitorous body trembled, aching deep inside where she hadn't ached since the last time she'd seen him. She moistened between her legs. How could he make her feel this way? After everything she'd been through, she'd been so sure that fire was extinguished forever. But it had only been banked.

Damien dragged her to the bed. He picked her up and threw her on the mattress, pouncing on her when she tried to slide off the far side. His big hands pushed down on her shoulders, pressing her into the bed. His angry face loomed over her.

"I don't want to have to do this to you," he said.

"Then don't."

"If I don't, someone else will. King's orders."

So that's all it was. He wasn't here in this chamber because of her, but only because his king had ordered him to do it. Anne burst into a new round of struggles. Damn him. If he didn't want her, he should have let someone else perform the ceremony.

A smaller hand caught one of her arms and unbent it, forcing it to straighten. She turned her head. It was Lorca, strapping her arm down with a padded restraint. She wasn't any bigger than Anne, yet she mastered her struggles with no apparent effort. All the Demon Kin were unnaturally strong.

The woman reached over her head and pulled a sling-like device down from the canopy of the bed. She picked up Anne's leg and strapped her calf into the sling. This secured her leg in a high, bent position. A humiliating position that opened her completely to Damien and caused the borrowed tunic to slide all the way back to her hips.

Damien got off her while Lorca repeated the procedure on Anne's other side. Now both her legs were high in the air, her sex utterly exposed. She pinched her eyes shut, trying not to think of all the men in those chairs. Watching.

"I'm going to close the curtains," Damien said.

"Very well." Lorca patted Anne's arm. "Damien will take care of you. There's nothing to fear."

What did she know about it? She was one of them.

The curtains were on small metal rings that made a chiming sound when Damien drew them closed. She made herself open her eyes. The draperies now enclosed them in a small nest-like space, dim and cozy. Or it would have been cozy if she hadn't been tied to the bed frame.

He knelt beside her on the bed, looking down at her with a somber expression. "You know I would never hurt you."

Anne said nothing.

Damien sighed. "I asked them to find someone else, but they couldn't."

Was that supposed to make her feel better?

He laid his hand on the crown of her head. A slight, tingling sensation passed from his hand into her scalp. Next, he touched her between the eyes, then at the base of her throat, between her breasts, just below her sternum, and below her navel. She flinched at that one, although each touch brought with it the same intriguing tingle. Finally, he put his fingers between her legs, pressing them lightly to her bare sex. Anne gasped and jerked in the restraints.

Damien removed his hand almost as soon as he'd made contact. He leaned down. Anne's heart began to gallop. Damien's face drew closer, his eyes gazing at her lips. He was going to kiss her.

His lips, full and soft, brushed against hers. "I take you, body and soul, so that we may know the truth that is in you."

Her whole body began to tremble. "Please let me go."

"Shhh." He kissed her again.

Anne held her lips tight. His attempted caresses just slid off her. They could force this on her, but they couldn't make her like it, no matter what the guards had said. She was a Novus Vitan and a member of The Army of God.

Damien's thumb brushed across her lower lip. "Relax for me. Open up."

"No."

"Anne. Do you wish to repeat the ceremony over and over until you do open up? That's what will happen if you don't cooperate with me."

To her embarrassment, her eyes began to sting with tears. "Of course I don't want that."

"Then relax your lips for me. I want to give you pleasure."

"But I don't want it."

"It's part of the ceremony. You must have it, just this once." He drew the backs of his fingers across her cheek. "After that, you can go back to being as upright and tense as you like."

But it wasn't true. Being with Damien would change her forever. She knew it. How could he not?

I don't have a choice. Unless I cooperate now, I'll have to do this again or else plead guilty.

"Your second time in the ceremony won't be with me," he murmured. "I've resigned. This is my last one."

Would a ceremony with someone other than Damien be better or worse? Her mind said better, but her heart said worse. Foolish heart.

He looked ruefully down at her. "I probably shouldn't have told you that. Now you'll hold out for the next man."

A single tear escaped her eye. "No. I won't."

Damien brushed the tear away. Then he leaned close and pressed his lips to hers, and this time she didn't pinch them quite so tightly together. The tender caresses of his mouth on hers only made her eyes sting again.

She'd been kissed by another once, behind the Teaching House after Meeting. A young man named Joe had talked her into letting him walk her home, only instead he'd led her behind the Teaching House and pushed her against the wall and stuck his tongue down her throat while he grabbed her breasts. She'd bitten him.

Damien's kisses were nothing like that. They felt gentle, exploratory. Persuasive. Memories of him flooded back and she found herself moving her own lips in response. And the soft pressure, lifting and then repeating, made her flesh tingle and ache. The place between her legs began to grow warm and heavy.

His big hands framed her head as he angled his mouth for a closer fit. His tongue slicked along the margin of her lips and without thinking, she opened for him. He slipped inside her. Anne gave a low moan of excitement.

He moved one hand down, along her neck and shoulder, then over her breast. She arched into his touch. What was wrong with her? It must be the wine, the spices, making her respond so wantonly.

Nimbly he worked the fastenings on the front of her tunic, until her torso was laid mostly bare for him, her nipples hard and pointing straight at the canopy. Damien pushed the fabric to the sides. He stared at her with a strange yearning in his eyes.

"Do you know how long I've waited to see you like this?" His voice was low and husky.

"No," she whispered.

"Ever since I first saw you." His mouth curled up on one side. "But you were always too pure for a creature like me."

He cupped one breast in his hand. The heat of him made her ache even more strongly. One thumb raked across her engorged nipple. Anne shuddered.

Not too pure. Too afraid.

He pinched the nipple, and rolled it between his thumb and forefinger. The sensations that produced—it felt good. Oh, God, it felt good, and she had to hold fast. Be strong. But he repeated the action and she moaned as sweet pleasure bloomed in her nipple and echoed somewhere deep in her belly.

"He'll fuck you," the female guard had said. "He'll fuck you and he'll make you like it."

"No," she whispered.

But Damien only lowered his head and took her nipple into his hot, wet mouth. He suckled her. Anne strained at the arm restraints. She wanted to put her hands on him, wanted to clutch his head to her. But she could only lay there, moaning, as he tormented her with delight.

He lifted his head. "Did you think I didn't notice the way you responded to me? All those years, Anne. But I never forgot." His head descended again, and the suckling resumed.

Something hot and restless took over her body, making her toss helplessly under him. She ached in her breasts and womb, and throbbed between her legs.

He slid his free hand down her body, over her belly, and she moaned more frantically, thinking "stop!" and "yes, please" at the same time. Lower and lower went Damien's hand. But then instead of descending to her sex it moved over, to the side, and cupped her hip, squeezing gently. Then downward again, or rather around the corner to the back of her elevated thigh and up, up her leg.

When was he going to do it? He was torturing her with fear and anticipation. He stopped to switch his attentions to her other breast. He had to climb over her because of her legs hanging from the bedframe. A human male would have looked slightly ridiculous, clambering over her like that, but Damien moved so fluidly he made the absurd maneuver look graceful.

And then he was toying with her and suckling her again and she forgot to think. Oh, God, he was doing something to her just by laying his hands on her. She didn't know what it was but it had to be unholy because it felt so good.

Then his hand, his other hand now, began that suggestive descent down her belly, across to her thigh, along the sensitive skin of her uppermost leg and she trembled and moaned. His mouth pulling at her nipple sent shocks of pure delight through her and his hand . . . . His hand skimmed her sex.

Anne jerked against the restraints. He brushed her again, still suckling. This time, she didn't jerk. Over and over he touched her, so lightly, petting her newly naked flesh. With a fingertip he began to explore her intricate folds.

She'd never felt anything like it, had never touched herself there except when the guard had made her apply the depilatory. But this was different anyway, almost unbearably pleasurable. A presence softly entered her mind and she hardly noticed it, she was so caught up in amazement at his touch.

The presence merely watched, anyway, making no demands, just waiting. But then his suckling turned fiercer, so hard she cried out at the weird combination of pleasure and pain.

The presence said, "show me."

Chapter 3

Damien gave Anne the command to reveal her inner self just as her cries became most frantic. The door in her mind began to open, just a crack, just enough so he could see the place beyond. Then it slammed shut in his face. Her body tensed under him.

Open for me.

No. No, I can't.

Damnation, why was she fighting him again? She knew this was how it had to be. Damien took a deep breath, scented of Anne, and forced himself to relax. There was time.

He returned to slow petting of her sex, while he pressed his mouth over hers and kissed her. She responded hotly, thrusting her tongue into his mouth and moaning into him. It seemed she'd lost some of that Novus Vitan reserve, then.

He kept his place in her mind, just waiting, letting her get used to him. When she once again writhed under him, he probed just a little deeper. The door inside of her remained closed.

He used his forefinger to trace the edges of her sex's outer lips. Anne shuddered eagerly, yet her mind remained locked. Damien met the petal-like inner lips, carefully teasing them.

Just beyond, her hymen awaited. He could barely see it in the dim light, a glistening pink barrier of delicate flesh. He'd had virgins before, several of them, but none had possessed a hymen so completely covering the vagina. Getting inside Anne was going to be difficult for both of them, but especially for her.

The lips of her sex swelled with excitement from his caresses, yet the door in her mind stayed shut.

He was going to have to use extraordinary measures if she couldn't cooperate better than that. Damien moved around her, crawling along the edge of the mattress until he'd positioned himself between her upraised thighs.

She opened her eyes and stared at him. "Are you going to—"

"Not yet. It's all right."

He sank down to the bed. The mattress was extra-large to give the controller plenty of room to comfortably service a subject from any position. Damien stretched out with his head between her legs. She stared at him wildly, her mouth open as if she wanted to protest. But she said nothing.

Gods of Belleren, her scent. It was all over her despite the fragrant oil they'd put on her, and here between her thighs it was overwhelming. It tied his gut into a twist and made his cock unbearably hard.

Her pussy was naked, all the hair removed. He'd always pictured her with dark reddish-brown curls, the pink flesh of her sex just peeking through. Yet her current nakedness allowed him an unobstructed view of her sweet little cunt, the intricate folds opening for him just like an exotic flower with a tempting little bud at the peak.

He lowered his head and kissed that tempting pussy. She made a strangled sound. Damien licked her. The tangy flavor of her brought an involuntary groan from his throat. His cock pulsed so powerfully it hurt.

Focus on the ceremony.

Using one's psychic powers to directly influence or control another's mind without that person's permission was forbidden except in the most extreme circumstances, even to controllers. They were supposed to go through the front door of the mind, using only the naturally opening powers of sexuality to get in. But he wasn't going to get in that way, not without using enough brute force to harm Anne.

So he snuck around the back way, melding his consciousness with hers without asking for permission or giving her notice. His tongue continued to play and delve at the entrance to her body while his mind sank deeper and deeper into hers.

And he saw.

He didn't need to go back very far, only about a year. He found her memories of obtaining employment with a charity called Open Hands, which was just a front for the Army of God. And she knew. She knew they were part of the A.O.G. and that they waged guerilla warfare against the Bellerenic occupation.

Damien reeled inwardly, but pressed onward, looking for more. All he could find was her rather mundane work as their secretary. They didn't share information about their missions with her, so she had no idea—as far as he could tell, anyway—that they'd deliberately murdered hundreds of Novus Vitans along with all the Bellerenics they'd killed.

On the day of the incident, they'd told her she was to hand deliver a data crystal to a contact she would meet in the square in front of the Bellerenic occupational government's headquarters. She would never have been discovered, until it was too late, if it hadn't been for a passing Bellerenic who had opened himself psychically for personal, unrelated reasons and caught the thought impressions laid on the object by the maker.

That incident had changed the way Belleren managed security. They now had guards trained to psychically monitor all sensitive areas. It went against Bellerenic tradition to be so intrusive, but it was for everyone's protection.

The A.O.G. hadn't told Anne the data crystal she carried was really a tiny bomb, so she was innocent of the possession of an incendiary device charge at least. But still, she knew for whom she worked.

He'd been a fool to even hope otherwise. Damien withdrew from her mind and body so abruptly that she gasped. He picked up a corner of the sheet laid over the bed and used it to wipe her juices from his mouth, flinging the material back when he'd finished.

"What is it?" she said, her voice sharp. "What's wrong?"

"What do you think, Miss Anne?" He grabbed the curtains and yanked them open, making the metal hoops ring. "I now know more about you than I ever wanted to."

"But—"

Snatching his tunic, he threw it on over his head. "You won't have to undergo the ceremony again, so you should be happy." Except now she'd be punished.

It's what she deserves, for collaborating with scumbags like the Army of God.

He slid off the bed and turned to Lorca, who was watching him with a concerned expression. "Did you get everything?"

She nodded. "Yes."

"Then I'm finished here." If the king wished to consult with him over this, his secretary would contact Damien, so there was no need to linger.

He turned and strode to the chamber door, feeling Anne's bewildered gaze on his back just as clearly as if it were her hand resting there. Idiot! He'd really hoped she was innocent, just because he'd been infatuated with her as a boy. And she was nothing but a Novus Vitan fanatic, violent and bigoted.

When he left the chamber, his body was trembling in reaction. At least he hadn't struck her. He wouldn't have been able to forgive himself if he'd struck her, even after everything she'd done.

What kind of a person did you think she was? You knew how she'd been raised.

When they first met, the look on her face as he came near her had proclaimed more clearly than a written declaration that she feared and despised him. The way she flinched away from him when he got within an arm's length of her. The way she turned her face from him when he tried to speak to her.

He used to tell himself she'd had to behave that way or her parents would punish her. She wasn't truly rejecting him. And she'd gotten over it and become his friend. Apparently some silly part of him had believed that nonsense. Otherwise, he wouldn't have reacted as if she'd betrayed him by joining the fanatics. She hadn't betrayed anyone. She'd made her loyalties known from the beginning.

❖ ❖ ❖

Lorca came to the bed and began to remove the restraints. Anne turned her head to watch her. The woman's face was carefully neutral, so neutral that it scared Anne. What had Damien found to enrage him so? There was nothing in her memories that she hadn't already told the interrogators.

No, that wasn't true. She'd left out how much she really knew about the organization whose employment she'd accepted, and minimized how long she'd worked for them. They had a front company, a non-profit charity called Open Hands, and she'd worked in that office, which was what she'd told the Demon Kin when they'd questioned her. But she'd known they were really the Army of God. That was why she'd applied for the job. She'd wanted to do something important to strike back at the Demon Kin who'd invaded and defeated her world.

Damien hadn't known that. It had made him angry. Why would he even care?

"What will happen to me now?" she said in a small voice.

"You'll be sentenced." Lorca glanced at her. "The judge will see you some time later today." She unbuckled the last cuff.

Anne sat up. Her body still hummed with the pleasure Damien had brought out in her, and deep in her belly she ached. He hadn't finished what he was doing to her. He hadn't penetrated her and had gotten no pleasure from the act himself, but besides that he'd left her strangely wanting.

"Will Damien report to the King?"

"No." Lorca patted her thigh. "I and the witnesses saw everything he saw. We will make our report."

She went hot all over. "Those men—they saw what Damien did to me?"

"Yes. We were linked with Damien's mind."

Dear God. Her skin burned even hotter. The curtains had just been an illusion, designed to get her to let down her guard. She'd just been mauled in front of an audience.

She buttoned up the white tunic, without looking over her shoulder to see if the hooded men were still watching. She didn't want to know. When she slipped off the bed, the chamber door opened. For a moment, she thought it was Damien returning, and her heart gave a little flip-flop. But it was only the female guard.

The guard returned her to her cell, where she whiled away several anxious hours wondering what they would do to her. They served her a tasteless lunch for which she had no appetite. Then a few more hours of pacing and waiting, until finally the guard reappeared and unlocked the door to Anne's cell.

The woman took her arm in her hard grip. "This way."

She escorted Anne down long, blank corridors with plain white walls and up a long staircase. Then another corridor, this one with paintings at intervals and better lighting. Another staircase, another corridor with even better paintings. These were desert landscapes, probably representing Belleren. Finally they reached an enormous, carved wood double door flanked by two guards.

"The prisoner Anne Paulsen," the female said.

The guards opened the doors, their faces completely blank. The female pulled her through and into a luxurious office. There was a Demon Kin male there, sitting behind a desk of satiny black wood. He had long, straight black hair that gleamed in the strong afternoon sunlight coming through the windows, and eyes the color of dark coffee.

Two chairs, also in black wood, sat on a gold carpet in front of the desk, but she didn't take a seat. She hadn't been invited to sit.

"Leave her with me," the man said, staring at Anne.

The guard bowed and left. The doors shut softly behind her. Anne stared back at the dark-haired man, who must be the judge. Although this office looked more beautiful than any judge's office she'd ever seen. There was a carved crystal statue of a rock lion on his desk, for example, that must be worth a fortune.

"Do you know who I am?" the man said.

"The judge?"

His lips curled slightly. "Yes, and no. I am King Night of Belleren."

She blinked. "The king?"

"You may address me as Your Majesty."

Anne swallowed. "Yes, sir. Your Majesty."

"What am I to do with you, Miss Paulsen? You collaborated with terrorists, knew the kind of work they did. In fact, Damien tells me you sought them out deliberately."

She lifted her chin, although a sharp twinge of shame curled inside her. It was hard to look this man in the eye and admit she'd worked to harm his people. "Yes, I did."

"I won't ask why. It seems obvious, and it doesn't matter anyway. I'm obligated to punish you. And you deserve it, for what you did. Helping the Army of God, even as a secretary, made it easier for them to murder hundreds of people. Are you aware of the attacks on the governor's compound in the Southern Sector of Novus Vita?"

"No, Your Majesty."

"They broke in and murdered mainly human slaves. Fellow Novus Vitans. What do you think of that?"

Was it true? She went cold all over. "I—I think it's awful."

"But it would have been all right if the victims had been Bellerenics? Demon Kin?"

Anne dropped her gaze. "No, Your Majesty."

"You seem contrite, but I can't help suspecting those are crocodile tears."

What in heaven's name were crocodile tears? She waited for an explanation.

"Miss Paulsen, you're a valuable commodity," King Night continued in a dry tone. "Did you know that? Your beloved Novus Vita sent a bioweapon to us three years before we declared war on you. That bioweapon was a plague. They meant, I think, to wipe out all of us, but it mainly affected our women. Ninety percent of our female population died."

Her head jerked up. "Ninety percent?"

"Ninety percent. We need women, and human women will do nicely, since Bellerenics and humans produce fertile offspring that, with gene therapy, can become fully Bellerenic. Therefore, I'm assigning you to the reparation program."

"W-what's that, Your Majesty?"

"It's a program I oversee myself. We assign Novus Vitan women to Bellerenic masters, for the purpose of making reparation for the harm Novus Vita has done to our world. You will be a sex slave, providing your master with pleasure and children."

Her knees wobbled, and she grabbed the arm of one of the chairs to steady herself. A sex slave.

"No. Please. Please, Your Majesty, don't do this to me."

"It's too late, Miss Paulsen. I've made up my mind. If you hadn't knowingly collaborated, I might have taken a more lenient position, but in the circumstances—"

"I'd rather be put to death!"

He smiled without humor. "I'm sure. However, you're too valuable for that. Belleren needs you."

"W-who will be my master?" She had to force out the last word.

"In a moment." He pressed a button on his desk console. "Send him in."

Chapter 4

Anne twisted her hands together. Some Demon Kin male would take her away and do terrible things to her, make her participate in who-knew-what kind of depraved behavior. Make her pregnant with babies who would grow up with horns on their heads.

Her traitorous sex pulsed with the thought of those depraved things he'd make her do.

The doors opened behind her. She didn't dare turn her head, but only waited, looking at the carpet. Someone walked up and stood beside her. Anne gave him a furtive glance out of the corner of her eye, and her knees once again almost failed her. It was Damien.

He'd changed out of the white tunic. Now he wore a pair of loose indigo trousers with a loose white shirt over them. His tail whipped back and forth as he stood there, not looking at her. The trousers must have an opening in the back to accommodate the tail.

He was the one. The king was giving her to him, Damien Fallyn, the one Demon Kin male she'd hoped never to see again. Her gut turned to ice.

Damien bowed deeply to the king. "Your Majesty?"

"On the occasion of your retirement from service as a controller, I'm making you a gift of this woman."

Damien sent her a startled glance. Then he scowled at his monarch. "Giving her to me?"

"As a slave. She'll warm your bed and give you children, Damien. Help you reestablish the Fallyn Clan."

The scowl deepened. "She's a traitor, Your Majesty."

"In her mind, she's a patriot. At any rate, Belleren needs her services, as do you. Take her." The king gestured at them. "My secretary will provide you with the proper documentation."

"All right. I certainly can't turn down your offer, can I?"

"No, you can't." The king's stern face showed a hint of amusement. "I assume you'll be at the wedding next week?"

"Yes, Your Majesty. I'll be there."

Another person entered the room. Anne kept her gaze forward. Heavy footsteps clomped across the floor and stopped at Damien's side. She peeked out of the corner of her eye. It was the female guard, smirking as she offered Damien a metal collar and black leather leash.

Anne flushed all over her body. Inside, she trembled. They were going to put that thing on her. Damien accepted the equipment. As he turned toward her, the guard waited. She wanted to see him put it on Anne so she could gloat.

That woman had been gloating ever since Anne had been brought to the prison.

"Leave us," the king said.

The guards lips tightened, but what could she do? One didn't argue with a king. She left the room, closing the doors behind herself.

Damien lifted the collar to Anne's neck. She couldn't help lifting her eyes to his as he did it. And he didn't look away. He didn't seem ashamed of what he was doing. But, of course, he wouldn't be ashamed, would he? He was Demon Kin.

His hands were warm, dry, and steady as he wrapped the chilly steel links around her throat and closed the clasp. A weird thrill went through her as the collar tightened against her skin. Her sex began to throb and her nipples tightened to hard needy points, complaining that he hadn't finished with her. Hadn't taken her all the way.

"Look at me," he said.

"No." Her voice came out in a whisper.

He took her by the chin and tilted her face up. "Look at me."

Slowly she raised her eyes. His were hard, the blue of his irises cold and angry.

"Who is your master, Anne?"

She swallowed hard. Heat rushed up and over her face. "You are."

The king still sat behind his desk, watching them. If she looked at him, she would die of embarrassment. So she didn't look.

"That's right." Damien's thumb stroked along her jaw, sending pleasure through her whole body. "I am your master. You will serve me and obey me."

She dropped her eyes again.

"Look at me and say it."

Oh, God. Anne shook her head. His grip on her chin tightened.

"Look at me and say it."

She looked, while her heart dropped down and down until it hit the floor.

"You are my master. I will serve you and obey you." Her voice was barely audible.

"That will do for now." He bent his head and kissed her, his lips soft.

Another wave of pleasure washed over her. Something was surely wrong with her, if she could respond to him that way even while he enslaved her.

Father was right about me. I am a slut. A pathetic slut.

There was a soft metallic snick. Anne jumped. She'd been so lost in her thoughts she hadn't noticed when Damien attached a leash to the ring on the collar. Just what she'd needed to complete her humiliation.

"Don't be too hard on her, Damien," the king said.

"Only what is necessary." He returned his attention to her. "When we leave, you will walk behind me and on the left side."

Anne nodded.

"Yes, take her home and get her settled," King Night said. "I'm sure you have a lot to talk about."

Damien gave him an abbreviated bow. "Thank you, Your Majesty."

With a gentle tug, he led her from the room. She walked at his left side, a pace or two behind as directed. The position gave her an unobstructed view of his back side and the way the linen of his trousers clung to the muscles of his ass. As shamed as she was, she still itched to run her hands over the hard curves of his body.

Did he want her? He'd been angry at the King's decision to give her to him. She would bet on it. Maybe all the years that had gone by had made an impassable breach between them.

What do you think, Anne? He's leading you with a leash.

Damien took her down a broad, sweeping staircase. Demon Kin males climbed up and down, passing them with open and curious glances and even a few smiles. Anne saw them out of the corners of her eyes. She wouldn't look at them.

They were looking at her, though. And everyone who saw her knew she was Damien's sexual property, that he would take her home and fuck her. The realization gave her a shamed excitement, almost as if she wanted them to know. That couldn't mean anything good.

"Well, Miss Slut, did you let him have you? Did he get between your legs?"

"No, Father."

A scornful glance. "The Doctor will discover the truth."

Miss Slut was her true name. Maybe she'd even known it ten years ago, although she hadn't wanted it to be true. She'd wanted to be a good girl, had tried so hard to get Damien out of her blood, yet he wouldn't leave.

They traversed a lobby floored in smooth, gray and white marble that felt cold beneath her feet. Ahead of them were glass doors leading to the sunbaked street, where more Demon Kin males walked or stood about talking, apparently impervious to the weather.

The doors slid open and they walked outside into a wall of heat and blinding light. The pavement of the sidewalk seared the soles of her feet, making her wince. She stepped gingerly on the balls of her feet and put a hand up to shield her eyes.

Damien strode along the sidewalk, oblivious to her pain. The leash tightened as she fell farther behind, then gave a jerk as it came up tight. Anne stumbled forward with a little cry.

He turned, scowling. "Don't fight me."

"I'm not."

"I'm not, Master. Say it."

She rocked from foot to foot. "I'm not, Master."

"What's wrong with you? Why are you doing that?" He glanced down at her feet, his tail flicking from side to side. "Where are your shoes?"

"I don't have any."

With an impatient growl, he stalked toward her and swept her into his arms. "You should have said something."

She kept herself rigid in his grip, but his body surrounded her and pressed against hers anyway, hard and hot and uncompromising. The scent of him, exotic and faintly spicy, teased her nose. She began to tingle and ache in places she preferred not to think about.

Damien carried her into the shade of a long, narrow pavilion that bordered the street. A public float car swept up to the pavilion and stopped, its doors opening on a soft hiss. Demon Kin began to disembark from the transport. All of them were men, dressed in loose, colorful tunics and trousers.

Some of them smiled at her and Damien, and spoke to him in Malefican. Probably congratulating him on the acquisition of a slave. Damien answered them in the same language.

One, an older man with silver threaded through dark hair, stopped and put his hand on her calf, rubbing the tight muscle there. She jerked her leg away from him. He responded by cupping her breast in his hand and thumbing the nipple.

"Damien!"

"Be still," her master said.

They chuckled together, their male condescension making her grit her teeth.

Then the exodus stopped, the older man went on, and Damien boarded the vehicle. He sat down in the a seat near the door, keeping her on his lap. The air inside was only slightly cooler than that on the sidewalk.

"You can put me down now," she muttered.

"Be still."

"I don't want to sit on your lap."

"And I want you here. Now be a good pet and be quiet."

Anne glared at him. He looked back at her, cool, his lips slightly quirked upward as if in amusement. Once again, she dropped her gaze. What was the point in fighting him?

"You shouldn't have let that man touch me."

"He's a friend. I was being polite."

A man sitting behind them watched her, his face unreadable. Anne flushed. To these people, she was a despicable criminal who'd attempted to blow herself and hundreds of others to hell. She had no right to complain about her treatment. But inside, she simmered.

The transport sped off and Anne stared out the window to avoid looking at Damien. The buildings were all white-washed stucco or sun-bleached adobe. They bounced the harsh sunlight back into her eyes and sent sharp black shadows across the dusty pavement. Doors painted cobalt blue, fuchsia, viridian or scarlet punctuated the pale walls every so often, and thick wooden shutters covered every window.

The finer buildings boasted potted agaves, cactus, and desert palms at their gates and front doors. The dusty green hardly softened the hard surfaces of the city at all. Yet there was a strange beauty in its stark patterns of light and shadow, masonry and plants, blue sky and sandy ground.

They went down three blocks, turned a corner and sped another three blocks without stopping. On the way, they passed three boys playing some kind of game with dice or small bones. They couldn't have been more than eleven or twelve years old, dressed in rags, squatting in the dust with their toys. One of the boys glanced at his friends and laughed, his face alight with youthful humor.

They looked so much like human children that her breath caught in her throat. She would have thought them human, if it hadn't been for the horns on their heads and the tails curled around their haunches. Her children might look just like that, some day. Damien's children.

Damien's thighs were hard beneath her bottom, and the place between her legs throbbed relentlessly. Her body wanted more from him, wanted everything he hadn't given her during the ceremony. Foolish body.

The transport stopped outside a tall building set slightly back from the street. Damien stood with her in his arms and left the vehicle to walk up the short, palm-lined path to the front door. A doorman stood there, under the shade of a generous arbor engulfed in scarlet and magenta flowered vines. He opened the door, bowing urbanely to Damien without so much as a glance at Anne.

Damien carried her through a generous lobby and set her on her feet in front of the lift. The floor here was some kind of stone, in a soft golden color. Its smooth, cool surface felt like balm on her bare soles.

Was this where he lived? She gave a surreptitious glance around the room before the lift doors opened. The ceiling had been painted to resemble the sky, with high, puffy clouds. A large chandelier dripping with rectangular crystals hung from the center of the ceiling, and two long benches, upholstered in cobalt-blue leather and flanked by lush potted palms, provided seating. The king must pay him well to be the court rapist.

The lift whisked them up nearly to the top floor. She followed Damien across a thickly carpeted landing to a carved door made of some kind of dark-colored wood. He pressed his palm to the ident-pad next to the door and it clicked open.

The foyer of his apartment was just as luxurious and beautiful as the lobby. It was floored in the same stone tile, and reminded her of the Malefican embassy back on Novus Vita, with its simple dark furniture and brilliantly hued walls and upholstery.

He closed the door. Anne clasped her hands in front of her and waited. He still had the other end of the leash in his hand. Would he beat her now? Would he punish her every day for her role in the bombing attempt? Did he believe she hadn't known about it?

It doesn't matter what he believes.

But she knew that wasn't true. He was now her master. He could do whatever he wanted to her and there would be no-one to stop him.

Damien took the neckline of her dress in both hands and tore, popping buttons and rending the fabric all the way to her waist. She gasped. Her hands clutched the ripped dress together over her aching, naked breasts. He stalked around her and tore the back of the garment, this time all the way to the hem.

"Take it off."

"It's the only thing I have. It's a proper, modest garment."

"And you're not a proper, modest woman, so you shouldn't be wearing it."

"You're not the Damien I remember."

He laughed harshly. "You and your family saw to that. Did you know your father had me beaten by a gang of thugs?" He pointed to the long scar on his face. "I have a souvenir."

"I begged him to leave you alone."

"Maybe you should've begged harder."

"You seem to have done well for yourself in spite of it. You are the court rapist, after all."

The look on his face made her regret her words instantly.

"Court whore is more like it." Damien shoved the dress of her shoulders. "It hurts my eyes to look at it. Take it off."

She released the fabric. The dress slid from her body into a crumpled heap on the floor. Damien smiled cruelly, his hand rising to cup her bare breast. He thumbed her nipple, which instantly cooperated by tightening to a hard and eager peak. Anne bit back a moan.

"Much better." He pinched and released her flesh, causing a thrum of excitement through her body.

"I hate you."

"The feeling is mutual, I assure you. Ah, but I have a duty to Belleren, to get children on you so our planet, our people, can survive. And I always do my duty."

If Damien hated her, why had he carried her over the hot pavement? Maybe he simply didn't want his valuable female slave damaged.

"The first thing you're going to do," he continued, "is take me in your mouth. In fact, you can start now."

Chapter 5

Anne's jaw dropped. Did he mean what she thought he meant? "I beg your pardon?"

"Get on your knees."

"You want me to—"

"I want you to take my cock in your mouth and suck it until I come."

Her traitorous pussy clenched even as she shook her head. "I can't do that."

"Yes, you can."

"No!" She grimaced. "It's disgusting."

"You may find me disgusting, but I am your master and you will obey. Now get on your knees." He put his hands on her shoulders and pressed.

She didn't find him disgusting, she thought as she sank to the floor. He was sinfully beautiful, like a fallen angel. It was just the thought of putting his cock in her mouth . . . .

He put his mouth on you.

Damien loosened the tie on his waistband so that his trousers opened. His cock sprang out, already thick and engorged. His sac hung heavy beneath it. Anne lifted her hand to cup his balls in her palm.

They felt warm and oddly tender. Vulnerable. His breath hitched as she stroked the soft, wrinkled skin and dark gold hair that covered them.

"Lick me." His voice was husky with need.

She grasped his cock, marveling at the steely core beneath hot satiny skin. His breath hitched again. Anne extended her tongue and gave the swollen head of his cock a firm swipe.

Damien moaned. "That's it. Do that again."

She repeated the action. There was a curious little slit in the tip. She licked it, too, working her tongue into it. He moaned again.

The floor was cold and hard under her shins. His hand rested on the crown of her head. Anne opened her mouth and took his cock inside. Was this what he wanted? She sucked on it and he groaned. Her pussy began an insistent ache, and she rolled her hips in an attempt to relieve it.

"Put your fingers around the base. That's it. Now move them."

He showed her how to stroke him with her hand while she suckled on the head of him. He tasted musky yet clean, the same way he smelled. The scent, the flavor of him, seemed to creep inside of her and make her desperate for even more. Her free hand came up, grasped the back of his thigh.

"Deeper. Take it deeper into your throat."

She whimpered. How could she get it any deeper without choking herself? He urged her head forward, and she tried to make her throat as open as possible. His thick length slid farther into her.

"That's right, Anne. Suck your master's cock."

She whimpered again as her pussy gave a desperate throb. It was wrong to like what he did to her, yet she couldn't seem to help herself. Anne gave the head of him an extra-hard pull.

"Gods of Belleren, that's good." He broke off with a guttural phrase of Malefican.

Damien threaded his fingers through her hair, holding it back from her face. She glanced up to see him watching her suckle him, his eyes heavy-lidded and hot, his face a mask of male lust and domination.

"You are mine." He growled. "My slave. Mine."

His hips began to thrust against the movement of her hand and mouth. He groaned again, a desperate sound, and his fingers tightened in her hair. His hips jerked, he gasped, his cock pulsed in her mouth.

"Swallow," he growled, as hot liquid squirted over her tongue.

Anne gulped it down. It tasted salty and slightly sweet as it ran down her throat. Not disgusting at all.

She glanced up at him. His face had lost its tense lines. For an instant he didn't look angry at all, and his hand stroked her hair gently, as a lover would. Then he closed up, the hard mask slipping over his features.

He smiled bitterly. "You learn quickly."

She released his cock from her mouth. Damien tucked it back into his trousers and fastened his waistband. Then he bent down and took her by the elbows, raising her up. He kissed her on the mouth, shoving his tongue in deep, mastering her all over again.

"Now we can go to the bedroom and I can finish what I started earlier."

"But you just . . ." She blushed. "And I won't have children if you keep doing what you just did."

God, what was she saying? She ought to keep her mouth shut. Forever.

Damien laughed softly. "You want my children?"

Her face grew even hotter. "I—I don't know."

"Well." He stroked her cheek with the backs of his fingers. "I needed to take the edge off my desire. Otherwise I might not be able to hold myself back, and I could hurt you."

She blinked, her eyes widening. "You don't want to hurt me?"

"No. Fool that I am, I don't want to hurt you. And you have a very tight hymen, Anne, so it will take some time to get you ready for me."

The butterflies in her stomach fluttered wildly. He was really going to take her and it was going to hurt no matter how careful he was. She'd been warned. Besides, he was huge. There was no way he could fit that thing inside her body without causing her pain.

Unfortunately, her pussy didn't seem to understand, because it still ached and throbbed in ignorant longing.

Damien pointed down to the leash dangling from her collar. "Hand me your lead."

She gave it to him. After what they'd just shared, he still wanted to lead her around like a dog, damn him anyway. He plunged further into the apartment without looking to see if she would follow. The leash went taut between them.

"Come," he said.

◆ ◆ ◆

Damien could barely hear her feet padding behind him as he led her to the bedroom. The sight of her on her knees, his cock in her mouth, had been one of the most erotic things he'd ever witnessed. Thinking of it now made him hard all over again, but at least he'd gotten some relief from his lust before he breached that hymen of hers.

The bedroom had an enormous bed with a canopy covered in gauzy white curtains—a traditional Bellerenic design. Now that he thought of it, it resembled the bed used in the Soul Opening. He'd never taken notice of that fact before since the style was so common all over Belleren. Would the resemblance make Anne more comfortable or less?

Who cares? She doesn't need to be comfortable.

There was an angry, vengeful side of him that wanted to strike out at her and hurt her for what she and her family had done to him. But when he turned on his heel, a mocking smile in place, the look of apprehension in her wide gray eyes drained the anger right out of him.

Damien held out his hand. When she didn't move, he began to draw in the leash, forcing her to him.

"You're not afraid, are you, Miss Anne? You who tried to blow yourself and everyone around you to pieces."

The muscles around her eyes tightened. "I didn't know about that," she said in a flat and quiet voice.

He continued to reel her in. "So you say. Are you scared?"

"Yes."

"You don't trust me."

"You said you hated me. And anyway, I know it will hurt. It always hurts the woman."

He raised his eyebrows. "Who told you that?"

"My mother." She lifted her chin. "And my Teachers. I know what you're going to do to me and I know it'll hurt, so let's just get it over with."

He couldn't help it. He laughed. "Is that what they tell all the girls on Novus Vita?"

Her face colored. "I imagine so. We tell our girls the truth so they'll be prepared, instead of filling them with all kinds of dangerous nonsense that turns them into whores before they even have a chance to marry."

She sounded so prim and upright that he laughed again. "Did you ever think there might be something wrong with Novus Vitan men that makes them bad lovers?"

The chin came up a little more. "Novus Vitan men do their duty before the Light. They don't wallow in sinful excess."

"Well, now we know what's wrong with them. No wonder you're afraid." He indicated the mattress with a movement of his head. "Lie down."

She went to the bed, her spine stiff and her movements awkward. He watched her climb up, breasts jiggling temptingly, and stretch out flat on her back, arms at her sides, eyes fixed on the canopy. As if she were waiting for an axe to fall on her neck. Or as if she were a sacrifice on the altar of some bloodthirsty god.

I think that's you, Fallyn.

Damien followed, leaning over her to unclip the leash.

Her eyes met his. "Are you going to tie me?"

"Not unless you fight." His cock twitched at the thought of chasing and subduing her. "Are you going to fight?"

"No."

Damn. "Then there's no need for restraints." He crawled onto the bed as his tail began to sweep lazily back and forth.

She tensed even more, her fingers digging into the bedcovers. He settled beside her and ran his hand lightly over her breasts, then down across her belly. She was firmer than he'd expected, with toned muscles under her pale skin. He cupped a breast, lifting and molding the soft flesh.

Her breathing became fast and shallow.

"Relax, Anne. I said I wouldn't hurt you."

"I can't."

"Yes, you can." He made circles on her abdomen, using the flat of his hand. "You're safe. We're going to go slowly, until you get used to me."

"Why?" She stared at him, her eyes going round. "Why would you do that for me?"

Damien shrugged. "What good would it do me to rush you? We're going to be together for a long time."

She stared at him, her expression gone unreadable. Probably wondering how many opportunities she'd have to murder him during all those years. She wanted to get the deflowering over with, and he might have obliged her if it weren't for the unusual hymen she possessed.

He slipped his hand down her belly to her pubic mound. Her muscles tightened as his fingers delved between the tender lips of her sex. He pressed the heel of his hand against her mound, rubbing in slow circles. Her breath caught.

He slid his body downward and parted her legs. Anne complied easily, but she threw a hand over her eyes as if to deny what they were doing. He allowed her to hide from him. She needed it now, but eventually he would make her watch.

Spreading her with his fingers, he drank in the scent of her. Clean, fresh female. Aroused female. She already glistened with cream. Damien licked her center, letting the flavor of her juices fill his mouth. She gasped and quivered, so he did it again.

"Please don't. Don't do that."

"Hush." He began to tease her gently with lips and tongue, while he inserted the tip of his little finger into her opening.

She was so extraordinarily tight that he would surely have caused her awful pain if he'd taken her straight out. He worked his finger back and forth, stretching her delicate tissues. Anne gasped again.

Damien paused. "Did that hurt?"

"No," she said breathlessly.

"Good." He pushed the finger as far into her as it would go and used the heel of his hand against her mound to soothe its entry. "Do you like that?"

Her hips began to move subtly in counterpoint to his hand. "No."

"Liar."

Maybe she wasn't aware of what she was doing. Damien switched to his forefinger, which drew a mewling sound from her throat and a downward jerk of her hips. Now she was trying to get away from him.

"It's all right," he murmured. "I'm just getting you ready for me."

How many years had he dreamed of having her spread for him like this? Of tasting her, making her cry out his name, making her beg for more? But he'd never dreamed she would be a virgin when he took her the first time.

She had a hymen so complete that it was almost like the head of a drum, with just a couple of perforations to allow him access. He pushed his forefinger back into the larger of the two openings and pressed, pushing outward against its edges. Anne squirmed, panting.

152

"Do you like it now?" he said.

"N-no."

He shoved the finger all the way in and crooked it against her inner walls. She cried out, but it was a cry of pleasure and not pain. He knew by the way she ground her hips against his hand.

"Say you like it, Anne."

"Oh!" Her hips surged. "I like it!"

"That's good. Good girl."

He licked around the base of his finger where it entered her body, pressing outward again, stretching her. She moaned, long and low. Damien began to insert a second finger.

A few minutes later, he had her writhing on the bed and clutching the sheets, her lower lip swollen from biting it. Didn't she know how much her cries delighted him? Maybe she did, and that was why she held them back.

Damien rose over her, his cock jutting straight out in its eagerness to be inside her. Anne's gray eyes widened. She scuttled backward across the bed, panting, her thighs closing tight to keep him out.

"You'll be all right," he said. "We'll take it slow." He reached for her.

"Don't!" She pressed herself against the headboard. When he once again reached out, she kicked at his hand. "I don't want you to! No!"

Grabbing her by the ankles, he dragged her closer again.

"No, please. Please, I'm not ready yet."

"I like the sound of your begging, slave, but you're begging for the wrong thing."

He forced her legs apart. She began to throw herself from side to side, until he laid on top of her to hold her still. With one hand he clasped her wrists above her head. With the other, he positioned his cock at the entrance of her cunt. Anne pinched her eyes closed, shutting him out.

He nudged his way into her. Gods of Belleren, she was still so tight. She made a strangled little sound and he paused to stroke her side, speaking softly in Bellerenic until she relaxed. Then he rocked his hips, pushing a little deeper. And a little deeper.

Anne kept her eyes pinched shut, closing her off from him. He trembled as he held himself over her, willing himself not to hurt her. Her lids lifted and she looked him right in the eyes.

"Will you just finish it?" she said in a cutting tone.

Damn her. "What's wrong, love? Are you so impatient for me that you can't wait?"

"I'm not your love. I'll never love you."

"Good."

Damien worked himself a little deeper. Something flickered in her eyes. It didn't look like defiance or hatred, especially when her lips softened and parted. He rocked his hips again, pushing his cock even farther inside her. A soft sound escaped her, almost a moan.

He plunged into her pussy, sheathing himself up to the hilt with a groan. She cried out and tossed her head back against the pillows.

"There. Now you have all of me," he growled.

He held her down on the bedding as his hips began to push rhythmically against hers. Gods of Belleren, she was tight and wet and hot. His own little piece of paradise. Even though he'd come in her mouth a short time ago, his lust boiled up inside him and turned to ecstasy and he pounded her, helpless to stop himself from hurting her and not caring anymore if he did.

With every brutal thrust, she cried out. Her eyes rolled back in her head, and her mouth opened on a long, broken moan. She might be a bitch, but she was beautiful in her bliss.

All the sensation in his body focused down on the joy of his cock in her hot, tight little pussy and it was good, so good; he'd waited so long, forever, for this. His balls tightened, his back arched, and he exploded into her, his voice a rough shout of exaltation as his seed burst out of him in torrents.

Damien shuddered in the aftermath of his orgasm. He'd nearly lost control of the situation, which was not good. Anne's eyes were closed again as if she couldn't bear to look at him. Damn her for a lying, fanatical little bitch. She was the one who'd tried to kill people, for pity's sake, and now she treated him like he was the criminal. The one who ought to be ashamed.

"You're not a virgin anymore, darling."

She said nothing.

He withdrew and levered himself off her. A smear of her blood decorated his now-shrunken cock. Anne turned her face toward the window, without opening her eyes. His momentary triumph drained away in the face of her indifference.

"I'm going to take a shower. I wouldn't try to run if I were you. Other Bellerenic men won't be as gentle with you as I am."

"I'm not stupid," she said without looking at him.

Chapter 6

Anne stared at the sheer white curtains covering the window. In the bathroom, the shower came on. She wanted to cry, but for some reason the tears wouldn't come.

She sat up and walked to the window, his ejaculate dripping out of her onto her thighs. Her heart ached, her throat ached, her pussy ached. She had tried so hard not to feel. But her slut nature asserted itself every time she looked at him, let alone when he touched her and kissed her and . . . all those other things he'd done to her.

Damien strode back into the room with an angry cadence and grabbed her by the wrist. "You're showering with me."

He dragged her unceremoniously into a luxurious bathroom. His grip on her was painful, and he walked so quickly she stumbled and he jerked her to her feet and kept going. At least he hadn't seen the skin on her back, where she still bore the marks of her humiliation and punishment twelve years before.

The room contained an enormous bathtub, but it was dry. Next to it was a little glass-enclosed chamber, almost large enough to be an entire bathroom in itself. Shower heads protruded from the wall at various heights on two opposing marble-tiled walls.

He kept her imprisoned with one hand while he opened the glass shower door. With a flick of his wrist, Damien turned on the water. He adjusted the temperature briefly before entering the enclosure and pulling her in behind him.

"You don't—I can bathe myself."

He didn't reply. Instead, he squirted some liquid soap into his palm from a dispenser mounted on the wall and began to rub it in languorous strokes over her breasts and under her arms. Water splashed down over her head, driving her hair into her eyes and blinding her.

Anne groped for the dispenser, meaning to take over the job of washing. But he only captured her hand and drew both arms over her head again, pinning her against the cold tile wall of the shower. Then he resumed washing her, without comment.

He went back for another squirt of the soap, then slid his hand impersonally into her crotch. Anne flinched away, trying to close her legs against him.

"No." He forced her thighs apart with one hard knee.

"I don't want—"

Damien shut her up with a hard kiss, forcing his tongue into her mouth in the same way as he forced his fingers between her legs. His cock, trapped between their bodies, began to lengthen again. He rolled his hips lazily against her belly.

Pulling an extendable showerhead from the wall, he aimed it at her pussy and rinsed all the soap away. Then he lifted one of her thighs and wrapped it around his waist. She had to come up on her toes to get her leg that high. Anne moaned her protest against his mouth, but he didn't give her a chance to talk.

He shoved his now-rigid cock into her channel, pushing it deep into her. She made a choked cry against his kiss. His tongue thrust into her mouth at the same time as he gave her a long stroke of his sex. His free hand came around and grasped the curves of her butt.

Damien held her in a cruel grip as he rammed her over and over, his tongue fucking her mouth as his cock fucked her pussy. It hurt. And yet it excited her unbearably. She felt the growing storm gathering in her sheath, in her belly, tightening with greater and greater force until she broke apart, screaming.

He tilted his head back and roared, his thick blond hair like the mane of a lion. His fangs flashed under the brilliant light of the bathroom as his hips pounded hers. Anne sobbed, caught in the fury of another pleasure storm.

She'd never known anything like it. Never even imagined it. His big body trembled against hers as he groaned and filled her with more of his come. Was the pleasure she'd experienced just like his?

Damien's movements slowed, then stopped, although he still shuddered in the aftermath. Anne shuddered, too, unable to hide how deeply he affected her. A stinging sensation flooded her eyes and she bit down hard on her lower lip to stop it.

He pushed the dripping hair from her eyes and gave her a lazy smile. "When I want to wash you, I'll do it, slave."

Anne glared at him.

"Ah-ah. That is not the look of a properly submissive slave."

"Get used to it. You're going to be seeing it a lot."

He grinned. Somehow, the expression failed to reassure her.

"I can see I'm going to have to teach you some respect. But first, you will wash me. Then, dinner. Afterward, we'll see how defiant you are when I spank you."

Her mouth fell open. "What?"

"You heard me. Now put some soap on your hands and get to work."

With an apprehensive sigh, Anne obeyed. She tried to keep her mind from dwelling on the smoothness of his skin, the warmth of him, hard muscle and bone and tender sex that could so easily punish and delight. But she couldn't. She was filled with him, body and soul.

When they left the shower for the dining room, food awaited them on the table. A servant must have come in and left it while they were otherwise occupied. Had he listened to them? Heard Anne's cries? She flushed hot all over again.

The food was simple fare, just some kind of meat and vegetable stew with fresh bread alongside. Wearing nothing but a pair of trousers, Damien portioned it into a couple of bowls, setting them on the table with a jug of red wine he brought from the kitchen.

He pulled out a chair and sat down, without a stitch of clothing on. With one hand, he held the leash. He pointed at the floor next to him. "Kneel."

Anne blinked at him. "I beg your pardon?"

"A fine beginning. However, I require your obedience. Kneel."

She stared at him until he gave the leash a tug downwards. Anne dropped to her knees. He smiled unpleasantly at her before turning to his food.

Anne watched him eat. The stew smelled delicious and her stomach rumbled. He'd eaten almost the entire bowl and half the bread before he seemed to remember her. Giving her a sidelong glance, he dipped up some stew and held the spoon in front of her mouth.

"Eat."

She was too hungry to argue. She opened her mouth and took the bite he offered. It tasted spicy, unfamiliar, but good. When she'd swallowed it, she licked her lips. Damien scooped up another bite, holding it out to her. Next he tore off a small hunk of bread and placed it between her lips.

Then he took up his wine goblet and held it to her mouth, tipping it. She let the cool, tangy liquid fill her mouth and roll down her throat, easing her thirst. He looked pensive, distant, as he watched her take his offerings one by one from his fingers.

When they'd finished, he wiped her mouth with his napkin and rose to his feet. The leash tugged delicately at her neck. Anne got up. She reached for the stew bowl, thinking to take it into the kitchen.

"No." Damien stopped her. "I have a housekeeper for that."

"Where is she?"

"*He* is probably in his room behind the kitchen, minding his own business. He'll take care of the cleaning up. Your job is to serve me personally."

She dropped her head. "I see."

"I think you're beginning to. Come." He walked away, confident that she would follow him like an obedient dog. And she did.

Once in the bedroom, he closed the door behind them. He walked toward one of the big, overstuffed chairs on one side of the room. The lights flickered and went out, sinking the room into blackness. Anne gasped.

"It's all right." His voice sounded even and sure. "It's just a power outage. We get them all the time nowadays."

He pulled her across the room, still on the leash. Rustling and rattling sounds followed. Then a small, golden glow penetrated the dark. He'd lit an emergency light.

Damien set the light on the top of a bureau. He returned to the sitting area and sank into a generous armchair. She hesitated, pulling the leash to its full length. Damien used it to force her closer. When she got within arm's reach, he grabbed her and lifted her face down on his lap.

"Hey!" She struggled without thinking.

He controlled her easily with one hand and delivered a stinging slap to her butt with the other. It hurt. Anne cried out, wriggling in an effort to get off his lap.

"It's time you learned who is the master in this household."

"I know who is the master!"

Damien smacked her hard on one ass cheek, making a sharp cracking sound as skin struck skin. It burned.

"Ow! Stop it!"

"If you're still arguing with me, you obviously have no idea who is the master."

He smacked her again, this time on the other cheek. "This is what happens when you behave disrespectfully to me."

Crack! Anne squeaked. He began to spank her in a regular rhythm, first one cheek and then the other, while the burn in her flesh grew and grew and she whimpered and jerked at each strike. Each roll and sway of her hips ground her pubis against his thigh and sent a warm flush of pleasure through her.

She hadn't been spanked since she was a child. But she had been beaten, severely and often, for several years of her life. This was nothing compared to what she'd endured then. Nothing but love taps.

In spite of that, or maybe because of it, she wanted to shrivel up and disappear so Damien would never see her again.

He paused to pinch the burning globes of her ass. Anne panted, trying to push off his lap. Damien smacked her again, hard enough to bring tears to her eyes. She subsided, waiting, the energy for fighting drained out of her.

He shoved her down and pinned her with his forearm before sliding his free hand between her ass cheeks and running a finger along her creamy slit. Her pussy was sore from his earlier use, and yet a tremor of excitement followed everywhere he touched her.

"Oh! Don't." She wriggled even harder.

158

"You're wet, my slave. You want me to fuck you again, don't you?"

"No!"

He pushed a finger inside her pussy. "Yes, you do. That's what all this sweet cream is for." Damien withdrew his finger and shoved it into her mouth. She whimpered against the strange, sharp flavor of her own sex.

Freeing his hand, he used it to smack her on the ass. "I am your master." Smack! "Say it."

"Oh! You are my master."

Smack! "You are my slave. Say it." Smack!

"I am your slave."

Smack! "Will you speak disrespectfully to me again?"

"No. Please, stop. You're hurting me."

He chuckled. "That's the idea." And gave her two more cracks on the butt.

Her ass felt like it was on fire. Damien stopped hitting her and rubbed the sore skin. "You look so tempting bent over my lap like this. What do you think I should do next?"

"I-I don't know."

"I think I should fuck you. What do you say to that?" He continued massaging her ass.

She didn't want him to keep hitting her, regardless. Her pride couldn't take much more. If he continued to spank her, she would start crying like a little girl.

She was going to do it. She was going to capitulate. But only with her words, never in her heart.

Anne closed her eyes. "W-whatever you like, Master."

"What a lovely answer, slave. Get down on your hands and knees."

She scrambled off his lap and got on all fours on the cold tile, trembling. Damien stroked her from her nape to her ass cheeks.

"Good. Lean down on your elbows and put your ass in the air."

More humiliation, yet she obeyed. He pushed her thighs farther apart. In this position, her sex was completely displayed to him, the cooling evening air swirling over the damp folds. She tingled with the knowledge that he was looking at her most private place.

Anne suppressed a sudden desire to arch her back and push her ass even higher in invitation.

"I love the way you look from behind." Kneeling behind her, he leaned down to taste the slippery flesh.

She gasped.

Then he touched a super-sensitive part of her with a gentle finger. "This is the head of your clit." He drew the finger along one side of her opening. "You have special tissues all along both sides of your pussy that swell with blood when you're excited. Your clit," he wiggled his finger, making her jerk at the sharp delight, "is like the head of my cock. It's where the pleasure is concentrated."

"S-should I take notes?"

Damien kissed the small of her back, then licked her pussy again. "If it helps."

He mounted her, shoving himself inside her in one hard stroke. Anne cried out and he groaned at the same time. So hot, so thick, the position forcing him far deeper into her body than the one he'd used before. His cock seemed to press on every part of her insides, on secret places she'd never known she had.

"Please," she moaned. *Damn it, shut up, Anne.*

Damien held himself still inside her, hands on her hips. "Please, what?"

Anne shook her head.

"Please, what, slave? Say it. Tell me what you want."

She only shook her head again.

Damien reached around to tease her clit with his forefinger. She tilted her head back with a broken cry. He removed his hand.

"What do you want?"

"No."

He teased her a second time. The pleasure spiked, forcing her to rock her hips against his hand. But he withdrew again.

"Tell me what you want."

Her fingers pressed hard against the floor tile. "I want you to do it to me."

"Do what?" He flexed his hips. "That?"

"Yes!" She tried to push back against him, but he prevented her with a firm grip on her hips.

"Say the word, Anne. Tell me you want your master to fuck you."

"You really are the spawn of the devil," she muttered under her breath.

"I heard that." He slapped her hip lightly. "Do I need to give you another spanking?" Damien flexed his hips again and gave them a twist for emphasis.

"Oh, God! Fuck me, master, please!"

That was it. She'd just volunteered to degrade herself.

He laughed darkly. "That's what I want to hear."

With a triumphant groan, he worked his cock slowly out of her, then back in, keeping her still and passive. All the way out, then all the way in, the slippery glide of his cock in her aching sheath making her writhe. Anne knew she wasn't supposed to show a response, but she couldn't remember why.

The pleasure had taken over, erasing every other thought from her mind. Damien's breath roughened as he sped up the pace. She rocked back against his every thrust, crying and moaning in thoughtless ecstasy, her breasts jiggling against the cold floor, his pelvis slapping into hers. She had become an animal.

Sharp pulses of bliss exploded through her body and she screamed. Damien gave a loud growl. His breath caught and his fingers tightened on her hips. He shoved into her again, two fast hard thrusts, and then he stilled as a broken moan issued from his throat and his hot come filled her.

She came back slowly from the animal place. Damien picked her up, still seated inside her body, and carried her to the bed where he stretched out with her, his thick arm around her waist. His breath came fast, blowing the strands of her hair. After a moment, he drew the long strands away from her neck and kissed her there, right above the collar.

Anne put her hands over his, clasping him to her. If only they could stay this way forever, and forget about war and slavery and betrayal.

Chapter 7

They dozed for a while in the dim glow of the emergency light. Then Damien withdrew from her body and rose from the bed. She watched as he went into the bathroom. Water began to run heavily. Anne got out of bed, careful not to get any of his come on the bedcovers.

The leash still dangled from her collar. Damien poked his head around the edge of the door and beckoned to her. She could fight him, but she'd still be a slave. Even if she ran for the door, even if she managed to get out of the building, the first man she saw would snatch her up and use her, perhaps more brutally than Damien ever would.

She went to him. He bend down to grab the leash, but instead of using it to pull her, Damien unclipped it. He balled it up in one big hand.

"Time for a soak." He led her into the bathroom, laying the leash on the counter. Another emergency light illuminated the smaller room.

Anne glanced up at him. His face had lost most of its anger and tension. He looked so much like the Damien she remembered that it made her heart ache.

"We already had a shower," she said.

"Your pussy will heal faster and feel better if you soak. I put something in to help you."

An herbal scent emanated from the steaming water. Anne poked her toe into it, finding it hot but not unbearably so. "How is it hot when the power is out?"

"We have a solar water tank on the roof."

She got in, her mouth opening in surprise when Damien joined her.

The tub was more than big enough for the two of them. He sat behind her, pulling her back to recline against his chest and belly, his hands splayed over her abdomen.

His tail floated in the water along the side. The puff decorating the forked tip was a darker russet, similar to the color of her own hair. In the water, it looked almost black. What would he do if she took it into her hand and petted it?

She didn't have the nerve.

Instead, she rested her hand on top of his, the ache in her heart growing deeper and sharper. She had loved him once, and part of her still did. That part

162

wanted to confess everything to him, beg him for forgiveness and understanding. Beg him for love.

Anne opened her mouth. The words refused to leave her throat. He would scorn her, laugh at her, refuse to believe her.

Do you really think you deserve his forgiveness?

The strange thought made her breath catch. She'd deliberately set out to harm his world and his people by working for the Army of God. She knew that, accepted it. Yet until today she'd never thought of her actions as evil or reprehensible. She was a patriot of Novus Vita.

King Night had made her feel a twinge of guilt this afternoon, but nothing like what flooded her at the moment. The familiar stinging rose up in her eyes so suddenly she had no defense against it, and tears flowed down her face.

"Are you crying?" he said gruffly.

"No." She sniffed.

"Yes, you are." Damien released the valve on the bathtub.

He stood up and lifted her from the water, grabbing a thick towel and wrapping it around her dripping body. Throwing a second towel over his shoulder, he carried her back to the bed and laid her down.

After a brisk rub-down of his body, he climbed in after her and snugged himself up against her back. His arm wrapped around her, as before, hugging her tightly to him. She burrowed her face into the towel that still covered her, forcing the tears back with the strength of her will.

"Is it finally sinking in that you're a slave?"

She didn't answer. Let him think what he wanted. The truth would only earn his scorn or pity, and she didn't want either.

He gave a heavy sigh. "It won't be so bad, Anne. I won't mistreat you."

Putting a collar on her neck wasn't mistreatment?

"I'll keep you fed and dressed, surrounded by luxury, and well-pleased in bed. You'll have a better life than you would if you'd stayed on Novus Vita."

Her continuing silence earned another sigh from him.

"All right. Have it your way. Tomorrow we'll go shopping for your basic needs, so try to get some sleep."

* * *

In the morning, Damien wished he'd taken his own advice. Of course, he tried to sleep, but he wasn't accustomed to sharing his bed and the fact that his sleeping partner was Anne Paulsen kept him awake far into the night. He kept trying to justify his treatment of her, his keeping her as a slave, and coming up short.

Night had given her to him. And she had committed a crime. But it didn't feel like enough, somehow, to excuse enslaving her.

The soft, early light lingered on the planes of her face and the long silky lashes of her eyes. She had dark circles under them, but for now she slept. Her sweet, full breasts were nestled against her arm. He caressed the curve of her body where her waist dipped in and then flared out into her hips, using a delicate touch to avoid waking her.

The love he'd lost and thought never to regain had returned to him, and it was his duty to punish her. The gods ever had a perverse sense of humor.

The truth was, dominating and spanking her had given him the hardest cock he'd ever had. And she liked it, judging by the creaminess of her pussy. But play was one thing, real slavery something else. It was only the second day, and already it tasted bitter.

Her eyes opened. For a moment she regarded him with a kind of wonder, as if she hadn't expected to see him and was glad. Then wariness returned to her face, and she shrank back from him.

Her change of mood cut him. He frowned. "Time to get up and get to work."

"What does that mean?"

"We have some shopping to do before we can leave town." He sat up, running his fingers through his hair.

"We're leaving?"

"Some friends of mine are getting married and we're going to the wedding."

Damien went to his closet and pulled out some underwear, a pair of sandals and an ankle-length tunic that had belonged to his former lover, Julia. He threw the whole thing at Anne.

"Put that on. We'll get you some things of your own while we're out."

She sat up, looking at the garments doubtfully. Then she drew them on without a word, covering those luscious curves. Unfortunately it did nothing to calm his raging lust.

He could have her, right now. Whenever and wherever he wanted. But there were errands to run before they could leave, and he didn't want to disrespect his friends by dressing his slave in hand-me-downs at their wedding.

You're fooling yourself again, Fallyn. You just don't want to admit you could spend all day and night doing nothing but making love to a woman who betrayed you.

Making love? It wasn't making love; it was fucking, plain and simple. There was no love involved. Maybe he should have that tattooed on his forearm, so he could remind himself hourly.

When they were dressed, he took her down the street to a small café for breakfast. They took a table in the back, for privacy, yet Anne still drew stares from the otherwise entirely male customers. It made Damien want to snarl over his scrambled eggs.

Anne pulled her chair closer to his, so close their bodies touched. "Why are they staring at me?"

"You're the only woman in here. Probably the only woman they've seen in months if not years."

"So it's not because of who I am?" She said that last while staring at her plate, as if she couldn't bring herself to meet his eyes. Was she ashamed of what she'd done?

"No, I don't think so."

Anne nodded silently, and took another bite of her food.

When they left the café, they attracted even more attention. Some of the restaurant patrons followed them into the glaring outdoor sunlight—a table of young men who'd been staring at Anne throughout the meal. A block after leaving the café, three more young thugs joined the first crew.

He should have known this would happen. Bellerenics were highly sexual beings, even more sexual than humans, and the men of his world had been deprived of their women for too long. Some had turned to other men for comfort, but that would only satisfy a segment of the population. The rest were starving for women.

A man loitering in the shadow of an old adobe building across the street caught a glimpse of Anne and turned to stare, shielding his eyes against the glare for a better view. His mouth fell open as he looked at her. Damien stiffened, his jaw clenching hard.

Anne shrank against Damien's side as the gawker started toward them from across the dusty street. Shit. He slung an arm around her shoulders and placed his other hand on the butt of the flechette holstered on his right hip.

He steered her around a corner, heading away from the new arrival and back toward his apartment building. Retreat was the wisest plan now.

"Hey!" called one of the men. "She's pretty. Where did you get her?"

Damien kept walking, but his tail began to lash.

"I said, where did you get her?" The cub sounded belligerent as he caught up with them.

"She was presented to me by the king." Damien gave the other man a warning stare. "She's mine."

The fellow's companions crowded around them, jostling. One of them lifted a lock of Anne's hair, rubbing it between his fingers. He grinned down at her, making a display of his fangs.

"You like Demon Kin, pretty girl?" His Galactic Standard was laced with a heavy Bellerenic accent.

Anne refused to look at him.

By now, they'd made it half way back to Damien's building. His heart raced, his blood pumping fast in anticipation of a fight. He didn't want to shoot any of these young fools, but he would if he had to.

"What would you take for her?" the first one said.

"She's not for sale."

"Come on. Just once."

The man with the accent grinned wolfishly. "I want a turn with her."

Damien growled. "No."

"We all want a turn!" yelled someone behind them.

Everyone laughed except Anne and Damien. Heavy Accent grabbed her by the hand, trying to drag her away from him. She cried out. Damien drew the flechette and pointed it at the offender.

Heavy Accent threw up his hands, his deeply-tanned face gone ashen. "Don't shoot. I meant no offense."

The others backed off as Damien turned to face them, the flared muzzle of the flechette glinting evilly in the sunlight.

"This woman belongs to me. She is not a whore. She is not for sale. Is that understood?"

The men nodded. Some looked angry and resentful, some embarrassed. Damien drew Anne close to the stucco wall of the building and began to back away from the crowd of harassers. Her arm snaked around his waist and held on tight.

"Anyone comes within three meters, I'll shoot."

Chapter 8

People scrambled to get out of the firing zone. He glanced over his shoulder. No-one approached from that direction, and the door of his building was only about six meters off.

He and Anne backed along the wall of the building until they came to the front entrance walk and its rows of palms. They turned and ran between the trees, up the walkway to the front door. The guard standing there jerked out of his bored doze to stare at the gun Damien held.

"Sir, what is it?"

"A mob looking for a woman," he said. "You might want to call for backup."

The guard opened the door for him and followed him inside to lock up. He was speaking into his voice link when Damien made it to the lift. They were going to have to get better security for the building, or he would have to move somewhere else.

The country house. Now that he was done with his job as controller, he could move back to his family seat. Anne would be safer there. They had a small army of retainers to defend her. But ultimately the woman shortage had to be solved, or Bellerenic society wouldn't survive.

The lift doors opened, revealing an empty car. They got in and both slumped against the back wall. Anne's eyes closed. Her hand came up and pressed against her forehead.

"I apologize," he said. "I didn't think about how attractive you are."

"You mean they'd leave an ugly woman alone?"

He smiled. "Probably not. But maybe they wouldn't have been so enthusiastic."

"I guess I'll just keep wearing these things, then, since it's too dangerous for me to show my face."

"When we get to the wedding, I'll have some things made up for you."

She peeked at him. "Why bother? I'm just a slave."

"Even a slave needs clothes."

She flushed. The pink color bloomed over her face and flowed down her neck, over her collarbones and into the curves of her breasts where they peeked out from the tunic's low neckline. Staring at those plump mounds made his mouth water at the thought of all the things he'd like to do to them.

He pushed her snugly against the back wall of the lift and tilted her chin up so he could take her mouth. Immediately she opened for him. Damien groaned as he slid his tongue into her. Did she have any idea how sweetly responsive she was? She'd never been made for the narrow, dry life of a Novus Vitan.

The lift pinged and the doors opened. Another Demon Kin male got in. Anne tried to pull away from Damien, giving a gasp of dismay.

He put his arm around her shoulders. "It's all right. We have to get out anyway."

The male nodded and smiled at him, and looked speculatively at Anne. Damien got her out of the lift. The doors closed, shutting away the interested look of the other male.

"I'm going to have a long talk with Night at the wedding." He strode so quickly to his door that Anne stumbled trying to keep up with him.

"About?"

"Getting more women on this planet. If we don't, the situation is going to get worse and worse for the few who are here."

He opened the door and they slipped inside. Damien locked up with a sense of profound relief. Home was sacred to Demon Kin and no-one would think to attack either of them here. At least, not yet. Give the mobs a few days to form and become enraged, and the situation might get ugly.

"We'll leave early tomorrow morning from the roof. That way no-one will see you."

❧ ❧ ❧

Anne nodded. Given the circumstances, she was more than happy to get out of the city. Kelzenec was apparently a hostile environment for women. How did that prison guard and Lorca, the ritualist, survive?

Damien's gaze turned predatory. He gave her a slow smile that heated her blood and made her heart race. She took an unthinking step backward.

He stalked her, his tail flicking back and forth in a lazy arc. Anne fetched up against a sideboard holding an expensive-looking glass vase and had to stop. He loomed over her, his blue eyes so dark with lust they almost looked black.

Damien leaned forward, supporting himself with his hands braced on the sideboard so he blocked her in, trapping her in a cage of his body. She reared away from him, heart tripping in a rhythm that was half fear, half anticipation. Slut.

"I-I'm sore." Her voice came out breathless and eager. As if she wanted whatever he planned to do to her.

"I have an alternative plan." He ran a finger along the edge of her neckline, lingering in the valley between her breasts.

"Oh?"

"I've fucked your mouth and your pussy, but there's one orifice I haven't had yet."

She frowned, puzzled. "What else is there?"

His smile broadened. "Your ass, sweet slave."

Her jaw dropped. "That's not possible."

"You have led a sheltered life, haven't you? I assure you it is possible."

"No!" Surely he didn't mean this. "It isn't . . . made for that. You can't!"

"I can and I will." He leaned even closer. "And I'll make you like it."

Anne shook her head so hard her hair whipped back and forth. "No!"

"Oh, yes." He moved one large hand to cup her butt, squeezing the muscled curve of it.

"You'll hurt me."

"I won't hurt you. Trust me, Anne. Do you trust me?"

"No."

She could have sworn she saw a flash of pain in his eyes. Then it was gone, covered by a cocky grin. "You will. Because I'm going to demonstrate to you just how much you can take and how good it can feel for you to submit to me."

"No, I don't want—"

He squeezed her butt again. "Remember you're a slave. What you want isn't relevant."

Damien picked her up and carried her into the bedroom. She looped her arms around his neck, more because being carried felt insecure, as if he might drop her. It wasn't because she wanted to be closer to him or have as much of her own body pressed to his as possible. It had nothing to do with that.

He set her down and divested her of her clothes, then took her mouth in a searing kiss that made her moan and whimper in spite of herself. His hands found her breasts, cupping and kneading them, thumbing and pinching the nipples. Every time he squeezed and then released an eager peak, she moaned at the flood of delight that resulted.

Damien fondled her ruthlessly, driving her to rub herself against him like a shameless cat. She couldn't help it. She seemed to lose all sense of self-possession when he touched her. Even the thought of him driving that huge cock into her ass couldn't stop her from becoming drunk with his kisses, couldn't stop her from clutching his hard narrow waist, couldn't stop her from rolling her naked hips against his thigh.

He sat down on the edge of the bed and took a nipple into his mouth, teasing and suckling it with his hot, wet tongue. Anne cried out. Her knees buckled and she grabbed onto his shoulders for support. The insistent pull of his mouth sent sharp arrows of pleasure shooting from her nipples to her pussy. A trickle of cream moistened her inner thigh.

Again he cupped her butt, yet this time his fingers slipped between the globes of muscle and found the tight rose of her ass and pressed gently on it, drawing a shamed and excited whimper from her. His finger circled her anus, teasing, caressing, until it pressed again, harder this time, pushing for entry while his mouth remained on her breast, suckling.

Damien broke off the erotic play to open a drawer in the bedside table and pull out a small jar made of pale carved stone. He lifted the lid. Some kind of scented ointment filled the vessel. He scooped some onto his fingertips and smiled at her, drawing her back into his embrace.

"Come here."

"What is that for?"

"It's to grease you so I don't hurt you."

His smile turned wicked as he found her asshole again. He dabbed some on before pushing his finger slowly inside of her. Anne bit her lip at the brutal invasion. It did hurt, damn him!

"I—don't! It's too much."

"Hush. I've hardly even started." Damien pressed her down on the bed and spread her legs, settling between them. She looked down at him in alarm. Now what was he going to do?

As if in answer, he lowered his head, licking and kissing the creases of her inner thighs, teasing eager gasps and moans of pleasure from her until she was almost begging for more. When he moved on to lick the lips of her pussy, she bucked so hard he threw his arm across her to keep her still.

Oh, God, the bliss of that wet tongue gliding over her most intimate place. She couldn't bear it. She needed more. He made her come once before slipping a thick forefinger into her sheath and crooking it, pressing on some secret place inside of her that drove her to a screaming, head-thrashing orgasm.

While she was gasping, panting for breath, he slipped the greased finger past her sphincter and into her ass. Anne twitched as he stretched her, invaded her, but she was too overwhelmed in bliss to pull away.

He crooked the finger in her pussy. She arched her back with a husky moan. Damien had one finger in her sheath and one in her ass now, completely possessing her. He began to fuck her with those fingers, working them in and out of her while his mouth descended on hers and his tongue plunged deep inside of her.

He tasted musky like the scent of sex. Anne moaned and shuddered and came helplessly on his hand.

Damien withdrew. She watched, her eyes glazed in submissive lust while he scooped up more of the scented ointment and spread it on his rigid cock. Then he pounced on her. She looked up at him, breathless.

"Don't you want me to turn over?"

"No, I like you this way. I want to look into your eyes while I fuck your ass."

She colored. Damien drew her legs up, bent, until they touched her chest and her asshole was lifted and displayed for him. He positioned the head of his cock at her hole. Fear shot through her and she struggled under him and Damien held her down and shoved the head of his cock into the ring of her anus.

"Ow! No!"

"Shhh. Settle down and relax. It only hurts if you fight me."

Relax? Was he kidding? "How am I supposed to relax? This is unnatural."

He laughed, soft and deep. "No, it isn't. Just let out a long breath. Let your body go limp. That's it, darling. My sweet slave."

He pressed forward with his hips, forcing his cock deeper into her . Damien was panting, too, his eyes half-closed, his lips parted. He captured her mouth again in a fierce kiss, and when her tongue moved to meet his, he plunged all the way into her ass.

Chapter 9

Anne sobbed against his mouth. His cock was so big in her, overwhelming, utterly possessing her, stretching her tight ass impossibly wide. He began a slow thrusting rhythm, his hips bouncing against her open pelvis with every push. A strange pleasure that she could not have imagined earlier started to unfurl inside her body.

Damien stopped kissing her to pull back far enough to watch her face with predatory intent. "I'm deep in your ass, Anne." His voice was hoarse.

She groaned wordlessly.

"And you like it, don't you?"

"Mmmm—yeah—"

The drag as he pulled out filled her with forbidden delight and the thrust in filled her ass so full she could hardly breathe or think. He'd greased both of them so well there was no pain. It didn't hurt, but she was helpless, pinned beneath him, unable to move or even thrust up against his hips. All she could do was hold on to his waist while he violated her ass.

He supported himself on one arm and reached between them to tease her clit. An orgasm rocked through her. She gasped, then screamed and shook at the dark all-consuming pleasure of his possession.

Damien seemed to lose control then, pumping ferociously, his hair falling forward and hiding his face from her. The golden strands tickled as they brushed against her skin. Another orgasm threatened, and Anne dug her nails into his skin.

He tilted his head back, exposing his throat. His lips pulled back in a grimace that almost looked pained. His fangs seemed impossibly long and threatening from her perspective beneath him. Anne cried out as she came, and Damien roared, shaking, as he poured his come into her helpless ass.

It seemed like hours before she was able to lift her head. Damien lay next to her, one heavy thigh between hers, an arm flung across her waist. His eyes were closed, his dark lashes thick and curved against his golden skin. He was so beautiful it made her ache to look at him.

His lips lifted up in a slow smile as he opened his eyes. "Spectacular."

"I'm glad you're pleased, Master."

Damien laughed softly. "Trying to make me feel guilty?"

"I thought you wanted me to call you Master."

He pushed some hair from her eyes. "You're determined to fight me any way you can, aren't you?"

He didn't believe her. *Told you he wouldn't. He's too angry to believe.*

"I'm just trying to please you."

"Hmm. Well, you're doing a good job." He kissed her lightly. "Time to get cleaned up."

They took a quick shower together and returned, naked, to the bedroom. Anne went to the window to have a look outside, glad her wet hair hung far enough down her back to conceal it from Damien. The longer she went without him knowing, the better.

Pushing one of the curtains aside with her fingers, she peered out. Facing them was another building, with balconies decorated with potted plants and flowers. More buildings flanked those two and in the generous square between them was a garden with a trickling fountain, glossy-leaved trees, and arbors covered in flowering vines like the ones at the front of Damien's building, half hidden in late afternoon shadow.

It was a private space for the residents of these buildings and their guests. What a lovely surprise after all the heat and glare of the desert streets, and like everything else the Demon Kin made, it was beautiful. They seemed to have a knack for creating loveliness everywhere they went.

The Army of God wanted to destroy them. Gazing down at that hidden garden, Anne couldn't remember why. They hadn't asked to be created, hadn't chosen to be the way they were. They'd been made that way, by a human being who thought he knew better than the Light. It wasn't the fault of the Demon Kin.

Novus Vitans didn't care about that, however. The Demon Kin were evil in their eyes and must be destroyed. That was the mission of the Army of God, a mission she had embraced. And why?

So I would never have to look at Damien again and know that I wanted him, like the slut I am.

She didn't know whether to be more ashamed of her uncontrolled response to him, or the terrible plot in which she'd participated. Even if she hadn't known she carried an explosive, she had knowingly worked for the A.O.G., and now that choice looked like a black mark on her soul.

"Do you like the view?"

Anne jumped, spinning around to put the curtains at her back. He moved so quietly that she hadn't known he was there. Had he seen? But he was looking at her face without a hint that anything was wrong, so he must not have.

She cleared her throat. "Yes. It's lovely. You have a beautiful home."

He regarded her with somber eyes. "You don't have to stay with me. I can speak to Night about finding another master for you."

Something cold and slippery seemed to run its fingers down her spine. Anne frowned. "You want to get rid of me?" She'd thought he was pleased with her.

"I didn't say that. But maybe we have too much personal history for this to work. If you can't even look at me, that does not bode well for our future together. There will be other human women coming here, so I can find a mate among them, and I assure you there are thousands of Bellerenic men who would leap at the chance to have you."

Other human women. She thought of Damien taking another, suckling that other woman's breasts, licking her, crying out over her, filling her with his seed. Her stomach threatened to rebel.

"No, I—I don't want—please, don't speak to the king."

He gave her a wry smile. "Better the devil you know, eh?"

She jerked her head up and down. "Yes."

"Well." He rubbed his hand up and down her upper arm. "Are you ready to make the best of the situation?"

"Yes." Her voice came out flat again. As if she didn't care one way or the other. But she did care. She did.

Damien began to draw away from her. She caught him by the forearm, and he looked back at her with a questioning lift to his brows.

"I-I want to say—I want you to know that—I'm sorry. I'm sorry for what I did, for working with the Army."

He stared solemnly at her. "Are you?"

"Yes." Anne forced herself to hold his gaze. "I wish I'd never heard of them."

"Why did you do it?"

"Because I—" Anne hung her head. "I thought it would make up for what I'd done."

"And what was that?"

He sounded utterly unsympathetic. Cold. Almost as if they'd never known each other, never touched before the Soul Opening, never loved.

"I . . . cared for you." Her voice was thin now, and weak. "And they said . . . they called me a whore. They said you were evil, and so was I for feeling the way I did about you."

"And you believed them."

She nodded miserably.

"Do you think I should believe you now? Should I believe that you've suddenly had a change of heart and become remorseful? Or maybe I should believe that you're just trying to manipulate me into letting down my guard."

Anne stared at him, stricken. "That's not true."

"Isn't it? I'm glad to hear it."

174

Her shoulders sagged. He'd never believe or trust in her. She'd gone too far, participated in something so horrible that Damien couldn't forgive her.

"If I could undo what I've done, I'd go back in time this instant and fix things."

"It's convenient for you that's not possible."

"I thought I pleased you! Why are you being so hateful?"

He closed his eyes briefly and heaved a sigh. His lips parted as if to speak. Then he shut his mouth and shook his head. "I'm just tired and hungry. I'm going to call for lunch now."

In the morning, Anne tried to burrow under the covers so she wouldn't have to wake up. Her pussy was still a little sore. Besides, if she could stay asleep a little longer, she wouldn't have to think about what Damien had done to her yesterday morning. The way he'd made her feel.

He'd shamed her, excited her beyond bearing, given her one orgasm after another. Made her think she loved him. And then he'd thrown her into despair all over again.

Damien chivvied her out of bed, gave her the same tunic and sandals to wear, and hustled her to the roof of his building, where a float car waited. The car had a driver and heavily tinted windows. Anne climbed into the back compartment, which featured heavily padded upholstery and an opaque screen between them and the driver.

Damien locked the door, pressed a button, and the car whooshed off over the roof tops of Kelzenec. He gave her a cool smile. "We have food and drinks on board."

Was he looking for her approval? She didn't answer.

Turning her face to the window, she watched the capitol city of Belleren speeding by beneath them. Much of the city had been destroyed, especially the outer fringes. Buildings lay in rubble, streets were obscured by piles of fallen masonry, and ramshackle tents and shanties bloomed all around the decimated structures.

Malefica—er, Belleren—suffered during the war, too.

She'd heard about the ground strikes. They'd been all over the news on Novus Vita, but seeing them in person brought the destruction home to her. War was ugly, no matter which side you were on.

There was nothing to do in the float car except stare out the window or talk to Damien. She didn't want to talk to him, so she kept her eyes on the landscape. Soon they left the city and passed over klick after klick of orchards. Hadn't Damien said long ago that they grew a lot of lemons on Malefica? She peered down at the silvery-green trees, but couldn't make out a single lemon.

"Those are olive groves," he said.

She glanced at him briefly. It was too hard to hold his gaze. "Olives?"

"Yes. Belleren has an excellent climate for growing olives."

Oh. "What about lemons?"

"We'll see those, too." He studied her as a smile crossed his face. "You remembered."

Anne flushed. "Of course I did."

"I thought you put me out of your mind when you stopped visiting."

"I tried." She returned her attention to the window, ignoring the stab of pain the memories always brought. "Believe me, I tried."

"Should I be flattered I'm so unforgettable?"

"Take it however you like. Sir."

They fell silent. The olive groves disappeared, quickly replaced by trees with darker, greener foliage. These didn't have any lemons, either. Damien reached into a cabinet at the front of the compartment, producing cheese, berries and cold drinks, which they ate in silence.

The orchards fell away and they flew out across arid grassland. The ground stretched away in monotonous, gray-green hills for klicks in every direction, under a brassy blue sky that already shimmered with heat. In the distance, a line of low blue mountains separated ground from sky.

Float car travel could be hideously dull, Anne decided. Especially when the only thing you had to look at was jumbled rocks and scrubby-looking bushes. She leaned back against the cushions and closed her eyes, dozing.

A deafening boom exploded on her left side. Anne's eyes flew open as the car rocked heavily. Boom! Another explosion, this time on the right side. She screamed. The car faltered, listing to the side before righting itself and speeding on its way. A third explosion rocked them from behind.

Anne threw herself at Damien. His arms came around her, holding tightly as she clung to his narrow waist.

"What's happening?"

"Some tribesmen shot at us."

A beep sounded. "Are you all right back there?" the driver said.

Damien pushed a button on the right wall of the compartment. "We're fine. How are you?"

"I'm good. We're lucky this vehicle is armored, though. A regular car would have been shot right out of the air."

Anne stared up at Damien. "What did he mean? Why were they shooting at us?"

"You, probably. There are very few women in the back country, even fewer than in the cities, and they're in high demand. The tribesmen have been shooting float cars down lately on the chance that one will contain a female."

She trembled. "What do they do with the women they capture?"

"Fuck them, presumably. Pass them around."

God. She trembled even harder. "That's awful."

"They probably treat them very well in other ways. Women on this world are precious now."

"Then why do they shoot them down? Women could be killed in the crashes."

He settled back against the cushions, his arms still around her. She nestled into the warmth and safety of his embrace. "People aren't always rational when they're desperate."

"I'm surprised anyone travels without military escort." Anne drew in a surreptitious breath. He smelled so good she wanted to bite him. And he was being kind, for the moment, his previous bitterness apparently forgotten.

"This car is armored, including the windows, and it has a high-powered engine so it's pretty fast. I hired it especially because of the danger of back country travel."

"Is your friend's estate safe?"

He stroked her hair. "Yes, it's safe. Merek and Jace are ex-military and employ a small army of highly trained guards. Their house is like a fortress, too. Surrounded by high walls."

"I don't know anything about fighting."

"Didn't the Army of God train you?" There was a smile in his voice.

"No. I was just a secretary. Besides, they don't train women in combat."

"Fools. They should use every resource they've got. Not that I'd suggest it to them."

She huffed a short laugh. "I wonder what they'd say if you did?"

"They'd think it was some kind of trick." He kissed the top of her head.

Did he really hate her? It didn't seem so, when he held her and joked with her. Kissed her. Those weren't hateful actions.

And what about me? For years she'd told herself she hated him for trying to ruin her. For taking advantage of a naïve girl's infatuation. For tempting her into behavior that had bought her terrible punishment. But with his body cuddled next to hers, the beat of his heart in her ear, she couldn't lie to herself anymore.

She didn't hate him and never had.

I'm probably just fooling myself. He has every reason to despise me and no reason to forgive. We're enemies. He made that clear yesterday.

The thought saddened her. Anne pulled herself out of Damien's embrace and took her former position across from him with a stiff little smile. They were going to have to live together somehow.

It ought to be easy to figure out how to coexist with a man she hated. After all, she'd done it during her growing-up years, living in her father's house. But this was different.

"Do you still enjoy reading?" he said after a long silence.

Anne looked up at him, startled. "Yes. I mean, I don't know. I haven't done it in so long."

He frowned. "Why not?"

Her face grew hot. "My parents wouldn't allow it, except for Teaching books. Not after—"

"After what?" His tail began to twitch restlessly.

"Nothing. It's only that my parents disapproved of the kinds of books I was reading, so they forbid it."

If she looked at him, would she see doubt on his face? That was all right. Doubt was better than horror, or pity, or satisfaction—whatever he would feel if he knew the real reason they'd forbidden her to read.

"Well, if you'd like to start again, I have a reader you can use."

She risked looking at him. He merely smiled at her, fangs hidden, the kind of smile one might give an acquaintance or business associate. Impersonal. Safe.

"I was getting pretty bored until those people shot at us."

"Unfortunately the reader is in my bags. I'll get it out when we arrive, which shouldn't be long."

"You don't have to do that. I'm just a slave."

"That is your official position," he said gravely. "But you'll never be just a slave to me."

"The object of your revenge, then?"

"Why would I want revenge on you, Anne?"

"Because I belonged to the Army of God." *Because I left you, ignored you, tried to hurt your people.*

"I admit I was furious when I discovered what you'd done and how much you knew. But I don't want revenge."

She raised her brows. "No?"

His lips pressed together. "I may not trust you, but that doesn't mean I'm trying to get revenge. My position as your master is a duty my king has laid on me."

Anne couldn't hold his eyes. "You hate me."

"No. I don't hate you."

"You spanked me. And—and did that other thing."

"Are you telling me you didn't enjoy it?"

"No, I did not!"

"Your body said otherwise. And then there was all the begging you did."

She had begged. Pleaded. Cried and moaned. Her pussy throbbed at the memory of his cock inside her sheath, inside her ass, the way it had pressed on every sensitive point in her body. She'd never known it was possible to feel that way.

"I don't pretend to understand it," she said finally. "I only know you said you hated me."

"You said it first."

She glanced up to see him smiling at her. Her lips twitched. "Maybe I did."

"I don't want to hate you or be hated by you."

"Then what do you want?"

An expression of sorrow crossed his face. Then he smiled again, but it looked forced. "I thought I wanted us to be friends. Lovers. Now, I just don't know."

"A slave and her master can't be friends."

"You might be surprised."

Anne turned away from him. Looking at him was dangerous to her inner equilibrium. She looked out the window instead. But what she saw there disturbed her more than anything she could observe on Damien's face.

Chapter 10

Just ahead, men on horseback were pouring over a low rise. She could see their horns emerging from the many-layered head wraps they wore, their narrow tails flying out over the tails of their mounts. Some of them raised their fists in the air and shouted. One stopped and lifted some kind of weapon to his shoulder, aiming it upward. At them.

"The tribesmen are still after us," she said.

Another explosion boomed just under the vehicle. The float car bucked and twisted, then dropped so fast it felt like her stomach had detached itself and was floating up into her mouth. She pressed her hand to her lips. They were going to crash.

A second boom, then a third. Smoke poured from the left side of the car. The engine made a whining sound, then sputtered and died.

"Get on the floor!" Damien opened a compartment in the wall and withdrew a pulse rifle and flechette gun. He stuck the flechette in his belt and checked the pulse rifle.

Then he glanced at her, his eyes hard as glass. "I said get down. They have better weaponry than we thought, and we're going down. It's going to get rough."

Anne dropped to the floor, huddling against the front of the bench seat. The float car still dropped, the ride jarring like an old farm wagon on a rutted country road. They were going to be overrun with tribesmen intent on gang raping her. She closed her eyes and began to pray.

Thump! The car jerked and shuddered, thumped again, then bumped along with a deafening scraping sound. Her eyes flew open. The float car must have hit the ground.

They slid sideways, dust and sand boiling up around the windows. The car slowed, skewing a little more, and came to a halt against some thorny desert bushes. From somewhere nearby, a wild ululation arose.

"Stay down no matter what happens," Damien barked. His tail flicked sharply.

"I will." She had no intention of showing herself.

"I'm opening the door to the cockpit. You stay back here." He gave her a narrow-eyed stare.

She nodded wordlessly. He jerked the door open and entered the cockpit, talking in low-pitched Malefican to the driver. The driver opened the cockpit door on the right side and the two men slithered out, leaving Anne alone in the float car.

What were they doing? Why had they left her? She couldn't see what was going on from her position behind the seat in the passenger compartment. But she'd promised Damien she'd stay put, and she wasn't going to go back on her word to him.

The thundering beats of horse hooves sounded, nearer and nearer. The shouts of the tribesmen, the flash and sharp crack of pulse rifles made the hair on the back of her neck stand on end. It was like living the invasion all over again. She began to tremble, but she didn't know if it was from fear or rage.

She ought to be able to fight, damn it. After all, it was her life on the line here. Her pussy, her womb. If they lost, the tribesmen would take her as their prize. She'd be their brood mare, and probably never see civilization again.

Pulse rifle fire snapped out from just outside the vehicle. *Please let that be Damien or the driver.*

There were some answering cracks from the tribesmen. More fire from Damien. Anne clasped her hands together and began again to pray, but she kept her eyes on the window.

She could see the tribesmen now, sitting restive horses that pranced wildly and tossed their heads, the tassels and metal ornaments on their bridles shaking, catching the sun and flashing shards of light into her eyes. They were so close.

Rifle fire snapped out from behind the float car. One of the tribesmen yelled and slumped in his saddle. He slid slowly sideways and tumbled to the ground. Another burst of fire from both sides. Another tribesman fell. On the right side of the float car, a man screamed.

Damien!

To hell with her promise. She crawled on the floor, through the compartment door into the cockpit. The long dress she wore caught under her knees, impeding her, and she yanked at it. Damn impractical thing. But she didn't have time to change into something more suitable.

She snorted back a laugh. Ten years ago, she'd have been paralyzed with fear. Even a few minutes back, she'd thrown herself at Damien because they were firing on the car, and here she was moving into the fray. Her father was right again. She was not only a slut, but a hoyden to boot.

It's more important to stay alive and free than to be a proper lady.

The cockpit door was open. She huddled next to the wall and peeked out. Long legs clad in blue trousers were just visible, as their owner leaned around the nose of the float car to fire. Had to be Damien. He'd worn blue today, and the driver was in brown.

Working a little farther forward, she spied the driver laying on the ground beyond Damien, with only a small boulder for cover. He groaned, clutching his thigh. Blood seeped from between his fingers and ran over the thirsty ground.

He was going to die if someone didn't help him. His position was just too exposed, the boulder insufficient cover to protect him against plasma fire.

An instant after she had the thought, plasma fire struck a glancing blow to the boulder. The bolt sent a spray of incandescent rock chips into the air and annihilated the boulder, leaving only a smoking, melted lump behind. Anne picked her skirt up in her hands and crawled out of the cockpit. She dashed toward the driver, the leash attached to her collar dragging along the ground.

"Get back, damn you!" Damien hollered.

She ignored him. The tribesmen wouldn't fire on her, would they? Not if they wanted a healthy, working broodmare, they wouldn't. Now why hadn't that thought occurred to her earlier?

Rifle fire whined around her, sending up sprays of rock chips and dust and bits of melted slag. One of the natives shouted. The weapon fire ceased.

She grabbed the driver under his armpits. Luckily he wasn't nearly as large as Damien, or she wouldn't have been able to drag him at all. Digging in with her butt muscles, she hauled him backwards toward the float car until she stopped just under the fuselage.

Damien fired his rifle again. "What the hell do you think you're doing? I told you to stay down."

"They won't fire on me. Remember? They want to fuck me."

"They have other weapons besides plasma rifles, and you don't need legs for fucking." He squinted and fired again.

God. She hadn't thought of that. She pushed the horrific notion out of her mind as she bent over the driver. He had passed out and his hand had released the wound on his inner thigh. There was a chance a major artery had been severed.

The trousers were in her way. She would have to cut them off. A knife. She needed a knife. Fumbling with the man's belt, she found a utility knife and drew it. Perfect. She stuck the tip into the driver's trouser leg and cut it away from the wound.

It wasn't burned, so he hadn't been hit with plasma fire. There was a strange hole in his leg, relatively tidy considering it might kill him. Blood pumped out of the hole with frightening speed, so Anne simply stuck the heel of her hand in the wound and pressed. The man whimpered.

"Shhh. It's going to be all right," she said. "We're going to get out of here and get help for you."

"He called for help as we were going down," Damien said. "They should be here any minute."

"You hear that?" she told the driver. "Help is on its way. You just have to hold on a little longer."

He didn't seem to hear, but you never knew with people who were unconscious. During the invasion, she'd worked in a hospital tending wounded soldiers of all kinds. She'd seen people wake up from comas and other unconscious states and repeat things that had been said while they were seemingly unaware of their surroundings.

Her hand was beginning to tire. She let go of the wound and took the hem of her dress in both hands, ripping until she had a long strip of fabric. Working as fast as she could, she wrapped it around the man's thigh just above the wound. She twisted the ends together, tightening it until it dug into the flesh of his leg, muttering prayers under her breath that the man's bleeding stop and his life be saved.

Plasma fire hit the nose of the float car and melted it.

"Gods of Belleren!" Damien scuttled backward. "We have to get back."

"I can't move him. I have to keep pressure on his wound or he'll bleed out." *And die.* She stopped herself just before blurting the fateful words. She didn't want to tell the poor man he was about to die. What if he believed her and gave up the fight?

The low drone of float car engines came from somewhere behind them. A monstrous blast hit the ground in the middle of the tribesmen, throwing roasted horses and their riders in every direction. A second blast hit farther afield. The remaining horses screamed and kicked, men shouted, hooves thundered as the riders retreated, dust boiling up to cover their movements.

The engine drone grew louder. Anne looked up to see a huge float car descending just to their right. Judging by the cloud arising on the other side of their vehicle, another was coming down over there.

She looked down at the driver's leg. The blood flow had lessened. Her simple tourniquet seemed to be working.

Men in light gray uniforms swarmed out of the nearby float car and ran to them. Anne tied off the tourniquet to make sure the pressure stayed on long enough to completely stop the blood loss. Then she let go and allowed the newcomers to pick the man up and carry him to the rescue vehicle.

Another man took her by the upper arm. "We're from Demon's Lair. We'll take you there."

Demon's Lair? Whatever. They were rescuers, and that was good enough for her. She nodded, getting to her feet. Next to her, Damien arose, still clutching the plasma rifle. The three of them ran to the waiting float car and climbed aboard.

The passenger compartment on this vehicle was nothing like the one Damien had hired. It was bare bones inside, just a mostly-empty shell with hammock-like net seats for the soldiers who sat against the walls. There were only a couple of tiny windows.

A float pallet against the back wall held the injured driver, with a drip already in his arm. A medic was slowly undoing the tourniquet she'd applied.

Damien grabbed her and squeezed her in a crushing, desperate hug. "You scared the hell out of me. I thought I was going to lose you out there."

"I couldn't leave him."

"I know." He kissed the top of her head. "I know."

"Buckle in!" yelled one of the guards.

Damien guided her to one of the net seats. She collapsed into it, leaning her head against the wall and closing her eyes. The float car shuddered, then rose swiftly into the air and zoomed away. Thank God, they'd all survived. Some of the tribesmen hadn't been so lucky.

Then again, they'd been the aggressors. They must be truly desperate to take such risky action to acquire women.

He clasped her hand in his and squeezed. Anne turned her head, opening her eyes to give him a shaky smile. He smiled back. The roar of the engine was deafening in this uninsulated space, and she didn't have the energy to yell above the din. But she hoped her relief and admiration showed in her eyes.

He'd held the attackers off by himself. She hadn't known he was so capable—not in a military sense at least.

Damien raised her shaky hand to his lips and kissed it. "Thank you," he mouthed.

About half an hour later, they began a quick descent. Anne craned her neck to peer out one of the windows. Just ahead was a house that looked more like a desert castle. A high, crenellated wall of golden stone surrounded it. Tall palms planted in intervals softened the harsh edges of the walls, and greenery peeked out from some of the open spaces inside the compound.

Damien leaned toward the glass. "That's Demon's Lair," he shouted over the engine noise.

She looked at him sidelong. "They named their house Demon's Lair?"

"On Belleren, we believe in taking pride in our demonic heritage."

"You aren't really descended from demons, are you?"

He cocked his head. "What do you think?"

"I think you're pulling my leg. You're the product of genetic engineering, not magic."

"Maybe you're right. But if foreigners are going to call us Demon Kin, we might as well wear the label with pride."

She must have had a strange expression on her face, because he grinned at her, flashing his pointed teeth. He truly looked devilish, with his fangs gleaming, his curling horns rising out of golden waves of hair, reddish-brown tail doing that lazy swish that seemed to indicate he was in a good mood.

He wasn't angry with her anymore.

The float car came gently to rest in the courtyard of Demon's Lair. A moment later the door slid open and the soldiers began to unbelt themselves from their seats. Anne and Damien followed suit.

When she stood up, her knees wobbled. He put his arm around her, urging her to lean against him at the same time as he took hold of her leash. Anne looked up at him and he smiled at her again.

"You're a bit unsteady," he said.

"I guess I'm having a delayed reaction."

"You can lean on me."

It was not the response she'd expected from him. His attitude kept changing so quickly it gave her whiplash. Did he love her? Hate her? Not care one way or the other? Even he didn't seem to know the answer.

They walked together down the ramp and onto the cobbled stones of the courtyard. His tail was still sweeping gently back and forth. Every time it flicked to the left, it swept across her calves, making her tingle all over. It should have repulsed her or horrified her, but instead she found it. . . seductive.

Demon Kin males wearing colorful tunics and trousers rushed forward, talking rapidly in Malefican. Damien answered them in the same language, while Anne leaned against him. Her legs were so shaky they felt like they might collapse underneath her.

"Thank the Gods you made it!" said a deep, male voice. A tall black-haired man with silver horns made his way toward them through the crowd of servants.

"Thanks to your men," Damien said. The two embraced, slapping each other's backs.

The black-haired man glanced at her and raised his brows. "And who is your lovely companion?"

"This is my slave, Anne."

"Your slave, eh? I hadn't heard you'd acquired one."

"She was a gift from Night, just yesterday."

"Lucky." Black-hair grinned. "She looks familiar, too. If I didn't know better, I'd say she's the terrorist. Anne Paulsen."

Anne dropped her head. Her hands clenched into fists.

"She is Anne Paulsen," Damien said.

"Perhaps not so lucky, then?" Black-hair said.

"Very lucky indeed. If it weren't for her, our driver would have died."

Anne blushed as Black-hair gave her a closer look.

"Really. I didn't know a Novus Vitan was capable of such compassionate action."

Damien snorted. "Merek, you should know better than that. Your wife to be is Novus Vitan."

Hmm. That was interesting. There must be quite a few N.V. women on Belleren. Were they all here as part of Night's program, or were some of them volunteers? It seemed incomprehensible that any Novus Vitan woman would volunteer for such a life.

You would have, ten years ago, if Damien had asked you.

Two more people approached them from the shadows of a colonnade along one wall of the courtyard. One of them was a tall, red-haired Demon Kin male and the other a slender blonde human woman. They were holding hands. Was this the engaged couple?

The blonde looked familiar. Anne studied her face, which lit with a big smile as soon as she saw Damien. Where had she seen this woman before?

The three of them surrounded Anne and Damien, the men slapping him on the back and talking rapidly in Malefican. Even the woman spoke the Demon Kin language, leaving Anne completely out of the conversation. But that wasn't surprising. After all, she was only a slave.

The blonde's gaze rested on her. "And who is this, Damien?" she said in Galactic Standard.

"My slave, Anne. Night awarded her to me just yesterday."

"Your slave?" the red-haired man said. "You got lucky."

Damien shrugged and smiled. "Yes and no. He gave her to me as a retirement gift."

"Ah, yes. Retirement. How is that working for you?"

"It's only one day old. It was working well until we came under attack."

They laughed.

"She's beautiful," the red-head remarked. "Retirement gift or not, I agree with Merek. You're lucky."

Anne stiffened. They were talking about her as if she weren't there, or too stupid to understand them. Plus, how had the redhead known what Merek had said? He'd been across the courtyard at the time.

She swallowed. Now Damien would explain to the red-head and the blonde just how she came to be in the position of slave in the first place. He'd tell everyone exactly who she was and what she'd done.

"Why don't you can go up to your room and get cleaned up first," the blonde said.

"Good idea." Damien smiled.

The humiliation was postponed, then.

They walked under an archway framed in colorful tiles and into a grand entrance which featured an equally grand staircase curving up to a gallery above. A servant came to lead them to their room on the second floor, and they left their hosts in the entrance hall.

Chapter II

Their room turned out to be a suite, including a large bathroom, a sitting room on the gallery, and a bedroom directly overlooking a garden courtyard, which featured its own outdoor gallery. The bed was so much like Damien's—and the one used in the Soul Opening—that Anne wondered if it was the official bed style on Belleren. Its filmy white curtains were drawn back in graceful sweeps to display the crisp white coverlet and piles of colorful pillows.

"Take off your clothes," Damien said as soon as the door shut.

He certainly didn't waste any time. Anne untied the laces on her ruined tunic and slipped out of it while he divested himself of shirt and pants just as quickly. But instead of leading her to the bed, he strode into the bathroom and turned on the shower.

She still trembled with reaction. She'd never been a resistance fighter, but there had been plenty of fighting going on all around her for a year or two on Novus Vita. It was supposed to be over. The war was over, and foolishly she hadn't expected that kind of violence to invade peacetime.

Damien drew her into an embrace under the stinging water. "I'm sorry. I never thought they'd attack twice, or that they'd have a weapon powerful enough to bring down an armored float car."

Anne nodded, her face sliding against his slippery chest. "I know. It wasn't your fault."

"Yes, it was. I should have hired guards as well. Next time, we'll have a cavalcade." He stroked her damp hair. "You were amazing. Brave and valiant."

She snorted. "I only did what I had to do."

"But you didn't have to. That's my point. You could have followed directions and left our driver out there to die."

"I thought you were angry with me for disobeying."

"I was. But I admire your courage just the same."

"You were brave, too. I didn't know you could fight so well," she said, tightening her arms around his waist.

"Hardly. Merek and Jace would have brought the whole company down."

She pulled back to look him in the eyes. "No, they wouldn't. Not if there were only two of them. You did what you could."

He smiled, bending down to kiss her lips. "Either way, I'm grateful to you for saving the man's life. It was a remarkable act for anyone, but especially for a former member of the A.O.G."

Reaching for a niche in the wall of the shower, he took a bar of sweet-smelling soap and rubbed it over his palms. Slowly he moved his hands along her shoulders, down her arms, then under the heavy curves of her breasts and up, across their tips. Her breath caught.

"You don't have to do that."

"Yes, I do." He teased her nipples again, pinching them until she shuddered. "It gives me pleasure to care for you."

Damien soaped his hands again, then worked them down her back and then her legs to her feet, carefully washing between her toes. Moving back up, he pushed her legs apart and bathed the lips of her sex. Her knees buckled. She sagged against the wall of the shower as he took the head down and rinsed her between her legs.

"Turn around and tilt your head back." He picked up a shampoo bottle.

By now, he'd touched more places on her body than anyone else ever had, except perhaps when she was a baby. Anne savored the feeling of his fingertips massaging her scalp, and when all the shampoo had been rinsed from her hair, she grabbed the soap and turned to face him.

"May I return the favor?"

"I hoped you would."

Anne soaped her hands. "Your wish is my command, remember?"

If she had to be a slave, at least she had Damien for her master. Maybe someday he'd come to forgive her for her mistakes.

Novus Vitan women vow to obey their husbands in all things. If they fail to comply, the husbands beat them. How is that any different than slavery?

It was strange she'd never thought of that comparison before. It seemed so obvious now.

"What do women on Malef—I mean, Belleren, do?" she said, slipping her hands across the scattering of gold hair on his chest.

"Do?"

"Yes. Are they housewives, like on Novus Vita?"

He studied her as if trying to see inside her soul. "It varies. Some keep house, some are professionals. Farm wives work the farm alongside their husbands. Why?"

Anne shrugged. "Just wondering."

"Some men stay at home. Did you know that?"

"They keep house like women?" She tried to keep her astonishment off her face.

"Yes." He laughed a little. "You find that strange."

"I do."

"Now that women are so scarce here, things will likely change, but we don't know how."

Anne walked around behind him to wash his back. "I think the women who are left will be locked up to keep them safe and controlled. The men won't want to risk losing them."

"You think so?"

"Yes. Look at how those tribesmen behaved." She ran her hands down to the small of his back and paused above his buttocks. His ass was so fine, just round enough and firm with muscle, and she wanted to touch it. Below, his tail hung still under the heavy flow of the water.

"Maybe you're right. I should let Night hear your thoughts."

She gave in to temptation and caressed his backside. "He won't care what I think."

"On the contrary, he'll probably find it interesting." Damien looked over his shoulder at her. "That feels good."

Did that mean he wouldn't mind her touching his tail? She ran her fingertips over the base of it and he drew in his breath. Anne snatched her hand away. "I'm sorry."

"Don't be silly." He caught her hand and placed it back on his tail. "I like it. All Demon Kin love having their tails petted."

"Oh." She clasped the muscular column of it in her hand. There were bones at the core of it. That probably should have been obvious, but she'd been wondering for years what those tails felt like to the touch and somehow she'd never imagined bones. Now she knew. They were firm, covered in sleek hair.

"Our tails are erogenous zones. Especially the bases."

"Ero-what?"

"Erogenous zones. Areas of our bodies that are highly sensitive and which provoke sexual excitement when touched."

Her eyes widened. "Um—"

She glanced down to see his cock fully erect and eager, watched as her hand stretched out to caress its hard length. Damien faced her, cradled her head in his hands and took her mouth in a blistering kiss. He crowded up against her, shoving her back against the shower wall in his excitement.

Anne cupped his ass in both hands, squeezing the heavy muscles, rubbing her palms over satiny skin. He moaned against her lips. When she stroked the base of his tail, he moaned again, his hips beginning a sultry rolling motion against her body.

"I want to be inside you," he growled, nipping the side of her neck. "I can't get enough of you."

She whimpered as his fangs lightly grazed her skin.

"Put your arms around my neck." He licked the place where his teeth had been.

She obeyed, and he grabbed her ass and lifted her. Instinctively she wrapped her legs around his waist. He held her aloft with only one hand as he used the other to position the tip of his cock at the entrance to her aching pussy.

How strong he is.

"So wet," he murmured.

She moaned. Water spilled over their heads, their shoulders, ran down their hot skin and between their bodies where they pressed together. Damien flexed his hips and filled her with one thrust. Pleasure stabbed her. They both cried out at the same time.

Her fingernails dug reflexively into his skin. "Yes!"

Damien groaned her name, clutching her ass as he began a pounding rhythm of thrust and retreat. She couldn't get enough leverage to push back into him. All she could do was hang on and take what he gave her, while soft animal noises issued from her throat.

He used his grip on her to work her back and forth on his cock against the movement of his hips. The water had darkened his hair and plastered it to his head, where it obscured his eyes from her view. But it didn't matter, because he lowered his head and kissed her again.

His tongue thrust deep into her mouth, then retreated, over and over, in imitation of his cock. Possessing her utterly. She sucked on it, nipped at it, drawing a groan from him.

Delight built inside her, throbbing faster and faster in the core of her body, pulsing harder and harder until it burst outward in a scalding wave of ecstasy. She wailed, thrashing her head back and forth against the wall.

Damien growled something in Malefican that she couldn't understand. He began to shudder and groan. His hips gave a spasmodic jerk as a look of bliss and pain came over his face. He whimpered, his big body trembling, quaking, as if the pleasure of orgasm were unbearable.

Finally his hips stilled. He kissed her between her brows and rested his forehead against hers.

I want to love him.

When he disengaged from her, Anne drew his head down for another kiss. Could there be love between master and slave? It wasn't an equal relationship. In fact, it was the epitome of unequal relationships. But she wanted to love him. More than anything.

She washed herself again, rinsing his cum from her skin and wondering if they'd made a child this time. Probably not. It was too early, too quick. Soon enough, though, she'd probably be pregnant.

The thought made a strange quiver of anticipation run through her body. Only a short time ago, the idea of bearing a Demon Kin child had filled her with horror.

All this sex with Damien has confused me, made me doubt my upbringing.

And yet, she hadn't been so happy in a long time.

He turned off the water, grabbed a towel, and began drying her with such tenderness it made her eyes sting. Anne combed his hair out of his eyes with her fingers. He stood up and handed her the towel, but it was damp. She threw it on the floor and pulled another one from the rack.

"You don't have to do that," he said as she rubbed the fluffy white towel over his chest.

"Damien, I think you're confused. You want me to be your slave and then you're uncomfortable when I serve you."

She glanced up at his face in time to see him blush. That was interesting. Anne gave him a pert smile and pushed the towel down his belly, past his navel and over his cock.

"I'm not uncomfortable," he said.

She walked behind him and toweled his back. "Yes, you are. I think you don't really want me to be your slave. You want something else."

Now, why did I say that? She hadn't meant to imply he wanted to marry her.

"What I want at the moment is more water."

"Where are you going?"

"*We* are going swimming."

She crossed her arms over her breasts. "With nothing on?"

"That's how it's done here."

"But I don't know how to swim."

Damien tugged on the leash. "I'll teach you."

He forced her to come to him. Heat swept her entire body at the thought of going nude in public.

"I don't think this is a good idea," she grumbled.

"That's because you've never done it before." When he'd brought her close enough, he slung an arm across her shoulders. "You'll like it, Anne. Trust me."

As if she had a choice. *I could start kicking and screaming.* But that would probably just slow him down. It wouldn't stop him. He'd been trying to get her in the water since the day she'd met him.

She gave a long-suffering sigh. "All right."

"I have a swimming pool we can use when we get home." He drew her out onto the balcony.

"You do? Where is it?" Maybe on the roof of his building?

"In its own section of the garden, just like here."

"I didn't see one."

He gave her an odd look. "Not at the apartment. In my country house."

"Oh. I didn't know you had one." She glanced around to see if anyone was watching them, but the courtyard seemed to be empty.

"Of course I do. The baronial seat."

She peered up at him. "You're a baron?"

"I am now. Both my parents died in the plague. It wasn't only women who were affected." He said the words easily, as if they didn't cause him pain, but Anne remembered how fond he'd been of his parents.

"I'm sorry, Damien. I didn't know."

He gave a half-shrug. "How could you? I'm sure you didn't keep up on Bellerenic news."

"No." She'd been forbidden. Then the invasion had come, her parents had died, food became scarce. News of Belleren society had not been on her mind.

They walked along the shady gallery and down two flights of stairs to the courtyard. The only sounds were the trickling fountain and a bird cooing somewhere in the shrubbery. Damien led her through another archway she hadn't noticed before and into a second courtyard.

This one was bordered by exterior walls on one side, the house on the other. It was open to the sky and blazed with heat and sunlight. In the center, a generous oval-shaped pool beckoned with glittering blue water.

Anne hung back. "It looks so deep."

"It's only deep on one end."

"I don't know, Damien." She'd never been immersed in anything deeper than a bathtub, and not very often even there.

He scooped her up in his arms, making her squeak in surprise. "I'll hold onto you until you get used to it." Then he waded in.

Stone steps led down into the depths of the pool. As he descended, chilly water lapped at her feet. She gasped. The water kissed her backside, then her thighs.

Damien smiled down at her. "How do you like it?"

"It's cold."

He grinned. "Give it a few minutes."

Now the water was up to her waist; now it tickled the tips of her breasts. She tightened her hold on his neck, her grip nervous as the water buoyed her up and made her float.

"If I wanted revenge on you," he murmured, "now would be the perfect time to dunk you."

Chapter 12

Anne's arms clamped down hard on his neck. "Don't you dare."

His eyes were even bluer than the water. "I wouldn't dream of displeasing you, my slave."

Right. Did he actually expect her to believe that? Damien lowered his head and sucked at her bottom lip.

She opened for him without hesitation. His tongue plunged inside her, the hot slick strokes distracting her from the disorienting sensation of the water. God, he tasted good. At one time, she'd thought she would never taste him again, never feel his body against hers or his hands on her bare skin.

And I believed I was happy about it. What a fool I was.

The brightly lit memories of her long-ago weeks with Damien were surrounded by nothing but the icy darkness of her life without him.

Her lower half began to float away from him, her legs dangling free as cool water sluiced over her skin. She broke off the kiss.

"You let me go."

"No, I didn't. My hands are still on your waist."

It was true. He still had her, but she now had the sensation of being fully immersed. And it wasn't so bad. It was kind of pleasant, actually. The water glided over her like a cool caress, and her whole body felt much lighter than it usually did.

"You can't drown, you know," he continued. "Unless you do something really dumb. The water would only come up to your chin if you stood on the bottom."

"Really?" She reached carefully downward until her toes and then her heels touched the bottom of the pool. "Oh! I can stand up." She laughed.

He grinned, his gaze warm. "That's the Anne I remember."

Her throat seized up. "Oh, God," she whispered, looking down into the water.

"What is it?"

She shook her head, unable to speak. Her arms slipped from his neck.

Damien caught the side of her face in his palm. "Tell me, love."

Love. He can't mean that.

"You'll think it's silly."

"Try me."

Anne made herself look at him. "It's just everything we lost. You and me."

194

His expression changed, softened, as a shadow crossed his face. "I didn't think you noticed."

She held his gaze. "I noticed before you did."

Damien frowned a little. "What do you mean?"

"The day you kissed me. I knew I could never go back and that I'd never see you again."

"Why? What happened after you left?"

Anne shrugged awkwardly.

"Tell me, Anne."

"Nothing. It's just that my parents forbid me to walk in the garden, and so I knew I'd never see you."

He gave her a searching look, as if he knew there was more to the story than that. But instead of questioning her, he merely gave her another kiss. "Well, whatever happened, you're seeing me now."

"Yes." She forced a smile. "Teach me to swim?"

That distracted him from the subject. She had to concentrate, however, to place herself so that he wouldn't be looking at her naked back with its pitiful scars. Anne gazed up at him as he held her in the water, teaching her to float on her back, and wondered why she didn't just tell him. Get it over with.

Because then he'd feel sorry for me.

Or—worse thought—what if he didn't believe her when she told him who was responsible? She closed her eyes, unable to meet his blue gaze. Everything between them was such a tangle. An awful, wadded-up mess of betrayal and pain, longing and mistrust.

If only I hadn't run from him that day. If only I'd stayed.

If only.

They'd forgotten to bring towels, so when their swim session ended they had to walk dripping wet through the two courtyards and up the stairs, leaving dark wet footprints behind them. The breeze blowing on her water-slick skin made Anne shiver. As soon as they got into the room, they found their towels from earlier and dried off as best they could.

"How did you like it?" Damien threw the used towels into the bathroom.

"It was very refreshing."

"Ready for a nap?"

Anne followed him into the bedroom, where he'd already stretched out on top of the coverlet before she caught up with him. He moved swiftly and silently, like a cat. Did Demon Kin have cat genes? Their lion-like tails suggested they might.

Damien patted the bed next to him. "Climb up."

She got up, not half as gracefully as he had, and laid down beside him, nestling her head against his shoulder. How quickly she'd grown accustomed to his nearness, the touch of his bare skin, the warmth of his body next to hers.

I've been waiting twelve years for this.

Anne sighed. She draped her arm across his midsection. *I love you.* But she didn't say the words out loud.

They dozed together and woke up when the sun was nearing the horizon. Anne's stomach growled fiercely as she sat up and ran her fingers through her hair.

"I could use some food myself," Damien said.

"Is it dinner time yet?"

"It's close, anyway. Let's get dressed and go downstairs."

"I'm afraid the tunic you gave me is ruined."

"That's all right. I packed some clothes for you."

She glanced at him sidelong. "Why do you have so many women's clothes, anyway?"

He grinned. "Jealous?"

"No." Anne shrugged. "Just wondering."

"Uh huh." He toyed with a damp curl of her hair. "I had a lover for a while, before I became a controller. We parted badly, and she died soon after of the plague. I never had the heart to get rid of her things."

"Oh." Not what she'd wanted to hear. "Did you love her?"

Damien shook his head. "No. I liked her a great deal, admired her, but I didn't love her. That was partly why she ended our affair."

"I see."

He gave her a wry half-smile. "Do you?"

"She wanted something you couldn't give her."

"My heart was already taken." He looked at her steadily until she dropped her gaze to the coverlet.

He couldn't possibly mean her. Could he? They'd been little more than children. And she'd abandoned him, at least as far as he knew. Run off one afternoon and never returned, refused to speak to him. Surely he hadn't loved her, hadn't carried that foolish attachment with him all those years.

Then there was all the anger and bitterness in him. She'd seen a lot of it in the last two days. Yet whatever was between them seemed altered since the attack on their float car. Her rescue of the driver had changed the way Damien looked at her.

He sat up and kissed her on the tip of the nose. "Get dressed and we'll see about food."

Their hosts were already seated at a table in the courtyard when she and Damien came down the stairs. The two men wore long tunics over loose trousers, like virtually every other Demon Kin male she'd ever seen. The woman dressed similarly, but her tunic was cut to follow the lines of her body and her long golden hair hung in a single braid down her back. She laughed and flirted with both of the men, each hand clasped in one of theirs on the table top.

Was she going to marry the redhead or Merek? She seemed equally fond of both.

Anne and Damien descended the last few stairs into the courtyard.

The high walls of the house surrounded it, with galleries on each floor. On the floor of the courtyard, palms cast striped shade over the stones and vines covered in masses of brilliant pink flowers climbed up the walls and half-obscured the lower balconies. In the center, a fountain trickled.

Their hosts looked up and smiled at them as they approached the table nestled under the shade of a vine-covered arbor. Servants were already there, placing trays of food and pitchers of iced drinks on the table. The blonde gestured to the food with a smile.

"I'm sure you're hungry and thirsty after that awful attack."

Damien gave her a short bow. "Thank you, Corinna. We're famished."

Corinna. She knew that name. Anne studied the blonde from beneath her lashes. Corinna. *Corinna Jerrix?*

She almost gasped aloud. Could this woman be the missing Corinna Jerrix? But she was thought to be dead, killed in a Malefican attack on her space cruiser.

"Where would you like your slave to sit?" Corinna said.

"She may have a chair."

"You are generous."

Anne steamed. She may be a slave, but she was still a sentient being with feelings of her own. Biting her lip, she refused to allow herself to give him a reproachful look.

Damien patted her on the shoulder and pulled out a chair. "Sit down, Anne."

She sat down. He took the seat next to her while Corinna began to pour drinks.

The others began to talk in Malefican again, leaving her out of the conversation. She gazed around the courtyard at the flowers, the patterns of sun and shade, the carved stone of the fountain. Someone was playing a musical instrument on one of the balconies. It sounded like a guitar, but she couldn't see the musician. There was laughter, too, both masculine and feminine. She and Corinna weren't the only females in the house.

Just as the music began to relax her a little, two people came out of a room to stand on a gallery across from where she sat. A man and a woman, both of them Demon Kin. They didn't seem to notice that there were others present and that they were easily visible from the garden, or maybe they didn't care. They were naked. And kissing.

The man pressed the woman against the wall of the house while his hands roved all over her breasts and hips. Anne's core grew heavy and warm as she watched them. The man picked his partner up, big hands supporting her ass, and she wrapped her legs around his waist.

Anne went hot all over. My God, were they going to . . . ? His hips began to move in an unmistakable rhythm. Yes, they were. In the exact position she and Damien had used so recently.

The woman's head fell back against the wall as he fucked her. She was digging her nails into the flesh of his shoulders. Although her face was hidden by the shadows of the gallery, every line and movement of her body communicated ecstasy. She enjoyed what he did to her.

Had she and Damien looked like that?

"Do you like what you see?" Damien murmured in her ear.

She started, tearing her gaze away from the couple on the balcony. "I can hardly believe what I see."

He laughed softly. "There will probably be more of that while the party lasts."

Her face must be the color of a hothouse tomato. She ducked her head. This was her life now, and some day she might get used to it. But to see people coupling in public—semi-public, at least—was too much for her sensibilities.

"They are also wedding guests," he added. "We'll meet them later."

"You will meet them. I will stand mutely and be ignored."

He grinned. "Feeling left out?"

"No."

"Your slave is unused to her position," the black-haired man said.

"She was only sentenced yesterday. Her training is minimal."

Red-hair raised his eyebrows. "Sentenced?"

"Haven't you been watching the news, darling?" Corinna said. "This is Anne Paulsen, the Novus Vitan suicide bomber."

Chapter 13

Corinna's companion stared at Anne, his face gone cold with censure.

"She isn't a suicide bomber," Damien said. "She is innocent of those charges."

"Didn't she have an explosive device on her when she was arrested?" Corinna sounded genuinely interested, not catty as Anne had first thought.

"Yes." He took Anne's hand. "But she didn't know what it was. She was told it was a data crystal."

He was standing up for her. She could have kissed him.

"That's what the news reports said, that she claimed she was ignorant. But it was an explosive, right?"

"She didn't know, Corinna. They were using her."

"How do you know that's the truth?"

"Because I performed her Soul Opening."

Corinna's dark eyes widened. "Oh."

"She's been sentenced to slavery as an accessory to the crime and because she was an auxiliary member of the Army of God. However, she risked her own life to save our driver. After he was injured, she dragged him back to the float car and made a tourniquet for his leg. He would have bled out if not for her."

The censure on the redhead's face eased. "That was brave and well-done."

Anne gave him a nod of acknowledgement.

The blonde gave her an apologetic smile. "I'm sorry for the misunderstanding. I'm a little oversensitive to Novus Vitan matters because I'm from there myself."

The pieces fell into place.

"You *are* Corinna Jerrix!" Anne flushed hotly as the words left her mouth. It wasn't a slave's place to speak so freely.

"Yes, I am."

"At home, they said you had died." Why couldn't she keep her mouth shut? But she wanted to know about this woman more than she wanted to be polite.

Corinna smiled more widely. "I'm sure they wish I had. But I was captured by Commander Merek."

"Oh."

"That's the scowling black-haired one." The red-head grinned at her. "I'm Jace, the friendly one."

Merek scowled more fiercely at his friend, but Jace only laughed.

"I don't understand," Anne said.

"Merek captured me. And now I'm marrying him. And Jace."

Her eyes must have gone as round as plates because everyone laughed at the same time. She flushed even more hotly. This woman, a Novus Vitan, was marrying not one but two Demon Kin males. At the same time.

"Why?" she said hoarsely.

"Because we love her," Jace said. "And she loves us, poor thing."

Corinna elbowed him and he dragged her off her chair and onto his lap, where he kissed her soundly. While this was going on, Merek quietly undid her braid and ran his fingers through her hair. Anne looked down at the table.

Damien slung his arm over her shoulders and grinned at her. "Don't be embarrassed. This is how we Demon Kin are. We can't keep our hands off the ones we love."

Her face flamed. He probably didn't realize there were two ways to interpret his words, given that he'd put his arm around her right before he'd said them. But he couldn't mean that he still loved her. Or that he'd ever loved her. He'd never said those words, not once. She needed to monitor her own thoughts, because she was in danger of fooling herself about his feelings for her.

The couple on the balcony had evidently finished with their lovemaking, or else they'd moved it into their room. They weren't there when she glanced up. She hoped Damien would never expect her to perform in public like that.

High-pitched giggles erupted from the far end of the courtyard. Two dark-haired Demon Kin boys charged into the space, one chasing the other and making shooting noises. They dashed around the table as if they didn't even see the adults sitting there, made two circuits of the fountain, and disappeared into the shadows under the gallery. Anne could still hear them calling to each other as they ran off somewhere else.

Like the boys playing dice in Kelzenec, they looked just like human children, except for the tails and the small horns peeking out from their curly hair. They behaved just like human children. How much difference was there, really, between Demon Kin and humans?

"My cousin's children," Merek said, looking at her. "They're a couple of wild cats."

Anne smiled. "They're cute."

Damien gave her a considering look. She glanced up at him and then looked away, flushing.

Servants brought in a second table and more chairs, along with platters of food and icy pitchers of water and jugs of wine. The balcony couple reappeared, fully clothed, and descended the stairs with their arms around each other's waists. The two Demon Kin boys were shepherded in by a servant, and another couple came down the stairs at the opposite side of the courtyard.

The man was a black-haired, olive-skinned Demon Kin, his woman a petite human female with pale skin and long mahogany hair. They, too, had their arms around each other's waists, and were looking so deeply into each other's eyes that Anne wondered how they managed the stairs without tripping.

Everyone spoke in Malefican, except Anne, who didn't speak at all. She supposed she ought to be grateful she was allowed to sit at the table and eat off a plate like a civilized person. Damien could have made her kneel at his feet like a dog.

The foreign conversation flowed around and over her, blending into the background like the tinkling of the fountain. She enjoyed the excellent food and the warm evening air and ignored everything else.

"Your slave ought to know," Jace said in Galactic Standard.

Anne brought her gaze around him. He looked serious for once, and he was watching Damien. Jace raised his brows and indicated her with a tilt of his head.

Her master turned to her. "Jace and I are going out tomorrow to investigate that weapon the tribesmen were using."

She could almost feel the color leaching from her face. "But that's dangerous."

"We'll be taking a full contingent of guards," Jace said. "They won't attack us anyway, once they know who we are. If they did, Night would send an army to squash them and they know it."

"Besides," Damien added, "you will stay here. Merek, Fury, and another contingent of guards will remain behind to defend Demon's Lair if necessary. You'll be perfectly safe."

She grabbed his forearm. "But you could be hurt. I wish you wouldn't go."

His face softened. "I'll be fine, Annie. We'll be back before nightfall." He leaned down and gave her a tender kiss.

Anne flushed again. Everyone was watching the two of them. Maybe she'd done something socially unacceptable when she'd expressed concern for his safety. Maybe a slave should keep her mouth shut. Yet Merek's and Jace's eyes sparkled with warmth and approval, so it couldn't be all bad.

She relaxed against the back of her chair. So she cared for her master and wanted to protect him. So what?

On Novus Vita, I'd be persecuted for loving Damien.

It remained to be seen what the Bellerenic people thought of it.

Damien took her hand, his long fingers folding around her smaller ones. Anne leaned against his shoulder. Something inside of her seemed to open up, blossoming with the release of tension.

"Damien, you must give Anne the language." Merek looked at her and smiled.

She looked up at Damien with a question in her eyes.

"I can use my psychic powers to speed your learning of Bellerenic," he said.

At one time, that admission would have frightened and repulsed her. Now, Anne merely raised her brows. "Oh. That's a useful talent."

"You don't think it's evil?" he said, watching her closely.

"No."

"Changing your mind so quickly, Anne? And here I believed you were completely committed to the Novus Vitan way."

She met his gaze straight on, trying to show him through her eyes that she meant everything she said. "Damien, I never thought you were evil."

He searched her face so long she began to squirm inwardly. Finally his face softened, his gaze warmed, and he put his arm around her shoulders and drew her in against his side. Anne let out a long, quiet breath. Maybe there were possibilities between them after all.

Chapter 14

He left so early in the morning that Anne didn't even see him. She woke to sun pouring through the glass and a strange bird singing outside the window.

"Too-*woo*-hoo-hoo-hoo," said the bird. "Too-*woo*-hoo-hoo-hoo." There was something both mournful and lovely in the sound.

Anne sat up, pushing the hair from her eyes. With Damien gone, she wasn't sure how to behave. Did she go to the kitchens and eat with the servants? But they were all men and it didn't seem like the best solution.

Someone knocked at the door.

Anne clutched the blankets to her chin. "Come!"

Slowly the door opened and a woman peeked around the edge. She had long, thick, dark hair and blue eyes. She'd been at the dinner the night before, with the swarthy Demon Kin male.

"May I help you?" Anne said.

The woman shut the door. "My name is Lily Sukay. We didn't get a chance to talk last night and I wanted to introduce myself."

Anne blinked. "It's—uh—very nice to meet you, but—maybe no-one told you, but I'm a slave."

"Oh, I know." Lily smiled. "You're with Damien."

She came in uninvited and perched herself on the edge of the bed. "My husband is close friends with Damien and Merek."

"Your husband?"

"Baron Sukay. Fury Sukay."

Anne shifted awkwardly. "I'm new to Malefica—I mean Belleren. I don't know many people."

"I know how that feels." Lily patted Anne's thigh over the blanket. "I'm from Novus Vita myself."

Her brows rose. "You are?"

"Yes. I was a slave, too, once. Fury rescued me."

Anne rubbed her forehead. "That's very—you're really a slave?"

"Was. Back on Novus Vita, in service to the provincial governor."

"I had no idea."

"I thought you might be more comfortable if I took you under my wing. We can go to breakfast together."

Anne shook her head. "No, that wouldn't be proper. I'm just a slave."

"Oh, pooh." Lily waved her hand. "No-one here cares about that nonsense, least of all me, or Corinna and Merek."

"Damien seems to care."

Her guest cocked her head. "Are you sure about that? He seemed very attached to you last night."

"He's angry with me." Anne watched the other woman. How well could she trust her? "We . . . cared for each other a long time ago, and my parents separated us. Damien blames me. And . . . I've done some bad things. I don't think he'll forgive me."

"If you're referring to your Army of God connection, I think he'll get over it. He must know you were fighting for your homeland."

"Yeah. Except it's a little more complicated than that."

"Well, I'll tell him I required your companionship today. If he doesn't like it, he can argue with me." Lily had a glint in her eye, as if she welcomed a spat with Damien.

"All right, Lady Sukay. I would be pleased to attend you at breakfast."

"Oh, it's just Lily. I can't get used to that Lady Sukay stuff. And you're not attending me, you're accompanying me as a friend."

❦ ❦ ❦

Damien stared out the window at the barren landscape below. There was nothing but sand and rocks for klicks in every direction. The desolation matched perfectly with his mood. "I don't know what to do with her, Jace."

"You looked like you were doing fine last night." Jace leaned against the seat back, his long legs stretched in front of him.

Damien glanced at his friend, then back at the scenery. "I can't trust her."

"Why not?"

"I hope you're kidding. She was with the Army of God for six months. A believer, Jace. She wanted to destroy us."

"Destroy us or drive us off Novus Vita?"

He snorted at the redhead. "Is there a difference?"

"Are you being dense on purpose? Of course there's a difference." Jace frowned at him. "I thought you did her Soul Opening."

"I did."

"Didn't that give you all the answers you need?"

"I don't know." He shrugged, sighing. "You're right. She never wanted to annihilate us, just get us off her planet. But to align with the A.O.G.—they're monsters. How could she?"

"Have you asked her?"

He winced. "What good would it do?"

"I think all that anonymous sex addled your brain, my friend." Jace slapped him on the back. "It's usually better to ask than to guess."

204

Damien had asked. He simply hadn't believed her answer. Had he been wrong in that?

The pitch of the engine's whine changed as they started to drop altitude. The float car descended into a narrow valley with no sign of civilization in evidence. The dwellings were hidden somewhere in the rocky foothills, where the wild tribes of Belleren had made their home for centuries.

The float car touched down, along with the two troop transports escorting it. The transports boasted heavy plasma cannon and short-range missiles. Only idiots would attack them. Still, Damien tensed as horsemen poured out of the hills and thundered toward them. If he died, who would take care of Anne?

The horsemen made a moving wall between their float car and the blue-shadowed foothills, their mounts kicking up puffs of dust that billowed out behind them in a huge gray cloud. Damien unlatched his flight restraints as Jace opened the float car door. They stepped out together, unarmed.

Jace wore the pale gray livery of Demon's Lair. As its seneschal, he was both entitled and obliged to represent the household in situations like these. Damien wore ordinary clothes rather than the black and magenta of House Fallyn. He was here to help Jace and Merek, not to conduct official business of his own.

One man rode forward out of the mob. His head wrap was made of many colors of cloth—red, canary yellow, indigo, lime green—twisted together, his horns just barely poking out at the top. The fellow had so many silver decorations and colored tassels on his mount that he nearly blinded Damien every time the animal moved. This might be the chief, or it could be his representative. The tribes were notoriously distrustful of Bellerenic city folk and Barons alike and sometimes they sent factotums instead of risking the chief.

Jace held his hands up in the traditional tribal greeting. "Well met, friends. I am Jace Riverton, seneschal of Demon's Lair."

The tribesman turned a hard gaze on Damien. "Who is he?"

"This is my assistant, Damien Fallyn."

Damien bowed.

"You come into our territory uninvited," the tribesman said gruffly. "You bring heavy weapons and two transports full of soldiers. What do you want with us?"

"They're guards, not soldiers, and the weapons are for our protection, as there seem to be brigands in the area."

The tribesman showed no reaction to this. "I say again, what do you want?"

"Our guests were attacked yesterday on their way to Demon's Lair," Jace said. "We merely wished to warn you that a band of criminals is active in your territory."

The tribesman's tail flicked back and forth. Just the tip. "What of it?"

"You yourself may be in danger," Damien said.

"These brigands possess a shock cannon, which they used to shoot an armored float car out of the sky." Jace smiled. "We thought to warn you, since the king will soon hear of the incident and we wouldn't want your people to be caught up in an . . . unfortunate misunderstanding."

The tail flicked more emphatically. The tribesman's lips tightened to a thin line. Then he grinned, making an expansive gesture with his hand. "Come, then, join us for a feast and we will talk."

Jace bowed. "Our guards will follow us."

"No!" The tribesman's gaze hardened. "No guards."

"Five guards only," Jace said, his voice calm. "The rest will stay here."

The tribesman's jaw clenched. "Very well. Five only."

"The others will remain in constant communication with Demon's Lair," Damien said. "Just in case the brigands return."

The tribesman looked as if he'd like to sever Damien's jugular vein with his own fangs. "Yes." The words came out clipped and angry. "Come. We will talk."

The man dismounted, his movements so smooth and graceful he looked as if he'd been born on horseback. A handful of his fellow tribesmen followed, moving to surround him like bodyguards. Jace motioned to one of the Demon's Lair guards, who gathered up his own group to surround him and Damien. They moved off, hiking away from both the float cars and the remaining horsemen, up a short rise and over the other side.

The tribesmen produced a blanket, sacks of food and jugs of wine, laying the refreshments out like a picnic. Then their leader took a seat on the blanket, while his companions ranged themselves behind him, their arms folded over their chests. They were hard-bitten men, their faces burned by the sun and bearing the scars of battle.

Jace and Damien sank cross-legged onto the blanket across from the tribal leader, and the talk began. Were any of the Demon's Lair guests hurt in the attack? No, but they could have been, and we know many tribesmen were killed or injured. Do you know of any tribes or bandits possessing shock cannon? None of our people would use such a weapon. On and on it went, swinging around the subject at hand, passing lightly over its surface, then back around for another pass without ever approaching the real question: did you fire on our float car?

Damien wished he could shake the information out of the man. He needed to get back to Demon's Lair as soon as possible. He was already feeling the effects of enchainment and separation.

His skin crawled. An empty pit had opened up in his belly, an ache that couldn't be soothed until he rejoined Anne. Jace was probably feeling the same thing for Corinna. It made both of them irritable and restless, a state which didn't bode well for these talks.

The sun was approaching the horizon when the tribal leader pointed at the sky behind Jace and Damien's heads. "A storm comes. You will stay here overnight."

Chapter 15

They both turned to look over their shoulders. Dark clouds with an odd yellowish tinge were massed just behind the hill at their backs, moving fast. A gust of wind picked up Damien's hair and blew it back into his eyes.

The two men exchanged a glance. Damien could see without opening his mind to his friend that Jace was reluctant to spend the night in tribal territory. As was he.

He shoved the unruly locks out of his eyes. "If we start now, perhaps we can beat the storm."

"You will never outrun it," the tribesman said. "If you fly in that, my friends, you'll never see Demon's Lair again."

"We'll spend the night in our float car," Jace said.

"Indeed, that will not be necessary. You will be our guests." The tribesman grinned, his teeth bright white in the failing light. "We have many beautiful young men to keep you company. You will have your pick of them."

Damien and Jace looked at each other sidelong. He couldn't be sure about the redhead, but Damien wasn't interested in fucking any of the tribesmen no matter how beautiful they might be. Telling their leader that, however, would be to refuse his hospitality and give grave insult. He opened his mouth to give some vague, diplomatic answer.

Jace slung an arm around Damien's shoulders, pulling him against his body. "We thank you for your gracious offer, but my assistant and I are life partners."

Damien blushed. He could feel his face burning, and due to his damned fair skin it was probably obvious even in the twilight.

The tribesman looked from one to the other with raised brows. "Are you, indeed? I had not suspected."

"We have an exclusive relationship," Jace added.

Damien cringed inwardly. He'd done many things in his life, and had experimented with other men, but to fuck Jace would be wrong. They were friends, not lovers, and he wanted it to stay that way.

"I think you jest." The tribal leader scowled. "You disdain our young men."

"Not at all." Jace gave him an easy smile. "I can see that you do have some attractive men among you. But I don't share Damien."

208

Damien resisted the urge to glare at his friend. Instead he gave the most convincing smile he could muster. Refusal of tribal hospitality could be grounds for violence, so they had to make their "love affair" look realistic.

The tribesman looked unconvinced. "If you are life-partners, then give him a kiss."

Jace frowned. "You doubt my word?"

"I find that your words conflict with the evidence of my eyes."

Jace put his free hand on the side of Damien's face, leaning in to press his lips to Damien's. They were soft, in contrast to the calloused hardness of his palm. They clung briefly and released. Then Jace captured his mouth again, tongue questing, looking for entry. Damien gave it to him.

He tasted like wine. Jace grabbed him, pulled him around and into his body, and all the bottled-up lust for Anne that he'd fought that day overtook him. He groaned against Jace's mouth. His arms went around the other man's body as Jace's tongue plunged deep. Damien's cock thickened, shoving against his trousers.

The redhead ended the kiss, but didn't release him. They were both breathing hard, staring at each other like they'd never really seen each other before. Jace smiled. Damien dropped his head to his friend's shoulder, unable to meet his eyes anymore. The gods only knew if he'd ever be able to look at Jace again without blushing.

"You see what you started?" Jace had a smile in his voice.

"I should not have doubted you," the tribesman said. "You should remove to your float cars now, before the storm hits. My men have an hour's ride ahead of them, so we must bid you good evening."

Jace let go of Damien to give the leader a short bow. "Thank you for your generous hospitality. I will inform the king when I see him that he has nothing to fear from your people."

Damien lifted his head to see the tribesman give them a bland smile. "We are King Night's friends, as he is ours. However, there are men in these hills who would kill to acquire even one woman. Our numbers are quickly dwindling without females. Tell your king that."

"I will tell him."

The tribesmen rolled up their blanket and walked back to their waiting army. Damien and Jace followed behind, their arms still slung around each other's waists. They stood that way while the tribesmen mounted up and wheeled away, kicking up clouds of dust as they rode toward the sunset.

When they'd disappeared over the nearest rise, Damien dropped his arm. "Tell me you were just playing."

"I was just playing."

He gave Jace a doubtful look. "It didn't feel that way."

"I'm faithful to Corinna and Merek, Damien. Just as you are to Anne. It was just for show. Although if you want to pass the time with me while we wait for the storm to end, I wouldn't complain."

He grinned at Damien, giving his shoulders a little shake. "You should see the look on your face. I'm not going to force you, boy."

"Will I be safe tonight?"

Jace laughed. "Completely."

* * *

The cravings began around lunch time. Anne had missed Damien since waking, but suddenly she ached all over her body, and it seemed that only his touch could satisfy her. There seemed to be a gigantic hole inside of her, a hole with ragged and painful edges.

She got up and began to pace the courtyard. Corinna and Lily stopped talking to stare at her. She didn't care. Walking eased the ache a little bit and made it possible for her to remain upright. If she'd stayed in her chair, she'd be curled up in a ball by now.

Probably with my hand between my legs.

She suppressed an embarrassed giggle. Really she had no idea how to pleasure herself and had never known a person who admitted to doing it. Not that she'd ever asked. On Novus Vita, one didn't speak of such things. Even to oneself.

On Belleren, masturbation was probably a public sport.

This time she giggled aloud.

"What's so funny?" Corinna said.

Anne flushed. "Nothing. Just an embarrassing thought."

The two other women looked at each other.

"Anne, are you all right?" Lily frowned in a concerned way.

"I'm fine." She forced a smile. "Why do you ask?"

"Because you're pacing like you're about to jump out of your skin."

"Oh." She turned on her heel for another lap. "I'm just full of energy, I guess."

"Do you hurt all over?"

Anne's eyes widened. "Yeah. How did you know?"

Lily propped her elbow against the table where she sat. "Do you feel like your body would stop hurting if you could hold Damien?"

She didn't want these women to know just how much she craved her Demon Kin slave master. But maybe they could help her. "Yeah."

"Enchainment," Corinna and Lily said together.

"What's that?"

210

Lily waved her hand vaguely. "It's when you and your lover become addicted to each other. Demon Kin are highly addictive."

"I'm addicted to Damien?"

"Yes," Lily said.

"He's probably addicted to you also, if that makes you feel any better," Corinna added.

"It does, actually. At least it's not one-sided." She rubbed her hands across her upper arms. "How long will this feeling last?"

"Until he comes home."

Anne groaned. "I don't know if I can stand it."

Corinna got up and patted her on the shoulder. "He'll be here before dinner. You can go upstairs and satisfy your appetite before you eat."

Anne blushed.

The other woman laughed. "Lily and I have become much more Bellerenic during our time here. You'll get used to us, eventually."

But Damien and Jace didn't come back by dinner time. The servants held the food for over an hour, waiting for the two men and the troops to return. Finally they laid the meal on tables in the courtyard because the other guests were famished.

Anne couldn't eat. Lily didn't have any trouble because she had Fury with her, and Corinna had Merek to comfort her. She spent the whole meal practically on his lap, eating out of his hand and sharing kisses with him between bites. It would have been highly embarrassing to Anne if she hadn't been so green with jealousy.

I've come down in the world. I'm reduced to yearning for the presence of a man who keeps me in a collar and leads me around on a leash.

Toward the end of the meal, a servant came running into the courtyard and shouted something in Bellerenic. Everyone looked at each other with wide eyes, clearly startled. Then they jumped to their feet and began to help the servants clear the courtyard. Although she had no idea what was happening, Anne pitched in, working as fast as she could because whatever it was seemed to be urgent.

As they worked, the sky darkened to a weird and ominous grayish-tan and the wind picked up, tossing the fronds of the palm trees wildly. The gusts had a gritty feeling to them, like they were carrying fine sand and using it to scour her.

She grabbed the edge of the last table and began to drag it across the cobbles to a sheltered area under the gallery. A Bellerenic servant grabbed her by the upper arm and yelled at her.

"I can't understand you!" she shouted back. The wind howled so loudly it drowned out her voice.

He tugged her arm and pointed to the main building, yelling. Anne nodded and allowed him to take her to shelter. The other servants had already closed and latched all the shutters, and the house had a huddled appearance, as if it were hugging itself for comfort.

The man hustled her into the house, then turned and closed the thick wooden doors that led into the courtyard. The howling noise cut off, leaving them in eerie silence. Another man slid home a sturdy metal bolt. Everything here looked ancient, like it had come from thousands of years ago on Earth.

I hope it's strong enough to withstand the storm.

"Well," Corinna said with a bright smile. "We'll just have to continue our entertainment inside."

Anne shivered, wrapping her arms around her torso. Any desire for entertainment she might have had disappeared in worry about Damien. Was he caught out in the storm? Would he be safe inside the float car? Surely an armored car could withstand a storm. But what if the tribesmen attacked, or a tree fell across the door of the car, trapping the men inside? What if they were buried underneath blown sand and couldn't get out?

Thunder rumbled in the distance. Rain hammered against the shutters, loud even through the wood and the window glass. God, there was going to be a flood out there. Damien might be drowned, not buried in sand.

She began to pace again, back and forth across the central hall of the house. The hole inside her seemed bigger and more painful than ever. Little skittering sensations moved through her skin, as if she had tiny creatures embedded there and they were crawling around. She rubbed her arms.

Corinna touched her elbow. "I have something for you."

"What is it?"

"A drug that can take some of your pain away. I'm using it, too. Otherwise, I'd be crazy with Jace gone so long."

"But you have Merek."

"Yeah, but whenever one of them leaves me for more than three hours or so, I start feeling the pain."

Anne tilted her head. "How does anyone on this planet ever get any work done?"

Corinna laughed. "It's not easy. We have to take frequent breaks to visit our partners." She gestured toward the staircase. "Let's go upstairs."

Merek was herding the guests into one of the downstairs room. Strains of harp music floated out of the open doorway. Anne allowed Corinna to lead her up the stairs and along the gallery to a room with huge, carved double doors.

Inside was an enormous bed, even bigger than the one in Anne and Damien's room. Its size made sense, given that three people shared it. Corinna went to a cabinet on one wall and opened the door. She produced a small pill bottle and extracted one pill, offering it to Anne.

"What is it?"

"Super-codone. It's fast acting. Addictive, too, so you can only have a small dose. But it should allow you to tolerate Damien's absence better for about ten hours. After that, he'll be home."

Or she'd need a new dose. She accepted the pill, hoping it would be the only one she'd have to take. "Thank you."

"I'm sure they're all right," Corinna said. "Jace has been out in these storms before. He and the men know what to do."

"But what about the tribes? What if they attacked?"

Corinna smiled, but she looked uneasy. "I don't think they'd do that. Night would massacre them for attacking a Baron and a Baronial seneschal."

"I hope you're right."

"Let's go downstairs. It's best to distract yourself at a time like this."

But she couldn't be distracted. It took almost half an hour for the super-codone to begin working, and even after she noticed her body relaxing, her mind continued to work at the problem of Damien and Jace's whereabouts. She curled up in a chair in a dark corner of the room and worried while everyone else sang, told stories and played board games.

※ ※ ※

Dawn was peering over the horizon when Damien, Jace and the guards returned to Demon's Lair. The palms outside the compound looked half-naked, while fronds littered the ground at their feet. The float transports descended into the courtyard, revealing more denuded trees as they neared the ground.

There weren't any guests around, and the windows of the house were still tightly shuttered against the storm. One servant appeared at the front door and waved to them as they disembarked. Damien and Jace walked shoulder to shoulder across the courtyard. Damien ached for the woman he'd left behind, so he imagined Jace must be uncomfortable too.

The house was even quieter inside than out, but the rattle of pots and pans could be heard coming from the kitchen. The thick doors leading to the courtyard were shut and barred. How bad had they been hit? It seemed the storm had been much more severe here than it had in the tribal valley they'd left.

"I'm going straight up to Corinna," Jace said.

"I'm right behind you."

When he opened the door to the room he shared with Anne, he found it dark and stuffy. The shutters were closed and barred, and very little light filtered into the room. Anne lay on her stomach on the bed, her eyes closed, one arm clutching a pillow against her side.

He went to the windows and opened the shutters, allowing fresh light into the room. Then he opened one of the doors that led onto the balcony. The courtyard was a mess, the fountain clogged with palm fronds and bits of flowering vine, the cobbles strewn with more of the same. The vines that had been so thick and colorful yesterday morning looked ragged and dull now.

Turning from the window, he watched Anne sleep. Her auburn hair was spread across her back and part of her face, like a veil. He sat down on the edge of the bed and pushed the heavy locks away from her face. She had dark circles under her eyes.

His cock throbbed insistently as he caught her scent. Damien brushed his hand over her back. He was trembling. He'd been enchained before, but never like this. Never so deeply that he couldn't bear one night away from his woman.

Chapter 16

Damien pushed the thick weight of hair from Anne's back, meaning to kiss her there, and froze. Gods of Belleren, the scars. She was covered with scars from the nape of her neck to the top of her buttocks. Some of them were thin, white lines and looked like they'd been made by a whip. Others were thicker, less even, twisting in unpredictable patterns.

The raging lust in him cooled, turning to anger as he stared at the damage. He scowled, tracing some of the lines with his fingertip. Who had done this to her? Why? It couldn't have happened in prison. The lines were white, old, as if they'd been made years ago.

Maybe it had something to do with the Army of God.

She took a deeper breath and murmured in her sleep. She turned to her side and opened her eyes. Blinked. Then she focused on him and a smile came over her, crinkling the corners of her eyes.

"Damien! You're back." Anne pushed herself up.

"Yes." He gathered her into his arms and held on tight. She felt tiny against him. So vulnerable.

Anne hugged him back. "I missed you."

"I missed you, too." He began to rub her back, feeling the contours of the scars beneath his fingers.

After a few minutes, she pulled away, her eyes widening. "You saw them."

"Yes." He couldn't help frowning. "What happened, Anne?"

Anne shook her head. "Nothing. It was a long time ago. I don't like to talk about it."

"I want to know."

"It isn't important anymore." She pulled the sheet up around her, clutching it as if it could protect her.

"Tell me."

"Damien, please, don't. It won't help to talk about it."

He caught her chin. "I need to know. Tell me. Was it the A.O.G.?"

"What?" She sounded startled. "No. Why would they beat me?"

"I don't know. I don't know why anyone would beat you. If it wasn't them, then who? Who, Anne?"

She began to shake her head and didn't stop, even when he pulled her into an embrace Her body quaked in his arms. He stroked her hair, his mind racing with questions, fears, possibilities.

"I won't be angry with you," he murmured. "No matter what your answer is."

She looked up at him. "Promise?"

"Of course I promise. Tell me who did this to you."

Her chin trembled. She pressed her lips together. "My father."

Her father had mutilated her? Damien went completely still inside. "Why?"

Anne's gaze dropped. "He found out about us."

"When? How? Did you tell him?"

"No, of course not," she said, still looking down. "He saw us that last day. When we were . . . ."

"Kissing." Gods of Belleren. This was his fault. If he hadn't kissed her, if he'd left her alone, she never would have been beaten and whipped.

"I did this, didn't I?" His voice had turned hoarse.

"No." She gave her head an emphatic shake. "You had nothing to do with it."

"If I hadn't kissed you, he wouldn't have been so angry."

She looked up at him, her blue eyes sad. "It wasn't your fault. I wanted to be with you."

Could it be true? Could he have been wrong?

"You wanted to be with me," he repeated. "Are you saying that only to make me feel better?"

"No. It's true. I'm the one who came through the gate, remember? I did it because you were there."

His stomach hurt. "I thought—damn, I was such a selfish shit. I thought you were rejecting me. That you were disgusted by me. But that wasn't it, was it?"

"No." She bit her lip. "I heard footsteps on the other side of the wall and I was afraid we'd be seen. That's why I left. But it was too late. My father already knew, and he was there when I came through the gate. He dragged me into the house and gave me a whipping." Anne clasped his hand tightly. "I couldn't get back to you. I'm sorry about that."

"Did they watch you after that?"

She gave a short, humorless laugh. "You could say that. They locked me in the attic, in a room on the other side of the house. I couldn't even see you from the window anymore."

Locked in the attic like a criminal. His muscles tensed with anger at the way they'd treated her. "How long did they lock you up?"

"For six months, I couldn't leave the room. After that, I could leave if I was supervised, but I couldn't go out on my own for six years. I think the only reason they relented was because of the war."

"Oh, Anne." He dropped his head and kissed her on her crown. "Annie. I had no idea. I didn't know."

She put her arms around his waist. "I know that."

"I wish you'd told me how bad it was. I would have done something. Given you shelter at my parents' house, gotten you off-world. Something."

"And caused an interplanetary incident? There was nothing you could have done, Damien. You weren't much more than a boy at the time."

"Still." He tightened his hold on her. "No wonder you hated me."

"I didn't hate you."

"No?"

For a long while, she didn't answer him. Her breath sounded uneven, as if she might be crying. Damien held onto her, threading his fingers through her hair, rubbing her back. Wishing he could take the years away.

She cleared her throat. "They sent teachers in to me every day. That's what they called them. Teachers."

"What did they do?"

"They talked. They said the same thing over and over. The Demon Kin are evil, you were trying to soil me. They made me repeat it." She met his gaze, her gray eyes wide and solemn. "At first I fought them and argued with them. But they wouldn't stop and nothing I said ever made a difference to them. Finally they got mad because I argued once too often and they beat the soles of my feet because my back was still too injured to receive more punishment. For a long time after that, I couldn't walk."

"Why was your back so injured? Was that from the whipping your father gave you?"

"Yes. He gave me several beatings. For the first six months, he whipped me once a month to remind me of what I'd done."

"I'd like to wring his neck." And he would have, if the man had still been alive.

"It's too late for that."

Damien growled low in his throat. "Give me the Teachers' names. I'm going to press charges."

"Please don't. I don't want to see them ever again."

"Annie—"

"No." She had a note of panic in her voice. "Please. I can't."

He sighed. "All right. But they shouldn't be allowed to get away with it."

"My parents died in the war, so we can't confront them anyway."

"I know." He continued stroking her hair. Her parents had been despicable to treat her the way they did, but she must have loved them. "I read that in your file. Mine died in the plague."

Anne lifted her head to look at him. Her eyes were red-rimmed. "I'm sorry. I didn't know."

"How could you? I'm sure it didn't make the news on Novus Vita." Damien kissed the tip of her nose. "After the wedding, we're going to my country house. It'll be safer there for you."

"You don't hate me?"

He cupped the side of her face in his hand. "No, love. I don't hate you."

"Even though I worked for the A.O.G.?"

"I still don't understand that, but I'm willing to listen."

Anne sighed and wiped her eyes. "They convinced me. The Teachers, I mean, convinced me that your people were bad. No matter how much I argued, no matter what I said, they just kept repeating that Demon Kin are evil. They made me repeat it, too, and if I refused, they beat me. Starved me." She hung her head. "I'm sorry, Damien. I'm so ashamed of that now."

"They brainwashed you."

"For a long time, I believed what they taught me. I believed all your people were evil. Even you. When your world invaded Novus Vita, I despised you. I wanted revenge."

"Anne—"

"No, hear me out. I want you to know how bad it was. I believed I had to purge you from my thoughts, cut all emotional ties to you. When the Demon Kin came to my world, I saw it as proof that the Teachers were right, and I wanted to do whatever I could to make life difficult for Bellerenics. I wanted to make up for the harm I thought I'd done by..." Her breath caught.

"By what? Kissing me?"

Her eyes glittered as if with unshed tears. She pressed her lips together. His thumb traced a gentle line back and forth along her jaw. Willing her to say the words. Afraid to hear her say them.

Anne closed her eyes and took a breath. "By loving you."

Damien's throat closed up and he bent his head again to hers, silently, continuing to hold her. His heart pounded, his thoughts tumbled over themselves in a clumsy mixture of joy and relief, guilt and shame. He'd blamed her—Gods, how he'd blamed her—for things that weren't her fault, things that had been forced on her with violence.

Finally she opened her eyes a sliver and peeked at him. He tilted her chin up and pressed a gentle kiss on her lips.

"And now?" he said, his voice husky.

"I still love you."

"Gods of Belleren," he whispered. "I love you too. I've been telling myself not to be a fool, but I can't help myself."

"You still don't trust me."

He sighed. "Were you aware of the A.O.G.'s methods?"

Anne pulled back and met his gaze, frowning. "What do you mean?"

"They're terrorists. They attack their own people as well as ours. Fury and Lily almost died when some of their operatives broke into the governor's compound in Vineyard South. The A.O.G. was killing the governor's human slaves, not just the Bellerenics."

She gave him a troubled look. "Your king told me the same story. I— wasn't sure whether to believe him. I knew the A.O.G. used guerilla tactics, but I had no idea they attacked our own people. They never mentioned anything like that in front of me."

"It's a true story. Ask Lily if you don't believe me. Her best friend was injured in a firefight."

"I believe you."

He wanted so badly to trust her. "You know I could find out everything if I wanted to?"

Anne met his gaze squarely, without flinching. "I know, Damien. If you need to do it, go ahead. I won't fight you."

It was a risk to trust her. But not trusting her was risky, too. Could he live his life with a woman, slave or free, whose loyalty he continually questioned? How would they raise their children in such an environment?

He'd seen no evidence during the Soul Opening that Anne knew the full extent of A.O.G.'s activities, and she'd proven her loyalty when she'd saved the life of the float car pilot. Jace had advocated trusting her, and he considered Jace to be a good judge of character. With a deep breath, he made the leap.

He took her face in his hands, bent down and kissed her on the lips. "I'm going to take your word for it."

She put her arms around his neck and kissed him, her soft lips clinging seductively to his. The lust and yearning resurfaced with a roar and a deep ache in his groin. Damien licked her, teasing her to open for him, and when she did he moaned and plunged his tongue into her warm wet depths as he crushed her to his body.

They kissed feverishly, as if they were starving, as if the touch of their bodies together was the only thing keeping them alive. Their hands moved frantically over each other's skin, tearing at clothes, caressing and holding and penetrating. Damien found her pussy, found it soaking wet.

She dropped her head back on a throaty moan as he stroked the creamy folds. When he plunged his finger inside her, she yelled, her hips jerking against his hand. Damien pushed her back onto the mattress and tore at his pants, shoving them down his thighs. His cock twitched in its impatience to get inside of her.

Anne spread her legs, welcoming him in, and he positioned himself and entered in one long thrust. They both groaned. The pleasure of their joining blazed into his mind, searing out all other thought, all other sensation. There was nothing but him and her, his rock-hard cock in her hot tight sheath, her arms around him, her breath panting against his chest.

Damien moved his hips. He needed to take it slow, to be gentle, to give her as much pleasure as possible before he lost control, but the instant he moved, the need overwhelmed him. He found himself pounding into her, groaning mindlessly, unable to stop or slow down, and Anne dug her nails into his hips, yelled out his name, shoved herself against him as if she, too, had no control.

The orgasm caught him unawares. He was fucking her as fast and hard as he could when he felt the tingle, the tightening in his balls, and his back arched and everything in him contracted and he screamed, spilling himself, his life, his hot come into her until it seemed that all of him had drained out through his cock.

He collapsed on top of her, panting and covered in sweat. Anne pushed a languid hand through his hair, spreading sweet delight across his scalp. She stopped at his horns.

Damien waited for her to pull away in distaste, but she didn't. She explored them. The horns didn't have much sensation, but they could feel pressure and he knew she was stroking them from base to tip.

"I'm too heavy for you." He withdrew from her body, rolling to the side.

Anne nestled into him, resting her head on his chest while her hand stroked circles across his belly. "I was all right."

"You wouldn't have been much longer. I don't want to turn you into a pancake."

"I would have been a happy pancake."

He laughed softly and kissed the top of her head.

For a while, they lay together without talking. A cool breeze blew in from the window, along with birdsong and the scent of herbs crushed by the storm. The king should be arriving this afternoon, and tomorrow the wedding would take place. Then he could bring Anne home and they could begin a new life together. A life without the collar.

He felt around the band of steel links until he found the leather strap with the buckle. The leather had swelled from exposure to water, and the prong of the buckle didn't want to leave its hole. Damien forced it through, and the leather strap fell loose against her neck.

"What are you doing?" she said sleepily.

"Taking off the collar. What does it look like?"

"Why would you do that?"

"Because I don't want my wi—my woman wearing a slave collar all the time." His wife. He hadn't meant to say that, but now the word had left his mouth it sounded like the right idea.

Anne lifted her head, frowning slightly. "Why not?"

"Would you like me to leave it on?"

"Well. No." She rubbed the skin left bare by its removal. "But sometimes it was ..." Anne turned as magenta as one of the flowers in the courtyard.

"Arousing?"

She nodded. "Uh huh."

"For me, too."

She raised her brows. "You like to wear a collar?"

Damien laughed. "I've never done it, so I don't know. But I doubt that I would."

"Why not?" Anne poked him in the ribs. "Is it only for women?"

"No. There are men who enjoy it, too. I just don't think it's for me."

"You'd rather be the master."

He grinned. "Yes, I would."

Anne tilted her head, staring at him with a speculative air. "Some might say that turnabout is fair play."

He blinked. "Are you threatening me?"

"Not at all. I just think you can give it but you can't take it."

Damien laughed again. "You're not going to get me to agree to wear a collar, Anne, so give it up."

She grinned back at him. Damien lifted her hand and placed it against his cheek.

"I lied when I said I hated you." He turned his head and kissed her palm. "I love you, Anne. I've loved you since the day we met."

Her eyes softened. "I love you, too."

"Even though I—"

"Even though." She leaned down and pressed her lips to his. "I can't help myself."

"I'm going to talk to Night about getting your sentence commuted to time served."

She pulled back, her gaze suddenly serious. "Are you sure that's a good idea? The people might be outraged if he goes soft on a Novus Vitan terrorist."

Damien sighed. She was right. But a life as his slave wouldn't do anyone any good, including their children. He looked into her eyes.

"Maybe you'll have to remain a slave for a few more years, but from this moment on, you're not a slave to me. You're just Anne."

She gave him a wobbly smile. "Thank you."

"Except when you need a spanking." He glared at her in mock anger. "There will be times when you'll need some discipline."

Anne's smile broadened. "I hope so."

The End

To sign up for Tori's mailing list: http://www.toriminard.com/mailing-list/

Tori Minard has published twelve romance and erotic romance novels and three novellas, in addition to a handful of short stories, both under her own name and as Tessa Tremaine. Her series include The Amaki, Legends Of A Dark Empire, Avery's Crossing, Fortunata: The Jhidris Conspiracy, and Tales Of The Demon Kin.

Tori wrote her first story in elementary school, with a lamentable lack of punctuation. In high school, she spent more time writing fiction than doing homework. Her early stories featured demonic dogs, dolls possessed by evil spirits—no, she'd never heard of Chucky—and politically incorrect post-apocalyptic romance.

She discovered science fiction in the sixth grade, with her dad's recommendation of Edgar Rice Burroughs' **At the Earth's Core,** the first book in his Pellucidar series. Prior to that, her reading had included ghost stories, animal stories and adventure tales. Around the same time, she was discovering the joys of erotica by sneaking her mom's books and reading all the naughty bits. Her mom claims to have skipped those parts.

After a long detour for such grown-up pursuits as working boring full-time jobs (State of Alaska, U.S. Postal Service), getting married and having a child, she returned to her first love—storytelling. She was born and raised in Alaska, and now lives in the Pacific Northwest with her husband, son, and micro-dog

Discover other titles by Tori Minard

Tales Of The Demon Kin:
Novellas:
Malefica
Fury Enchained
The Devil You Know
Taken By Storm

Novels:
Lucifer's Castle
Mastered By Love

Short Stories:
Stainless Steel Vampire, story number one in the Skye Donovan series
Love Potion Number Ninety, Skye Donovan story number two
If I Should Die; a Legends Of The Dark Empire story
Price of a Rose, a sexy fairy tale (novelette)
Lemon Drop, a sweet erotic toy possessed by a sex spirit

Amaki Novels:
The Heart Moon
Dragon Moon
Blood Moon

Avery's Crossing Novels:
Rush
Bad Company: Gage and Nova Trilogy Book 1
Bedeviled: Gage and Nova Trilogy Book 2
Breaking Free: Gage and Nova Trilogy Book 3

Fortunata Novels:
Dirty Magic

Legends Of A Dark Empire Novels:
Temple Of The Heart
Darkness Awakened
Darkness Forbidden
Darkness Beloved
Darkness Embraced

Connect with Tori online
To learn more about Tori, visit her blog at http://www.toriminard.com
Twitter: http://twitter.com/#!/ToriMinard
Facebook: http://www.facebook.com/toriminard.paranormalromance
Pinterest: http://www.pinterest.com/toriminard/